Mistress Koharu

NOBORU TSUJIHARA

Translated by Kalau Almony

Honford
Star

This translation first published by Honford Star 2025

Honford Star Ltd.
Profolk, Bank Chambers
Stockport
SK1 1AR
honfordstar.com

ISBN (paperback): 978-1-915829-27-6
ISBN (ebook): 978-1-915829-28-3
A catalogue record for this book is available from the British Library.

Printed and bound in Paju, South Korea
Cover design by Bumpei Kii
Typeset by Honford Star
Cover paper: 250 gsm Vent Nouveau by TAKEO, Japan
Endleaves: 116 gsm NT Rasha by TAKEO, Japan

1 3 5 7 9 10 8 6 4 2

Contents

Part One

Upon returning home a little after 10 p.m., Yano Akira opened his bedroom door and, without turning on the lights, whispered, "I'm home" to Koharu, who was sitting up, leaning against the headboard. Koharu squirmed ever so slightly, glanced at Akira, and gave him a small nod. Akira shut the door with bated breath and walked to the living-dining-kitchen at the end of the hall.

Akira lived in an apartment in a five-story building. He did not own but rather rented it from a real estate corporation, which had acquired the apartment as an investment. It was, in Japanese real-estate parlance, a 1LDK—a single bedroom and a combined living-dining-kitchen space—and was far from large, just forty-five square meters, but for a single man like Akira, the layout was perfectly livable. On the left of the hallway leading from the entryway was his bedroom and a small spare room he used for various chores; on the right were the bathroom and shower, divided into separate rooms. At the end of the hallway was the combination living-dining room and kitchen about ten tatami mats in size, and in this living-dining-kitchen was a large closet.

Before turning on the room lights, Akira approached the aquarium on the left of the closet and asked, "How are you doing?"

The tank was lit by a small clip-on light. The two red and white sarasa comet goldfish waved their long, flowing tails and raced to the surface of the water, opening and shutting their mouths in anticipation of food. In response to Akira's call, the pure red ranchu emerged from his usual position in the crevice between the base of the heating cord and the corner of the tank, moving in a gentle, clockwise spiral. It was three years ago that he had brought these fishes home from the large plastic viewing tanks of Kingyozaka, a goldfish specialty shop in Hongo.

After Akira fed the fish, he watched the three of them swim back to their usual positions, and once they had returned, he shut off their light and covered the tank with a blackout sheet before switching on the lights of the living-dining-kitchen.

Akira approached the window and opened one of the sliding glass doors that led to the balcony, letting in the night air. The apartment had been shut up all day, and he wanted to air it out. He had left the front door half open for that purpose as well.

Below the balcony was a municipal park for young children. If one were to draw an oval within its rectangular grounds, it would probably produce a track of about 150 meters. Across the now barren and blackened park, the playground equipment and low trees cast tentative shadows. In the middle of the park was a pond with a fountain, but Akira had not once seen the fountain spitting water.

About forty meters away, on the opposite side of the park, stood a ten-story Leopalace apartment building. At this hour, Akira thought he could connect the dots of the few room lights still aglow and wind up with a constellation he knew. The wind blew through his apartment, and once Akira felt the air had freshened up, he closed the glass door and then closed and locked the front door as well.

Mistress Koharu

Akira had moved into this apartment in Nishi-Kanda five years ago, when he was thirty-four. Prior to coming here, he had spent twelve years in the company dorm for single men in Mejirodai, near his workplace. The super there called him "boss." Next year he would be turning forty, but he was still completely unattached. No one around him had brought up talk of marriage recently, and he had no intention of looking for someone to marry either, so it was probable that his life as a single man would continue. His father had lived for a long time as a widower in Minoh, one of Osaka's satellite cities, and would be turning seventy this year.

Akira took a can of Guinness from the refrigerator opposite the kitchen sink, checked his mail, and read the evening paper. After finishing the beer, he made himself a Tachibana Genshu on the rocks, a sweet potato shochu he had ordered from Kuroki Honten distillery in Miyazaki.

Sitting on the couch, Akira turned on the TV. The NHK-BS1 news broadcast had just started, they were announcing today's opening of a new extension to the Hokuriku Shinkansen bullet train line, which would connect Tokyo and Kanazawa. The trip would take only two hours and twenty-eight minutes! The newscaster added that the line was expected to be extended to Tsuruga in Fukui by 2022.

Akira remembered traveling around the Noto Peninsula one winter in his mid-twenties. Back then, he had taken the Joetsu Shinkansen to Echigo-Yuzawa Station and changed trains for the Hakutaka Express to get to Kanazawa. It had taken over four hours. He was shocked by how much faster the trains had gotten.

As the clock struck twelve, he turned off the TV, showered,

changed into his pajamas, brushed his teeth, and headed to the bedroom.

Akira turned on the floor lamp to the right of his bed, removed Koharu's dress, helping her strip down to just her lingerie, and positioned her face up on the mattress.

He climbed over her, and from her left side, leaned on top of her, his right hand massaging her thigh and buttocks as he rubbed his face in her breast.

Koharu was a life-sized love doll Akira had had delivered from a gallery in Koganecho in Yokohama's Naka Ward. Such dolls used for sex were once called "Dutch wives," but the term "love doll" had come into general usage to denote a Dutch wife made with realistic detail.

Akira graduated as a literature major from the humanities department of his university, with his undergraduate thesis on Chikamatsu Monzaemon, the playwright of bunraku puppet theater and kabuki plays. Even before this doll arrived, he had decided that he would call her Koharu—the name of the heroine of Chikamatsu's *The Love Suicides at Amijima*.

After he began living with Koharu, Akira made a discovery. Something unrelated to the workings of sex, something to do with sleep.

The expression "Dutch wife," the predecessor of the term "love doll," came from Dutch-occupied Indonesia, where Dutchmen sought to improve their troubled sleep in the hot tropical nights by sleeping with body pillows made of bamboo. These "bamboo wives" inspired the name of the dolls later made for sex. And what Akira discovered was that, when he slept spooning with Koharu, she served to drastically improve his sleep.

Mistress Koharu

He found that when he went to bed with any part of his body touching Koharu, he would fall into a deep sleep such as he had never before experienced. Moreover, he had completely stopped dreaming.

Akira's bedtime ritual began with petting then advanced to him telling stories. Problems at work, memories from his childhood, gossip about friends; the talk would continue endlessly, and Koharu, an excellent listener, would nod her head, give simple responses, and touch his body at just the right moments. Akira would grow relaxed, overcome by a warm and gentle feeling.

Akira worked in the editorial department at a large publishing house of both books and magazines, and tonight he couldn't help but let the complaints spill from his mouth.

"Printing ran late again today. The editor should have marked the author's corrections on the galleys and handed those over to the printers, but she just gave them the galleys with the author's notes attached. The operators had to do twice as much work, and the way they mark corrections isn't even the same."

"Is it that woman editor again?"

"Yeah, did I tell you about her? The new girl who started last year. I don't know who trained her, but they don't seem to have taught her anything ..."

Koharu pushed her right breast against his left arm, and Akira tried to continue his story with his eyes closed, but there was nothing he could do to fend off the sleep that suddenly overcame him. After dropping off for just a moment, he woke again, and though he felt aroused at Koharu gently stroking his penis through his pants, sleep came and dragged him back into its depths.

2

When he was a student, Akira encountered the work of manga artist Tsuge Yoshiharu. As with many Tsuge fans, he first read *Screw Style* and then began collecting all his major works. After landing his current job, Akira learned that Tsuge had once serialized his diary in a literary magazine, and so, for a hefty price, Akira purchased on Amazon a used copy of the hardcover edition of *The Diary of Tsuge Yoshiharu*.

The Diary covers five years, beginning in 1975 and ending in 1980, though there are at times significant gaps between entries, and the work is filled with the details of the manga artist's daily life. It begins with the birth of his son and goes on to capture on page his wife's battle with cervical cancer, the couple's disagreements, the deaths of friends, memories of a discontented and oppressive childhood, and complaints about his incapacity to create new work.

Tsuge was haunted by an incomprehensible anxiety, and beginning in the second half of *The Diary*, mentions of that anxiety grow frequent.

"It's not that I grow anxious about some imagined problem; rather I'm in a state where I'm anxious about anxiety itself. Sometimes I feel as though the only escape from this anxiety will be death."

One day, on a walk with his four-year-old son, Tsuge suffered a sudden episode of some sort and collapsed in the park grass. There, lying on his side, he followed his son's movements with his eyes, his own body stiff and trembling.

The Diary ends on sports day of his son's preschool.

Mistress Koharu

Akira read the book in one sitting. In the afterword, Tsuge wrote that he was encouraged by his editor's flattering claim that his diary "is actually an I-novel," but Akira felt that the work possessed a charm different in nature from the so-called I-novel of Japan. He remembered the feeling he had after reading the book: it was as if in one corner of a dark and gloomy sky there had opened a gaping mouth of blue.

When Akira discovered that the author Tomioka Taeko had written about this diary, he searched the office library for her essay.

The piece was titled "Personal Life and the I-Novel," and was in Tomioka's essay collection *The Scene of Expression*. In the opening she touched on how Tsuge mentioned his editor complimented him by saying that his diary was like an I-novel, and then she drew attention to Tsuge's understanding of his own work as an I-novel. She argued that unlike the I-novels that came before it, Tsuge's was not premised on the intention to express the self through fabrication, and she went on to claim that the unostentatious style of the work was the result of Tsuge's optimistic belief that one could both maintain the purity of their "personal life" while also making themself into the subject of an I-novel.

Additionally, she wrote, "Whenever I think about the 'novel,' I imagine a scale with 'I-novels' in the Tsuge style on one side and 'allegory' on the other. These two are polar opposites, and the 'novel' must not go to either extreme; it must fluctuate between the two sides. Maybe it is because his illustrations are a form of allegorical expression that his written work tends towards the opposite extreme."

As Akira looked over the other essays contained within

The Scene of Expression, he noticed a piece titled "Curses and Reproductions."

Tomioka Taeko begins "Curses and Reproductions" by citing an interview with a "Dr. S" published in the May 1984 issue of *Photographic Era*. After witnessing the suicide of a mother of a disabled child and seeing families collapse under the pressure of raising disabled children, Dr. S, a neurosurgeon, decided to create a Dutch wife for mothers and children. Dr. S proposed this unexpected solution after coming face to face with situations where the male child's sexual desire was directed at the mother.

After many prototypes and failures, Dr. S managed to produce one thousand dolls which he believed would be effective as partners for disabled people. Dr. S called those dolls his "daughters," and he is quoted as saying that "those who have requested one of my daughters must choose auspicious days for the occasion of receiving her" and that he truly felt as though he were sending daughters off to get married.

This was when Akira first developed a strong interest in the Japanese-made Dutch wives, called "sex dolls" in English, twenty-two years after Tomioka Taeko wrote this essay.

Tomioka noted the measurements of Dr. S's "daughters." According to the essay, they were 158 centimeters tall, with busts of 88 centimeters, waists of 60 centimeters, hips of 89 centimeters, and weighed 7 kilograms. Their skin was made from 100% latex, and the subcutaneous fat of rubber. When he looked this up online, Akira found that these types of dolls were now primarily made of silicone.

In terms of its texture, elasticity, and translucency, silicone was the material that most closely resembled human skin, and

Mistress Koharu

it could be used to reproduce even the most delicate features of the human body.

Further, contemporary dolls had frames made of stainless steel, industrial plastic, brass, and aluminum, and as their joints were made of fiber-reinforced plastic, their shoulders, groin, hips, and knees could all be moved freely.

Akira had imagined a love doll shrugging and smiling, and he thought to himself that at least once he'd like to see a real one.

While online, Akira had stumbled upon Orient Industry. Of the handful of love doll makers within Japan, Orient Industry was the oldest and largest, the premier brand. Because, at the time, Akira lived in a dormitory for single men, he wouldn't have been able to bring home a love doll. However, Orient Industry had a showroom and took reservations for tours. Out of curiosity, Akira had headed to their showroom in Okachimachi.

Over fifty dolls had been on display, dressed in a variety of fashions and striking a range of poses, and while Akira did find some charm in their deportment and construction, he did not find a doll whose face he liked. The heads were connected by joints and interchangeable, but they all looked like characters from comics or anime and were made up like popular idols; they had felt quite distant from his own preferences.

At the recommendation of an editor who joined the publishing company at the same time as him, Akira had watched the film *Cape Fear*, directed by J. Lee Thompson, starring Gregory Peck and featuring Robert Mitchum in the role of the unforgettable villain. Akira fostered a secret adoration of the actress Lori Martin, the only daughter of the lawyer played by Peck—and he had hoped for a doll with a similar, daintily featured face.

After the tour of the showroom, Akira continued to browse the webpages of love doll makers and maniac fans, and among them he regularly visited a certain connoisseur's webpage called Taa-bo's Dress Up Reference Room. And though his interest in love dolls never waned, he never encountered a doll that made him take the leap and make an actual purchase.

Then a few years after leaving the dormitory, in the fall of 2014, he had happened upon a youth magazine's special issue on love dolls. One of the articles in the issue said that Gallery Hitogata in Yokohama's Naka Ward held a biannual exhibition and sale of love dolls assembled from around the world. The owner of the gallery was the manager of a major restaurant in Chinatown, and he collected love dolls for his personal amusement.

So twelve months ago, mid-December 2014, Akira exited the gates of Keikyu Hinodecho Station and headed for Gallery Hitogata. As he had previously researched, the gallery was located below the Keikyu Main Line that ran alongside the Ooka River, halfway between Hinodecho Station and Koganecho Station. This area used to be a red-light district, overrun with prostitution and drug trafficking. However, the commencement of a construction project to repair and reinforce the elevated Keikyu Main Line in case of earthquakes triggered evictions of the shops and residences under the rail line, as well as the establishment of the Koganecho Area Management Center, a non-profit organization with the goal of beautifying the area.

As part of their activities, in 2011, the organization established a new facility called Konagecho New Studio Beneath the Rails in the one-hundred-meter space below the train tracks between Kogane Bridge and Suekichi Bridge. The facility combined gallery spaces, shops, studios, and meeting rooms.

Gallery Hitogata was housed within that complex. Akira walked along the footpath between the tracks and the river, searching for the gallery.

Konagecho New Studio Beneath the Rails was a long, two-story, rectangular glass box stuffed beneath the train tracks, and Gallery Hitogata was on the second floor. On the first floor was a used bookstore, Artbook Bazaar, which specialized in art books.

Akira climbed the wooden stairs, then, walking along the glass wall, made one pass of the hallway before opening the door of the gallery. There were no other visitors. A small, fat man built like a penguin who, like Jean-Paul Sartre, had a lazy right eye approached him. He said something to Akira, but as a train passed overhead just as he began to speak, Akira couldn't catch what he was saying.

The man introduced himself as the gallery manager and politely led Akira to the display space. The floor was covered in the same wood as the hallway, and aside from the entrance, all the walls were glass, with off-white lacquered boards positioned to block the sun—and people's glances—from the outside. Soft downlighting illuminated the small space, where fifteen or so dolls striking various poses lay in wait.

"Our specialty is foreign-made dolls," the man said in a whisper. "These are mostly from America, from Abyss Creations in San Marcos in Southern California. This company doesn't call their products love dolls, but 'RealDolls.'"

Akira looked at the dolls one by one. Both the build and

makeup of these dolls, which were clearly made for American tastes, made Akira deeply uncomfortable. Their breasts and butts were emphasized to the extreme, and all together they felt forbidding to him, the thickness of their eyebrows and plumpness of their lips simply abnormal. Were they supposed to look like some Hollywood actresses?

After looking over about two-thirds of the dolls, Akira had begun to lose interest. Then, when he arrived in front of a doll sitting on a stand in the corner of the display room, he stopped in his tracks.

This doll had an entirely different aesthetic from those made by Abyss—she had short, black hair, and looked undeniably Asian. In English, one might call someone with her clearly defined features a handsome woman. Yes, she was without question a handsome doll.

She was wearing a purple cotton dress. It fit her loosely, and the hem came down far enough to cover her ankles, but the sleeves were short and tied back at her elbows. The whole dress was embroidered with colorful flowers and trimmed with white lace; it made Akira think of the traditional clothing of some Eastern European tribe. The fabric had faded slightly, which exaggerated the yellowing of the lace.

"The gallery owner purchased this one. According to him, this doll was made in a studio in the suburbs of Budapest, Hungary. Supposedly the posthumously discovered work of the legendary doll-maker Giuseppe. The ancestors of the people of Hungary were originally Asian nomads, so I imagine that explains how she acquired such a face.

"This doll had been sent to St. Petersburg in Russia as part of a special exhibition; the owner picked up whatever dolls didn't sell. He got her along with two French dolls. Here, the French dolls sold right away, but this one ..."

Once again, a train passed overhead, cutting off their conversation.

"The owner said she had a nickname in Russian, and that name translates to something like 'leftovers.'"

Here the manager's story veered further off the tracks.

"I've heard there is a small village north of St. Petersburg, where every year they host a Dutch wife river race. Contestants race inflatable dolls down the rapids of the local river. Occasionally, there are even deaths."

Akira hadn't just liked the looks of this doll. With just one glance he had felt somehow that they would be able to talk to each other, that they'd get along. He was drawn in by the intense magnetic force she was emanating, but he did not mention this to the manager.

"Why hasn't anyone wanted to buy her?"

"A black-haired Mongoloid in Russia? And in Japan, it's her size. She must be about 165 centimeters tall. They make all the dolls smaller here. There are optimal proportions for dolls, you know. At Orient Industry, all the dolls are between 148 and 155 centimeters tall, their busts are ..."

Akira recalled a television show he saw on Animal Planet about dog shelters in America. Since it's generally assumed that big, black dogs don't find owners, they are all put down.

After taking a perfunctory look at the remaining dolls, Akira returned to the Hungarian-born doll. He took a photo of her and then asked, "Can you please take off her clothes?"

3

Upon deciding to purchase the doll, Akira asked if there was anything to prove it was actually the work of the famous artist Giuseppe, some sort of product guarantee. The manager said that unfortunately he had no such documentation, but proceeded to take out a handwritten memo left by the gallery owner. Indeed, the name "Giuseppe" was written where the manager indicated. The manager attached a red ribbon saying "Sold" to the embroidered breast of the doll and whispered, "Congratulations."

After processing the payment on Akira's credit card, the manager handed him a pamphlet for first-time doll purchasers, clearly just put together and printed out on the office computer, titled "Dear New Love Doll Owners."

Akira returned home, and, using the photos he took in the gallery, identified the embroidered pattern on the doll's dress as a traditional Hungarian design known as Matyo embroidery. He learned Matyo was the name of a region approximately 130 kilometers east of Budapest, said to be the poorest area in all of Hungary. There, the majority of residents worked in agriculture and were, uncommon in Hungary, primarily Roman Catholic. The patterns of the embroidery were known for their use of roses, birds, tulips and other sumptuous motifs, and in 2012 it was registered with UNESCO as a form of intangible cultural heritage.

Akira began to read "Dear New Love Doll Owners."

<u>CAUTION!!!</u>
1. Tight-fitting clothing and wire brassieres may damage your doll's supple skin.

Mistress Koharu

2. Dark-colored fabrics (black, red, purple, brown, blue) may transfer color to your doll's skin.
3. High-heeled shoes increase risk of falls.
4. Changing your doll's clothing is a constant challenge. Front or back fasteners are fine for clothing on the upper half of her body, but you cannot use side fasteners. However, skirts that fasten to the side present no problem.
5. When posing your doll, poses such as holding the doll's arms above her head, standing the doll straight up or at attention, squatting the doll excessively low (or raising the knees high in a sitting or lying position), or squeezing the doll's breasts together may put excessive force on the silicon, causing rips or damaged joints.

[...]

Recommended Clothing

- Camisoles and fabric brassiere sets. Stretch fabrics, thin knitwear, and jersey items.
- For sexy options, consider a set with an open top and mini-skirt or string bikini swimsuit.
- Only use fingerless gloves. It is difficult to insert the doll's fingers in regular gloves.

The Hole/Misc.

- Included in your purchase are two types of Japanese-made holes (genitals): opened and closed types. Please consult with a love doll maker for specific questions about their use. All makers offer a wide selection of parts which can easily be purchased individually.

[...]

Thank you for your purchase. We appreciate your patience as you wait for your doll to arrive.

Sincerely,

Gallery Hitogata Manager

It would be over a week before the exhibition ended and the doll would be sent to Akira's apartment, so he spent the time with fashion magazines and mail-order shopping catalogues spread across his coffee table. Until now, he had never paid much attention to women's clothes. In all his time working in magazines, he had never once handled a woman's magazine.

He used the magazines and catalogues to gather basic information, and then on the weekend he went out to department stores and boutiques to make his actual purchases. He purchased a cashmere tunic coat, a wool one-piece dress, lingerie, panty stockings, socks, shoes, scarves, accessories such as earrings and necklaces, a parasol for the sun, and considering the possibility that he might take her for a drive, sunglasses and masks as well. Once, he even paused for a second in the department for menstrual products.

In two or three of the stores, female staff gave him strange looks; they must have been wondering if he was a crossdresser. Akira also bought thicker curtains to replace the ones in his bedroom, which had been hanging there since he had moved in, and replaced the mattress and sheets of his king-sized single bed.

At the end of the year, a large, heavy, rectangular cardboard box arrived. The box was plain, and the packing slip listed the product name as "furniture."

After much struggling, he was just barely able to get the box through the door to his bedroom. From within the thick, double-layered cardboard, emerged Koharu, still dressed in Matyo embroidery. Akira lifted her up, laying her across his arms, and carried her to the bed.

Paying careful attention to the range of motion of her joints, he delicately bent and arranged her arms and legs, removed her dress, carried her to the bathroom, and gave her a shower.

Her skin was smooth, youthful, and a brilliant white. He dressed her in the lingerie set of lace-covered silk shorts, a brassiere, and a slip and leaned her in a relaxed position against the headboard of his bed.

In the pamphlet he had received from the gallery was a warning that if you leave the doll in a position that creates wrinkles in the crotch, stomach, side, or back of the legs for an extended period of time, it may cause cracks to form when repositioning, so it was best to leave the body in a wrinkle-free position as much as possible. Take care not to forget that her body is made of silicone, the pamphlet reminded.

There were tears and frayed spots on Koharu's dress, and it smelled of mold. When he tried washing it by hand in the sink, the water turned blackish red from the dirt and dye. After he dried the dress out, he sent it for the most expensive cleaning option at the dry cleaners, and when it was returned he hung it in the closet along with her other clothes.

Akira did not dislike these little chores. In fact, they allowed him to demonstrate his attentiveness and dedication, and he took them up eagerly.

He was, however, soon met with a surprise. About ten days after her arrival, some oil-like substance began to leak from the surface of Koharu's skin, dirtying her shorts and underclothing. When he emailed the experts at Orient Industry asking what was wrong, there came an immediate reply. This was a phenomenon known as "bleed"; the oil added to soften the silicone was leaking from the surface of the doll. The oil should be removed with a cleaning product such as Magiclean. The doll should then be showered, thoroughly dried off, and dusted with baby powder to prevent further bleed. The baby powder will not only give the doll's skin a human-like feel, but also prevent the buildup of static electricity and the collection of dust. The response from Orient Industry included a postscript mentioning that when all the oil had left the doll's body, the silicon would harden and the doll would have reached the end of its life.

The love doll's eyes could be moved, as could its tongue. The mock genitals were called a "hole," and there was an empty space to insert that hole in Koharu's nether regions. There was also a part called a "hole cap" that was to be inserted to prevent wrinkling in the crotch area when a hole wasn't in use.

When she arrived, the empty space in Koharu's crotch was stuffed with high-grade cork. The standard-type holes included in the packaging were so carefully constructed, Akira found himself transfixed.

Usually, there was only one empty space in a love doll's crotch for inserting a hole. To create another one in the rear to replicate an anus was considered technically difficult for structural reasons. Inclusion of such a space would inevitably lead to weakening of the groin region and the hip joints.

Koharu, however, had two spaces. This, Akira had seen with his own two eyes when he had the manager of Gallery Hitogata undress her.

From the beginning, Akira's sexual relations with the doll were simple, vanilla. While he found pleasure in missionary and doggy style, he did not attempt any risky positions such as cowgirl.

In his first few days of living with Koharu, a sense of familiarity of the sort he'd never felt before took shape within him, and Akira was struck by a premonition that their relationship would grow to be a close one. His sense in the gallery that they'd make a good match must have been correct.

While he bathed the doll, patted her down with baby powder, and changed her clothes, he would talk about whatever trivial matters came to him. That was good for his mental health, and he discovered the importance of having someone who would listen to his troubles.

"There's a branch of a university hospital near my office, and in the lobby there, there's this coffee vending machine. It was on that variety show *Tokoro-san no Me ga Ten!* on Nippon TV. Sometimes on my way back from lunch I get a jumbo-sized mill-ground coffee mocha for 180 yen. There's one with eleven grams of sugar, and one with sixteen grams. I always get the eleven gram one with cream. For a vending machine it takes a while for the cup to come out, but while you wait it plays that song 'Coffee Rumba' by Nishida Sachiko: *'Long ago, a great Arab monk gave a sad man who'd given up on love an amber drink so rich in smell it tingles …'* It's nice to listen to that song while you wait for your coffee. There are a couple of other fans of this vending machine in my office as well."

One night, about three weeks after Koharu had arrived, Akira stopped by a bar in Jimbocho before heading home. After he showered, he laid on the bed and while touching Koharu's chest said, "Last night on NHK they played an episode of the travel documentary *Shin Nihon Fudoki*, I think it was the one called 'Osaka Babe Ruth.' I had it recorded. The backing song was by Ueda Masaki, and it was about the people living near Osaka Harbor, people from Okinawa and barge families, fishermen who worked in the mouth of the Yodo River. I thought it was a good show."

Unprompted, he started telling a story he had heard from his father.

"My family is originally from Ikeda City in Osaka," he began. "When my father was in elementary school, sometime at the start of the third decade of Showa, my grandpa took him to see his great-grandfather's house in Fushiodai in Ikeda. It was this enormous house, all fenced in, and with this great kabukimon-style gate, a wooden one with a crossbar on the top that sticks out on both sides. On the other side of the trees in the garden, my father could make out the second story of the wooden house. Then they went to see a nearby temple where my grandpa played when he was a child. But the temple was abandoned and no one was there. There was a placard with a list of all the people in the neighborhood who had donated money to the temple, and they found my great-grandpa's name there and how much he had donated.

"My grandpa passed away when I was eight, in Minoh, Osaka. When I was three or four he'd let me sleep in his arms, and he always sang me Osaka bedtime songs or lullabies or whatever you want to call them. '*Akira / Starts with A / Anjuro / Ants a-hoisting / Aren't they? / Aren't they?*' And it goes on, but that's all I remember. It was like a spell or a curse or something, when I'd hear it I'd get so, so sleepy."

Koharu, who had been lying beside him, lifted up her body and repeated,

"*Ants a-hoisting / Aren't they? / Aren't they?*"

Akira was drunk. He broke into a full grin and said, "Amazin'. You memorized it!" in his Osaka dialect. In the moment, he did not find it the least bit strange that Koharu had risen and begun speaking on her own.

4.

Yano Akira began working at the publisher in 1998, just two years before what was widely perceived as the end of the twentieth century and the start of the new millennium. The following year, the publisher would begin publication of a partwork—a publication released in sections—called *Record of the 20th Century*. They planned to release one volume a week for each year of the century, covering the history of the twentieth century in both Japan and the rest of the world.

Incidentally, the twentieth century actually started in 1901, not 1900. The first century began in year 1, and thus its final year was year 100—the year zero did not exist, and thus the new millennium would actually begin in 2001.

After completing his three-month training period, Akira was assigned to the editorial department, as he had requested upon hiring, and began working as the assistant to the two editors in charge of *Record of the 20th Century*. His work consisted of proofreading—comparing the proofs against original texts and correcting any typos or other errors, while also keeping an eye on the factual accuracy of the content.

Akira acquired basic editorial skills such as how to use correction symbols and handle first and second drafts. He also learned how to collect the necessary materials for editing and fact checking historical texts, registering as a user of the National Diet Library in Nagatacho for this purpose. He would keep note of the content that he couldn't satisfactorily check with the materials in the company library and, once a week, make his way there.

As this particular partwork was a graphic magazine using photographs to illustrate wars, disasters, changes in customs, and other important incidents, the quantity of photographs they could collect would be key in determining the quality of the work. Therefore, the editor of each issue worked with specialized staff gathering photos, and they amassed an enormous collection of historical images. On occasion, rare, once forgotten photographs were rediscovered through the process.

Once, Akira discovered a black and white photo of a meeting of the Imperial Council at the Imperial Palace printed backwards in a second draft, and he just managed to replace it in time, averting certain catastrophe. The writer of that article had joked that "a car full of far-right protesters were already on their way," and was so relieved the mistake was rectified that he took Akira to a restaurant in Kagurazaka and treated him to dinner.

That same writer also shared with him several stories of his hardships searching for photos, including one occasion he worked on a column in *Record of the 20th Century* that was titled "Nippon from the Outside." This column was about how Japan and the Japanese were seen by people from other countries, and in the middle of each article there would be a photo of the face of whichever person's perspective was being described.

In the 1913 (Taisho 2) issue, the column's subtitle was "Shogun Nogi Through the Eyes of a US Newspaper Reporter." The topic was how Stanley Washburn, a twenty-six-year-old special correspondent for the *Chicago Daily News*, saw Nogi Maresuke, the general in the Imperial Japanese Army who famously led the 1904 (Meiji 37) attack on a Russian military detachment in Port Arthur.

Washburn's best-known work was the book *Nogi: A Man Against the Background of a Great War*, and the magazine writer explained to Akira how he had to find a photo of this journalist's face. However, no matter where he looked, he couldn't find any publication in Japan that had run a portrait of him. He could have reached out to American media, starting with the *Chicago Daily News*, but there was simply no time. The writer was under pressure and spent several nights visited by nightmares where the column, with an empty space where the photo should have been, came chasing after him.

One day, as he worried himself, he had a sudden flash of brilliance and recalled that he had heard the U.S. Embassy in Akasaka had a wealth of materials relating to America. Though he may have been grasping at straws, he called their publicity office. The voice on the other line asked if he knew the date of Washburn's death, and after answering, he was told to try checking the obituaries of the *New York Times*, as that paper was well known for publishing photos of the deceased.

Upon hearing that, the writer darted from his office and rushed to the Diet Library, where he finally found a photo of the young Washburn, and was also shocked to find that the library had complete archives of not just the *New York Times* but also the *Times*, *Le Figaro*, and numerous newspapers of record from around the world.

After his time on this partwork project, Akira worked on men's weekly magazines for quite some time before being assigned to a men's monthly, where he was faced with a certain situation that bothered him.

That monthly poured a lot of resources into their nonfiction pieces and wasted no effort on developing their writing talent. One day, when he was editing an article on the Glico-Morinaga Incident, Akira's eyes stopped on a passage. The Glico-Morinaga Incident began in Nishimiya City, Futamicho just after 9 p.m. on Sunday, March 18, Showa 59 (1984) when a group calling itself "The Monster with Twenty-One Faces" raided the home of Ezaki Katsuhisa, the forty-two-year-old president of food company Ezaki Glico, and kidnapped him.

The passage in question read, "The gang infiltrated the house through the servant's door using a spare key and quick as the wind raced up the stairs of the Ezaki residence to the bedroom on the left side of the stairway." However, this depiction, in a piece which attested to be nonfiction, sparked a deep suspicion in Akira. It described how the criminals moved through the house as they searched for Katsuhisa, who was on the second floor bathing with his children, but no one had actually witnessed this scene.

Mistress Koharu

There were several other sections that repeated this sort of imaginative depiction, and each time he found one he left a Post-it with a simple comment, but when Akira checked the revised manuscript, the writer had ignored all of his notes and the piece was published as it was.

For Akira, the question of whether a writer of nonfiction can use their imagination and insert such suggestive passages between the facts soon grew into a larger question. Whether nonfiction or otherwise, all writing must necessarily take the form of a narrative. Therefore, did this not then mean that the adding or subtracting from the facts to create structure and the incorporation of the writer's own biases and flourishes always happened somewhere in the background of a piece of writing? And was this authorial intervention not also a sort of black box, impenetrable to readers who have no means of evaluating the function and extent of the author's imagination?

An inspiration for this question were the crime novels *Incident* by Ooka Shohei and *Vengeance is Mine* by Saki Ryuzo. Akira harbored the suspicion that when the authors wrote these crime novels—both based on real incidents—they were actually doing the same thing as nonfiction writers. He felt that the presumption that the use of imagination increased as one moved from nonfiction to fiction based on true events, then further increased as one moved to wholly imagined fiction, was both naïve and contrived.

A case in point was Honda Yasuharu's *Kidnapping*, which carefully retraced the second half of the life of Kohara Tamotsu, the criminal behind the Yoshinobu-chan kidnapping case of March of Showa 38 (1963), and was considered a classic work of postwar nonfiction. In the final chapter, "Last Will and Testament," Kohara's kidnapping and murder of a child was described using Kohara's own testimony, and Akira had been moved by the seeming truthfulness and power of this section.

The author recounted how Kohara bundled up innocent Yoshinobu, who so completely trusted his kidnapper, in an overcoat, before quoting Kohara's own words: "I turned the boy to face me, wrapping his legs around my sides as I held him up." He then fixed a snakeskin belt around the sleeping boy's neck. This bloodcurdling scene achieved a sense of reality because it was based on fact, but Kohara's confession was depicted through a combination of the third-person, objective perspective, and monologue, and the use of such literary techniques transformed it into a first-class realist novel.

Four years ago, Akira moved from the monthly magazine to the educational books department, where he now spent his time pondering the ever-present fictionality of historical records of a supposedly more objective nature.

<u>5.</u>

While in university, Akira had a girlfriend three years younger than himself. After graduating from a women's college, she studied abroad at a language school at the University of Toronto. Six months later, she transferred to the University of Toronto as a third-year student, and, after earning a Canadian degree, chose not to return home but to remain in Canada, where she married a local man.

However, she and Akira had stayed in touch through email,

and they had even met up when she visited Japan with her children. But as she had never once explained her reasoning behind suddenly cutting things off with Akira and heading to Canada and he never found the chance to question her about it, he still held onto unresolved feelings.

In 2008, the year Akira turned thirty-two, Prime Minister Fukuda resigned and the Aso cabinet took power; outside of Japan, American financial uncertainty spread across the globe, and the value of the Tokyo Stock Exchange plummeted. Back then, Akira was editing a weekly men's magazine, and in April three new part-time employees, all women, were assigned to his editorial department.

In September, when Lehman Brothers went bankrupt, the magazine immediately put together a special feature on the collapse of the American financial giant. After finishing his read through of the first draft of that article, Akira spotted one of the new employees on the subway platform and chatted with her for a bit. Thereafter, they developed a relationship that consisted of them occasionally stopping by at a café for tea on the way home or going to see movies and dining together on days off.

Akira liked her carefree and positive personality and also considered her frankness and ability to talk without dressing things up a great virtue. Her parents had gotten divorced when she was still in elementary school, so she and her younger sister were raised by her mother, but her father paid child support and always kept his promise to meet them once a month. Her family had lived in a rented house near Chitose-karasuyama Station on the Keio Line, and her mother worked at a private girls' high school in Kichijoji doing clerical work. When it was a few days before payday and finances were tight for the family, "All we had to eat with our rice was stir-fried veggies," Akira's colleague had once said, smiling.

Akira heard from her that she had only been to the seaside city of Kamakura once, so one Sunday at the end of the year, they planned to meet at Kita-Kamakura Station to go for a walk on the Tenen Hiking Trail. He had invited his old girlfriend there before, but she had come down with flu just before they agreed to meet, and the hike had never happened. Since then, he had walked the trail several times by himself.

The course ran from the north to the east of Kamakura, along a series of short mountains about 100 to 150 meters tall, called sometimes, half in jest, the "Kamakura Alps."

The pair climbed the stone steps of Kenchoji Temple and tread over the thick layer of oak leaves as they clung close to the edge of the mountain ridge. Over their heads darted a group of ten-odd squirrels, practically flying across the treetops. Akira watched the woman follow the squirrels into the distance with her eyes and said, "This ridge goes all the way to Kanazawa Bunko," as he pointed to the east.

They walked to the peak of Mount Ohira and could see spread out below them the city of Kamakura as well as the mountains of the Miura Peninsula. Mount Fuji hid behind a veil of thin clouds, refusing to show itself. In a tea house on the Tenen cliffs, they drank hot amazake, blowing on it to cool it down.

Occasionally a hiker would appear from an unexpected side road or from behind an enormous tree and greet them. Akira wasn't much for these greetings between hikers. As a middle-aged man fully fitted in hiking gear passed them, he said,

"Some of the ravines in the middle ridge of the Miura Alps are still snowed in. It was quite the struggle," and then walked off.

"Snowy ravines in the Miura Alps?"

"He must be kidding around. He's just playing hiker I bet."

They walked to the Zuisenji Temple trail head, and after descending the mountains and praying at the Tsurugaoka Hachimangu Shrine, they stopped by a cozy little restaurant with counter seating called Yoshiro near Komachi-dori and then headed home. Akira clearly remembered that she had been a surprisingly strong walker who didn't break a sweat, and that at each rest spot or lookout she would stare endlessly at Sagami Bay.

Their company's hiring policy stipulated that part-time women could work for a maximum of two years; they would work for one year in one department and then another year in a different department. Also, each summer and winter they would be paid bonuses of approximately one and a half months' salary. During the Employment Ice Age following the bubble, these positions were popular with young women, but employment in such jobs required a recommendation from a full-time employee.

The following March, Akira's colleague was moved from the editorial department to the manga department, and Akira was also reassigned from the weekly magazine to the monthly one, so for some time they did not see each other.

Then one day in May, when he attended a union meeting in the company's auditorium, Akira sat next to another single man who had joined the company at the same time as him, Okitsu Yasutaka. This manga editor Okitsu was like a walking, talking manifestation of the phrase "Do your own thing." When he had joined the company, he was attending lessons at a Brazilian jujitsu dojo, and later Akira heard that he had taken up saxophone classes at a Yamaha music school. For his summer vacation he had gone to Bali and flipped his rented motorcycle, leading to broken bones. He was the sort of man always up to something and never without a story to tell, but he had few friends. For some reason he was especially fond of Akira, and when they would occasionally bump into each other, he would always invite Akira for a drink at the same izakaya he frequented on Jizo-dori in Edogawabashi.

That day too they headed to Jizo-dori and snacked on pike conger teriyaki from the island of Nushima, south of Awaji, as they drank shochu highballs. Okitsu couldn't drink much, and once he got a little tipsy he had a sharp tongue. When he started saying, "That new part timer who joined last April, she's so innocent. She's great, but ..." Akira had a bad feeling but listened on as though unbothered. "We were having tea in the cafeteria in the new building, and when I asked her if she liked fortune telling, she seemed really interested, so that Saturday night we agreed to meet at this café, Hato, near Shibuya Station. I told her to bring a deck of playing cards."

Okitsu also brought a deck of cards, and as he and the part-time woman sat facing each other across the café table, he had explained, "We're going to test our compatibility. The closer the cards' numbers and suits, the better our match."

Following Okitsu's instructions, they shuffled the cards, swapped decks with each other, and then spread the decks face down in two rows across the table.

They each picked one card at the same time and looked at it,

Mistress Koharu

and after gathering the decks back up together, placed the card they chose at the top and cut the deck. In other words, there was no way for the other person to know which card they had chosen. They traded decks again and searched for the card they had chosen in the other deck. Once they had found it, they showed it to the other on the count of one, two, three. Okitsu and the girl had showed the exact same card, the six of spades.

"I never thought she would have been so shocked. This is the very, very simplest of card tricks. Even a kid can do it. When you first shuffle, all you have to do is remember what the last card, the one at the very bottom, is. That one will wind up next to the other person's card after they cut the deck."

"You got the best possible match," Akira said.

"After that we went drinking, and, well, we had a good time. I invited her to Maruyamacho and she just came along."

Akria nodded limply and whispered, "That's great."

6.

Every Friday after work, Akira stopped by a bar in Jimbocho on his way home. Called Rosebud, the bar was located in Suruga-daishita, diagonally across from Chiyoda Municipal Ochano-mizu Elementary School, between a stationary store and The Asakusa Hanko Center, a name-seal shop.

The owner was a woman named Ukai Chikako, and she ran the place by herself. Two years older than Akira, she had first met him when she was training as a bartender at a long-estab-lished bar called Kohaku in Ueno-Hirokoji, after Akira had been taken there by an older colleague in the editorial department.

The colleague who took him there was a pleasant old man who had boasted about having read Iwanami Shoten's *Complete Works of Classical Japanese Literature* in its entirety three times over, and even after retiring, he came to the office three days a week, working on commission.

Upon completing her two years of bartender training, Ukai Chikako opened this bar on Kinka-dori in Jimbocho in April, 2009, and Akira had been visiting since then. Back when it opened, he still lived in the single's dorm in Mejirodai.

Chikako was born in Shiga Prefecture, in Takatsuki-cho, on the north side of Lake Biwa, a town known for Doganji Temple and the eleven-faced Kanon statue, a designated national treasure. After graduating from a prefectural high school, she moved to Tokyo and worked for fifteen years at a high-rise hotel in Ikebukuro. When she quit the hotel, she made ends meet with her severance pay and unemployment benefits while working as a bartender apprentice, until, in 2009, she was finally able to open her own bar.

Upon opening the heavy wooden door of Rosebud, one was greeted by a narrow entrance and a four-seater sofa and table. On the right side, extending to the back of the space, was a fifteen-seater counter made of a single piece of elm shaped like a half horseshoe. Behind those seats was an alcove-like area, designed so that five or six patrons could relax in a space separated from the rest of the customers.

Next to the alcove was the bathroom, the size and layout of which shocked most first-time customers. There was a large full-length mirror built into the wall—its frame decorated with countless tiny seashells—and an intricately structured chigaidana shelving unit made of rosewood. And at the end of the long pathway between those two was an off-white throne with a ceramic tank and a washlet. "I fell in love with the bathroom, so I took the place with all the furnishings," Chikako would answer before even being asked.

The downlights hanging from the ceiling were so dim one could safely call them ornamental, and customers emptied their glasses primarily by the light of smokeless, scentless mini oil lamps set throughout the bar. Music was played exclusively on vinyl.

Once Akira asked, "There aren't many people living around here, right?" to which Chikako replied, "People think that, but on either side of Hakusan-dori from Jimbocho to Sarugakucho, and from Nishi-Kanda 1-chome to 2-chome, there are actually quite a few apartment buildings. There are a lot of restaurants and convenience stores, actually. Even a gym."

Sometime after that, Akira was introduced to a real estate agent drinking at the bar, and after visiting several apartments around the area, he wound up moving into his current place in Nishi-Kanda 2-chome.

Chikako was convinced that she had bad luck with men. Two years after coming to Tokyo, she met a young man named Negi Shintaro at In the Still Night, one of the little bars at the east end of Shinjuku Golden Gai, near Hanazono Shrine. Negi said he was from Okayama Prefecture and was twenty-eight years old, that he had quit a private music school and worked as a studio musician while trying to make it as a songwriter. When Chikako started frequenting love hotels with him, it became clear that he was a regular user of amphetamines.

"You take one hit and inspiration for new songs just comes welling up, and you can't stop," he explained, though he didn't seem to have ever pitched any song he had written to a record company. There was something weak-willed yet kind about him, and Chikako saw that it would probably be impossible for him to sell himself, build up a reputation in the biz, and fight his way to the top of the industry, so she assumed the music was an excuse and the amphetamines were just to maximize his own sexual pleasure.

Negi, who had sensed Chikako's judgmental attitude, never once tried to get her to use. He was a fan of Aoyama Masaaki's book *Dangerous Drugs*, published by Data House, and would occasionally spill gems of knowledge like, "There are two kinds of uppers, methamphetamines and amphetamines. Methamphetamines were actually discovered by Dr. Nagai Nagayoshi of Tokyo Imperial University in 1893."

Sitting beside him on a hotel bed, Chikako had watched Negi administer intravenous injections on himself countless times. On the bedside table he'd prepare a bottle of mineral water and a cup, an ashtray, syringe, an ear scraper, a thin rubber tube, and a hotel notepad. He'd remove from the breast pocket of his shirt a plastic bag the size of a stamp that he called a "package." Using the ear scraper, which he had for this purpose alone, he'd scrape one hit's worth of uppers, which looked like rock sugar, onto the notepad.

He'd stick his needle into the cup of water, pull back the plunger to fill the chamber, and then eject the water into the ashtray. After he did this two or three times to clean out the needle, he'd remove the chamber and insert the drugs, and then after reattaching it, he'd again pull in a small amount of water from the cup. For about ten seconds, Negi would rub the syringe, waiting for the drugs to dissolve completely into the water. This whole process he carried out gracefully, each action flowing smoothly into the next.

He would then roll up the left sleeve of his shirt and tell Chikako to tie the rubber tube around his bicep. When she had finished tying, he would insert the needle into one of the swelling veins on the inside of his elbow, let the blood come into the syringe, and after confirming that the needle was in a vein, hold the syringe in place and tell her, "Loosen it." When she untied the tube, he would push down slowly on the plunger, his eyelids trembling ever so slightly, and inject the drugs.

While Chikako had considered breaking up with this man many times, she had never managed it because she received great sexual pleasure from him.

The effect of stimulants can generally be described as an increase in concentration and desire for activity, and in Negi's case, this meant he could have sex without showing any signs of fatigue, sometimes continuing intercourse for an hour and a half.

One day, two years after they had begun to see each other, a couple of detectives from the Ueno Police Department showed up at her apartment.

During the questioning by police at her home, Chikako was informed that Negi had died a suspicious death. They had contacted her because her phone number and address, as well as records of their frequent contact, were found on Negi's cell phone. Later, she learned that his death was classified not as a suicide or homicide, but rather an accidental death due to excessive use of amphetamines.

Negi taught Chikako to fear drugs, but he taught her something else as well, a sexual technique maybe best called "oral massage." After Negi's death, Chikako had relationships with three different men, and all three were startled by her skillfulness in the bedroom.

Once, when Chikako was working at the Ueno-Hirokoji bar and Akira visited alone, she asked him as they chatted, "Hey, you know those big shops they've got everywhere? The ones that sell brand goods for cheap. Why do they call them 'outlets'?"

Akira replied, "Well, in English there's this expression 'let out' that means getting rid of excess stock or damaged products. Outlet is just 'let out' flipped around. I guess properly speaking they're called 'outlet stores.'"

Chikako had never met a man who explained foreign words this way. She liked Akira. Several times after that she tried to seduce him, but he always remained noncommittal and would never play along.

When Rosebud first opened, not many customers came, and, perhaps to show his support, Akira would pop in two or three times a week. After about a month passed, sometime in the middle of May, Akira showed up one night after 10 p.m. He took a seat, looking different from usual, and without ordering anything, let out a tremendous sigh.

Chikako placed a wet hand towel in front of him and waited for him to speak.

"I just went to eat pike conger," he said. There was displeasure in his voice.

After eleven, a middle-aged couple left the bar, and the only ones remaining on either side of the counter were Chikako and

Akira. Paulinho da Viola's sorrowful voice flowed from the record player.

Chikako stopped wiping the glass in her hand and said, "You're not yourself tonight."

Akira looked down and said, "Don't worry about it," then went silent.

Closing time was midnight, but Chikako said, "I think I'll wrap up for the night. Want to go for a drink somewhere?" She made her voice cheerful.

Akira nodded noncommittally.

"Or would you like to come by my place for a drink?" This time she lowered her tone and made her voice smoky.

The two took the Hanzomon Line from Jimbocho Station to Mitsukoshimae, where they changed to the Ginza Line, and then got off at Tawaramachi Station. They climbed the stairs outside the ticket gate and returned above ground at the Kotobuki 4-chome intersection, where Asakusa-dori and Kokusai-dori meet. The streets were glittering with damp. It must have rained while they travelled underground, but as they'd climbed down the stairs at Jimbocho Station, they had seen the crescent moon overhead. Though they hadn't travelled very far, Akira found himself feeling as though he had been transported somewhere surprisingly distant. The shops in the area had shuttered for the night, but Akira saw several neon signs saying BUTSUDAN, SHINTO SHRINES, FESTIVAL GOODS still illuminated in the night.

"Sensoji Temple is that way," Chikako said pointing north up Kokusai-dori. "And my room is there." She looked straight across the street and towards a thirteen-story building on the northeast corner of the intersection. "It really is 'ultra close' to the station, right?" she said, mimicking the expressions of real estate advertising.

Chikako's room had no unnecessary furniture or ornament; it was organized and clean. Akira liked it.

"I know. It's boring. Unlike with the shop, when it comes to my room, I've got no interest in interior design."

Akira's eyes stopped on a wooden-framed, camel-colored leather sofa placed up against the window.

"That's the only piece I like. I went a bit overboard and bought it at Noce in Kuramae. The frame is walnut. Have a seat."

After taking out a bottle of Beniotome kaku sesame shochu from Kurume in Fukuoka Prefecture, Chikako put on music and then fixed some drinks.

"This CD's called *Slow Motion Bosa Nova*."

Akira took a seat on the sofa, and Chikako sat straight on the wood flooring, looking up at him with her glass in her hand. When Akira asked her about her income from the bar, Chikako answered frankly.

"With my current income, the rent here and for the bar is a bit tough. But I'm going to be in a couple of magazines soon. Two days ago I was just interviewed for *Sampo no tatsujin*, and next week *Otona no shumatsu* is coming for a photo shoot, so I guess things will be picking up."

"Apparently if you think positive thoughts, you'll attract good luck. That's what people say, anyway."

Chikako laughed. "What a line. You sound so old."

Akira did not remember when he fell asleep. He was lying on the sofa, using a cushion for a pillow, when Chikako told him, "It's morning. Time for radio calisthenics," and woke him up.

Mistress Koharu

Having just showered, Chikako was wearing a bathrobe. Silently, she handed Akira a towel and pointed to the shower.

In bed, Chikako took the lead, and Akira found himself submerged in a pleasure he had never before experienced. He was shocked to learn, thanks to the work of Chikako's tongue and lips and the careful movements of her fingers, that not only his penis but his nipples, scrotum, anus, and even the bottoms of his feet and tips of his toes were highly sensitive erogenous zones. He was overcome with tremors resembling seizures multiple times and ejaculated repeatedly.

The two slept with their bodies pressed together and woke again close to noon. Chikako's sweat gave off a smell resembling that of a salvia flower.

After leaving the apartment, they walked south down Kokusai-dori towards Kuramae, then cut across Kasuga-dori and entered a shop on their right. The first floor was a bakery, and upstairs on the second floor was a large and relaxing café space, with a long L-shaped counter and several tables.

Chikako went up to the waitress at the corner of the counter and said, "Two Early Summer Martinis."

As he looked at the menu, Akira asked, "What sweets are good here?"

"Their claim to fame is the seasonal choux crème."

At the rear of the café, they sat down in two red seats with elbow rests, and in front of each seat was a small table. Near the stairway was a large Bizen ware pot with a burnt-yellow plant as tall as a man in it.

"That's pampas grass. In Japanese it's called 'obake susuki,' ghost pampas. The flower spike is a faintly pinkish silver color, right? It so perfectly fits the mood of this café. I want to do something like that at my bar, but I can't just yet."

The Early Summer Martinis were brought to them. They weren't served in cocktail glasses but smallish, clear cut-glass cups.

"It has dry gin, dry vermouth, black tea, and pineapple juice. Their own original martini," Chikako explained.

"The bakery below and this café are run by the same person, and all the staff are young women. The owner is from Taiwan, a very charming woman. I think she's around my age. I recommend the oolong tea madeleine, galettes bretonnes, or the fig and caramel cake. The granola I serve at Rosebud is from here as well."

Akira felt a little drunk from his hair of the dog, and after a moment's hesitation, he placed some cash in a clear file he happened to have with him, printed with a color ad for one of his company's publications, and placed it on Chikako's lap. Chikako was surprised and looked back and forth at Akira's face and the file and then, without saying anything, put the file away in her bag.

From that day, Akira visited Chikako's apartment once a month on a Sunday morning. Late each Friday night, he would go to Rosebud, but always sat at the back of the bar, trying to hide his closeness with Chikako from the other patrons. Each time the bar made it into the media, the number of customers would increase, and he knew among them were several men who considered themselves "fans" of Chikako.

One day at the end of July, 2012, Akira visited Chikako's

apartment near noon, holding in his right hand a black shopping bag from the rental store Tsutaya.

"I've wanted to see this movie for a long time now. I just found it and borrowed it. Want to watch it together?"

"What's it called?"

"*Blue Mountain Range.*"

"Is it a mountain climbing documentary?"

When Akira first joined his company and was assigned to the editorial department and working on his first partwork, *Record of the 20th Century*, there was a column titled "Stars and their Famous Scenes," that covered a few major films from each year.

In the issue for Showa 24 (1949), the year Dr. Yukawa Hideki became the first Japanese person to win the Nobel Prize for physics, they covered three separate stars, Mifune Toshiro, Misora Hibari, and Hara Setsuko, and introduced films they starred in: *Stray Dog* directed by Kurosawa Akira, *The Sad Whistle* directed by Ieki Miyoji, and *Blue Mountain Range* by Imai Tadashi.

Blue Mountain Range was a Toho Studios adaptation of a novel by Ishizaka Yojiro, originally published serially in the *Asahi Shimbun*; Ide Toshiro and Imai Tadashi wrote the screen adaptation, and Imai took up the director's megaphone. The film's plot was simple: set in a bayside town in Tohoku soon after the end of the war, some students, a doctor, a female teacher, and a geisha who all believe in a democratic future band together to fight the corrupt leaders of the town. It was a massive hit upon release and set new box office records.

Akira went into the film expecting a simple propaganda piece touting the greatness of democracy; however, he was surprised at the light touch and deep pleasure with which it depicted the glory of youth, and he was entranced by Hara Setsuko's beauty, which he was witnessing for the first time. "I can't believe we had an actress like this in Japan," he said with a deep sigh.

For Chikako, it was her first time watching a black and white, 4:3 aspect-ratio, Japanese film. She watched the film from a different perspective than Akira, and at the time, she had simply listened to his impressions without sharing any of her own thoughts.

A few months later, when Akira said, "There's this famous okonomiyaki restaurant, Sentaro, and it's not even a ten-minute walk from here," Chikako suddenly recalled a shop with a similar name, "Umetaro." After Akira had left, when she searched her memory for where it was, she realized it was not a store but a person's name.

She filled the bathtub with lukewarm water, got in up to her shoulders, stretched her arms and legs, and recollected the plot of *Blue Mountain Range*.

Numata Tamao, the doctor of a girl's school played by Ryuzaki Ichiro, is attracted to the new English teacher, Shimazaki Yukiko, played by Hara Setsuko. He confesses his feelings to Umetaro, a geisha played by Kogure Michiyo, whom he is close with. Umetaro, who not only understands Numata but also loves him, hides her true feelings, and while fixing the button on his shirt which was about to come off, tells him, "You most certainly have a chance" with Shimazaki, to encourage him and lift his spirits.

Later, after having met with Shimazaki Yukiko, Umetaro drinks alone, and tells herself, "No matter what we geisha do, we'll never catch up," in reference to "decent" women as intelligent and full of life as Shimazaki. "I'll give up, I should just give up," she adds.

Chikako understood this geisha's loneliness and pain, and she found it incredibly strange that the doctor Numata was so completely oblivious to her feelings, but she also felt that Akira, who tried to rationalize his relationship with Chikako as a simple financial transaction, resembled Numata in some way.

She didn't want to marry Akira, and she didn't want him to acknowledge her as his lover either. She simply hoped that they could continue their current relationship. And in her entire troubled relationship history, she had never before wished for even such a small thing until now.

Chikako noticed a hickey in the dip under her collarbone and, covering it with the fingers of her right hand, got up and decided to take a cold shower.

7.

One day, Akira was double-checking the proofs of a history book and noticed there was something they had missed in the first draft. The same sort of mistake occurred again soon after. When he saw the red marks on another first draft left by the editor who had previously caught these same mistakes, Akira couldn't believe he'd slipped up like this. He was then struck by fear of some mental affliction, perhaps caused by a physical ailment.

However, the company physicals administered in April, 2014 found no abnormalities in Akira's health. And the only symptom he was aware of was a slight feeling of heaviness in his body.

Then, after the long public holiday at the beginning of May, Akira was contacted by an employee of the Minoh Municipal Elderly Welfare Center and informed that a social worker had visited his father, who lived alone, and reported that it would probably be best for his father to be relocated to a nursing home or some other such care facility.

Akira rushed to Minoh and after confirming that his father was unable to live independently due to his early-stage dementia, consulted with the local welfare center and went to visit several senior housing facilities in the Osaka metropolitan area. And then, upon returning to Tokyo after coercing his unwilling father into the arrangement and completing the paperwork for his entry to a facility in Nishiyodogawa Ward, he was notified that his father had applied to end his contract with the facility, and Akira had to immediately return to Osaka.

With all of this unfolding, Akira became aware that he was getting increasingly less sleep at night. He tried to resolve this issue with alcohol and increased the volume of his nightcaps, but his lack of sleep persisted, so he decided to meet with the clinical psychologist who visited the company once a month.

The doctor advised Akira to try the sleep medication triazolam, saying, "If you take this, you'll get at least six hours of deep sleep. There are cases where people wake up to use the restroom in the middle of the night and have no memories of it at all, so some do criticize it, but the effect, or should I say harm on your body, of consuming too much alcohol is certainly much greater."

Triazolam pills came in dosages of 0.25 milligrams and 0.125 milligrams; Akira received a one-month prescription for 0.25 milligrams.

Mistress Koharu

Akira had never struggled in his life until now, not even with college entrance exams or job hunting. His work as an editor suited his personality well, and he normally felt a sense of pleasure from managing his hard schedule. His only real hobbies to speak of were driving his Toyota Land Cruiser around the city and taking care of his goldfish, but he had no complaints about his lifestyle, though it revolved primarily around his office job.

Thus Akira felt a generalized nervousness at this, the first dysfunction to ever face him in his seventeen years since starting his job, and because his thoughts were so scattered—What had caused this situation? Was it because he was missing something? When would he be able to get out of this slump?—he could not come up with a solution.

Soon he was possessed by a strange delusion. Six or seven years ago an American film titled *Into the Wild* was released, and he had seen it at a theater in central Tokyo. The last scene of that film played again and again in his mind and eventually transformed into a sort of obsession.

The main character of the film, Chris, was born to a wealthy family on the East Coast of the US, and after he graduated from college he left to trek across North America without saying anything to his parents, sister, or friends. He hitchhiked and met many kinds of people, like a hippy couple and an old man without any relatives, and ultimately made it to the foot of the Alaskan mountains, where he advanced on through the great snowy wilderness. He took shelter in an abandoned bus and began to grow thin from lack of food.

The scene of Chris passing into eternal rest, starved and wrapped in a sleeping bag, haunted Akira, and gradually, through a successive chain of associations, this image of Chris transformed into a story in which he was the main character. When he wasn't at the office, he'd spend countless hours pursuing imaginary scenes where he was in his own version of *Into the Wild*.

From the center of the Kamikochi highland valley, he would set out for the peak of Tokugo Pass. He would begin walking from the Kappa-bashi Bridge, along the right bank of the Azusa River. Turning up a trail running next to a mountain stream, he'd somehow wander into a forested area and get lost among the improvised paths and, completely exhausted, collapse into a dense patch of windflowers. Having gone missing, lost in the wonders of nature, he would pass away, his undiscovered bones would bleach, and first tens then hundreds of years would pass.

For Akira, these ridiculous, dreamed-up stories were like sweet and precious memories, but he was simultaneously aware that this was a dangerous sign.

That year, he did not visit Chikako's apartment throughout July or August. He kept up his weekly Friday trips to Rosebud, so it wasn't as though they lost touch, but Chikako also made a point to avoid asking the reason he hadn't come over, and even when they did see each other in person, their conversations tended to fall flat.

He had been searching desperately for a way to get out of this slump, and then, when autumn came, he stumbled upon that special issue, sensed something, and took down the address and phone number of that gallery in Koganecho.

We look up at the night sky, find shapes and meaning in the placement of heavenly bodies that have no relation to each other, assign them names, and call them constellations. In the same way, we discover meaning in the connections between unrelated happenings in our day-to-day lives, and by choosing to act in accordance with those discoveries, our fates sometimes change.

When he had exited the Hinodecho Station gates and walked toward Gallery Hitogata, Akira had been overcome by the sensation that he was being pulled in by some strong magnetic force.

Opening the gallery door, the lazy-eyed little manager had appeared before him, and Akira recognized the series of events that led him here as a sequence of meaningful coincidences. And then, when he saw the many love dolls lined up, he was at first disappointed, but as he paused in front of Koharu, he was struck by a premonition that this would be the thing that changed his fate, and he decided to purchase her.

Living with Koharu, Akira constantly felt that she was a perfect match for him.

When he spoke to her, touching her skin, even if it was just meaningless talk about his day, the earnest expression on her face looked as though she were listening intently. When he bathed her and patted down her body with baby powder, he felt as though he could hear her speaking words of gratitude. And then, one night, Koharu sat herself up, repeated Akira's childhood lullaby, and began conversing with him.

There was now a woman waiting for him to come back home, and that woman was a good listener, was good in bed, and when he slept with her by his side, he would fall so deeply asleep that he didn't even remember his dreams. Just as he had predicted in the gallery, he had grabbed hold of the opportunity to escape from his troubles, and he learned what it had been that he was missing in his life. By developing the shared delusion between himself and Koharu, unspoiled by any third party, he had found peace.

He tossed the triazolam he no longer needed in an empty black tea can, and later, when Chikako complained she couldn't sleep, he gave it to her as a present.

Akira did not tell Chikako about Koharu. He thought that his monthly visits to Chikako's room to drown in a world of pleasure and his life with Koharu and the psychological relief she provided him were categorically different, and both were necessary for him to continue his life alone. He thought it would be impossible to make Chikako understand that Koharu was not just a tool for his sexual gratification.

Browsing the Orient Industry website, Akira learned that there were special makeup artists for love dolls. Koharu's features reminded him of a Westerner's image of an Oriental, and while undoubtedly beautiful, he felt they could be a little bit softer, maybe have a bit more of the feel of a Japanese woman, so he immediately reached out for the makeup artist's contact information and had the artist come to his home the following Saturday. The artist requested that Akira send photos via text message of Koharu's face from head on, above at an angle, and in profile. When Akira replied with five photos of her face, the response was, "Is she a Russian or Western European girl?"

The makeup artist who appeared the next Saturday afternoon was a large middle-aged woman with glasses. She closed the living room curtain, sat Koharu on the couch, and then turned on the spotlight she had brought. She took a black and white photo book out of her bag and opened to a page marked with a sticky note.

Mistress Koharu

"Have you ever heard of Marbell, the bromide specialty shop? This is a book of portraits of movie stars I found there," she said. "This doll looks like an actress called Kitahara Mie who worked at Nikkatsu, back when there was the Five-Company Agreement. Her sharp features feel quite strong. If you soften things up a bit …" she said, as she showed Akira an enlarged photo of an actress he had never seen before. "This is Ashikawa Izumi. She worked at Nikkatsu with Kitahara Mie. There's going to be a retrospective of her films playing soon at the Jimbocho Theater. I thought we could give this doll more of this sort of soft and innocent look. What do you think?"

Akira said he would leave it up to the artist. He stood next to her as she began her work, staring at the photo book, and he came to realize that the captions on the portraits were really very odd.

For example, the long caption on the page for Yoshinaga Sayuri began: "Sayuri-san entered Shibuya Ward Yoyogi Junior High School a full five years before I was even born." And then this "I" described how an underclassman in their junior high school flunked out before adding, "Yes, that's right, Sayuri-san is our true class president. Talented, cheerful, in control, and, on top of that, beautiful. One word from her and the whole class will come together. No fighting in this class."

Akira found this incredibly amusing, and upon looking at the other actresses' pages, he found another bizarre caption on Wakao Ayako's that must have been written by the same author.

"Wakao Ayako is a good woman. No complaints here. I'm a fan of hers."

It ended with the line, "I think I'd be willing to commit double suicide if it was with Wakao Ayako."

When he opened to Ashikawa Izumi's page, he found, "You think she's giving you an intelligent smile, then you're shocked to find that suddenly she's a dumb beauty. When she worked at Nikkatsu, she had the aura of a mercurial Venus. In her lead roles, her smiles are sweet nothings, but when she's in a side role, she reveals a morbid lasciviousness, and with her body trained for the stage by her time in the music troupe Shochiku Kagekidan, her borderless appeal is too hot to handle."

The lack of personal adornment actually made this one of the more reasonable captions, but if Ashikawa had read phrases like "dumb beauty" and "morbid lasciviousness," it seemed doubtful she'd consider them compliments. Overcome by these comments, Akira closed the book and looked at Koharu. She had been reborn, terrifyingly beautiful.

They moved to the dining room table and Akira made tea. The makeup artist took one sip and said with a smile, "Oh, Fauchon's Darjeeling."

"Makeup can really change the impression one gives. I never thought she'd look like an actress or a model."

"Beauties like this don't actually exist in the real world. You shouldn't let anyone else see her, man or woman. I think something bad might happen if you do."

Akira nodded and observed Koharu's transformed profile.

<u>8.</u>

Akaneya Kyoko woke up at 8 a.m. every morning. Her morning routine began with her, still in her pajamas, going to her window and opening her pastel-blue Morocco drapes and white lace curtains about ten centimeters. She wanted to check if she could see anyone on the third-floor balcony of the apartment building on the other side of the municipal park. She did this before turning on the lights.

Kyoko had moved to the fifth floor in this ten-story Leopalace apartment building in Nishi-Kanda 2-chome in December of last year, 2014. And as it was now May, she had for about half a year been observing the resident of the opposite building's third floor.

When she had first moved in, her target, Yano Akira, would wake up just before or slightly after ten, open the glass doors of the balcony, look out at the park with glazed eyes, and then sit on the couch and blankly watch TV.

Kyoko knew where he worked, even which department he was in, and was also aware that his company employed a flextime work schedule. Thus, she did not think it strange for a salaryman to wake up around ten and lazily gaze at the children playing in the park. However, as of February this year, he had begun to wake up earlier, and the glass door of his balcony would open around eight. Then when spring started to arrive, he began to head out on to the balcony and, perhaps under the influence of some sort of yoga or mindfulness practice, spend ten to fifteen minutes practicing his breathing, occasionally raising both his hands over his head to stretch his back, or twisting his body left and right, performing stretches for her to see.

Whenever she confirmed that Akira was on the balcony, she would take out from her desk her military-grade binoculars, which she had bought on Yahoo Auction, and through the 42-millimeter diameter lenses providing enlargement of up to

8.5 times, she would stare longingly at the shifts in his expression and movements of his body. Her Leopalace apartment building was approximately forty meters away from the building across the park, so through the binoculars she could view him as though she had been transported to just 4.7 meters away. Oh, just once Kyoko longed to see the area around his shoulder blades and his calf muscles up close.

Even at night and on holidays, Kyoko was often on lookout, and not even a small change to the interior of Akira's living-dining-kitchen, which she could see directly into, could get past her. To the left side of the door at the back of the room, he was keeping some kind of pet, and she needed to know what it was.

She had started spying on Akira as soon as she moved to Nishi-Kanda. Kyoko had hoped that after moving near where he lived, she could bump into him "spontaneously" somewhere, come to trade regular greetings, and then finally become more than just friends. However, after acquiring a tool as convenient as these high-spec binoculars, spying turned into a goal in itself, and she had fallen into a pattern of simply pursuing ocular pleasure and the satisfaction it brought.

Having spent a long time watching the scenes unfolding on the lower floor across the way, she noticed something. In a person's day-to-day life, aside from checking the sky for rain, they seldom ever bother to look up to the windows of higher buildings or the rooftops surrounding them. Akira had never once turned his eyes to the upper floors of the Leopalace apartments, and the probability of him ever returning Kyoko's gaze was practically zero.

Kyoko was aware that part of the pleasure she got from

peeping on Akira's private life owed to the fact that she would not be seen. If she were to ever find the gaze of her object turned to her, the pleasure of spying would vanish. People can either look or be looked at. They must choose between one of those two possibilities.

And, if the day was to come when she would be the object of Akira's gaze, what would make that possible? She was awkward and totally helpless when it came to men. Kyoko occasionally looked over the report on Akira she had received from a detective agency, and she spent lonely nights engrossed in the planning of their first meeting, wondering, for example, could she simply show up at the bar he frequented?

Kyoko had been working as a subtitle translator for ten years. She was born in the city of Matsue in Shimane Prefecture and had attended the English literature program of a private university in Tokyo.

The city of Matsue appeared to float on water—it stretched from the Sakai Channel to Lake Nakaumi and along the Ohashi River to Lake Shinji. Long ago it was a major port for shipping routes in the Sea of Japan, such as the kitamaebune route from Osaka to Hokkaido, and had prospered building and repairing wooden sails and fishing vessels. Those traditions had been passed on, and there were still fifteen or sixteen small ship-making companies in Matsue.

Kyoko's family operated, though small in scale, a shipyard that constructed and repaired wooden and fiber-reinforced plastic fishing ships. When her father died five years earlier, her brother had taken over the business. However, the economy for shipbuilding was poor, for shipyards both large and small, and her family business had since then been at risk of shutting down.

After graduating from university, Kyoko found a job in the city at a large manufacturer of prefabricated homes, but as there were no opportunities to use her English ability, she quit after three years and decided to become a subtitle translator, like she had always dreamed of. She found an internship program that allowed her to study abroad in Los Angeles for a year, and after returning to Japan, she worked at a temp agency while completing a basic course on subtitle translation for six months. Then over the course of a year and a half, she attended a subtitling seminar four days a week.

When Kyoko lived in an apartment in Nishi Ogikubo, on the weekends she would go to the Suginami City Central Library and read from cover to cover books on the history of film, film theory, and collections of scripts for stage and screen; then at night, she would watch both Japanese and Western movies rented from Tsutaya. While still attending the subtitling seminar, she did some translation tests for a large subtitling company and received two A grades and two AA grades, and as a result she began to get requests to do preliminary translations. After completing the seminar, she continued to take on work doing preliminary translations, as well as other minor projects such as DVD special features and small programs for satellite TV. Then finally, in 2006 she quit her job at the temp agency and began to make it on her own as a translator. She shelled out the four hundred thousand yen for the CANVASs SST Super Subtitling System software that had just been released at the time.

Along with the new subtitling software, Kyoko installed a

video player on her computer, and while watching the video, she could divide up the lines and narration of the Japanese script she had translated—a process called "boxing." Then she could "spot" the subtitles—decide the timing the text would appear on the screen. Since she could do this all on the subtitling software, her work could now be completed entirely on her computer; she no longer needed to use a TV or videotape. But Kyoko still always printed out the completed subtitles on paper to double-check. There were always mistakes and changes in nuance that she wouldn't have caught when looking at the text on the screen, and on the page the continuity of the story and flow of time were easier to grasp.

A viewer could read four characters per second on the screen, for example, "私は元気" or "I'm fine." Each Japanese character counted as one character, whereas numbers and things such as contracted sounds each counted as a half. Question marks and exclamation points were not counted towards the character count. Generally, commas and periods were avoided, but when they were used, a half space was needed after a comma and a full space after a period. Ellipses were treated as one character.

One set of subtitles would appear on screen for a maximum of five to six seconds, so if the viewer could read four characters per second, one set could contain twenty to twenty-four characters. In the case of a 120-minutes long film, there were usually about 1,000 to 1,200 sets of subtitles.

It was said to be possible for a translator to translate a maximum of ten minutes of film a day, so a 120-minute film would take a total of twelve days to complete. There was an incredible amount of work, so just before deadlines Kyoko was often glued to her computer from morning to night. Exhaustion was not uncommon.

Production companies paid subtitle translators per ten minutes of film, and pricing varied widely: based on the their experience, translators could be paid anywhere from eight thousand to tens of thousands of yen per ten minutes. Kyoko's pay varied depending on the genre, but generally she made between twenty to thirty thousand yen per ten minutes—placing her safely around the median rate for the role—and for the last two or three years, her yearly income had been about five million yen. She was the type who never refused a job, and not only did she take on subtitling, but she would also do translations for voice-overs whenever possible. At the moment she had projects for TV shows booked for the next six months, and two movies she had subtitled were currently being screened in both Tokyo and Osaka.

Last year she had been interviewed for a magazine on the subtitling industry, and when asked about her future dream she answered, "To subtitle a film starring Jude Law, and then work as his interpreter when he visits Japan to promote it." When she later discovered that Jude Law was a tremendous fan of the works of Kitano Takeshi, her passion waned.

There were several men interested in Kyoko. Among them, the most persistent was the heir to the president of a distributor of imported films who currently worked as the director of sound and subtitling production. They had gone for tea and dined together on several occasions, but the restaurants he would take her to, especially the cafés, did not suit Kyoko's taste, and on top of that, he loved coffee and cakes that were labeled "American." Kyoko simply went along as part of her job.

Mistress Koharu

As this implies, Kyoko had strong views about cafés. Aside from her collection of magazines and books on cafés, Kyoko had three notebooks containing information she had collected herself while visiting cafés in the city and the suburbs. However, Kyoko had no interest in sharing that information online or otherwise making it public.

Her suitor at the film distributor was a fan of *Star Wars* and always wanted to share his knowledge of the franchise, but Kyoko did not care for George Lucas's films. She would simply nod along without really paying attention, but the heir remained oblivious and would passionately yammer on about the "undeniably classic" film series.

Soon after Kyoko had started observing Yano Akira, one night after returning home late and taking a shower, he put on a DVD and took a seat on his couch with a whiskey glass in his hand. His television was up against the room's right wall, so no matter how she adjusted the angle of her binoculars, she was left with only an almost profile view of the TV. But despite that, while straining her eyes patiently at the horizontally contracted and warped image on the screen, she realized she had seen that film before. Tom Cruise was entering a large space where some sort of strange ritual was being carried out, and there, in the middle of a circle of women wearing black capes was a man standing in a red cape.

"It's *Eyes Wide Shut*! What was the password to enter this mansion? 'Fidelio'?"

Akira was absorbed in the film. Kyoko wanted to sit down next to him and explain in detail the technical precision and appeal of the work of Stanley Kubrick. She found herself muttering in the exaggerated tones of film critic Yodogawa Nagaharu, "*Eyes Wide Shut*—what a frightening film."

9.

Back in university, Kyoko had belonged to the English-speaking society and strived to qualify for the All-Japan Student English Debate Tournament. She knew an older male student who had won one of the top prizes.

Kyoko admired him. On checking the club registry, she found that he lived in Yoga in Setagaya Ward, so one day in August during summer vacation, she made an unannounced visit to his home. He knew who she was, but having never really spoken to her he did not know how to react to her turning up at his house, and totally befuddled, he made simple conversation while trying to figure out what it was that she wanted.

Her excuse for visiting was that she wanted him to tell her how to prepare for the debate tournament, but the boy's mother who brought them both tea in the living room thought her suspicious and worried that she might have been trying to lure her son to join some sort of new religion.

After university, when Kyoko worked for the manufacturer of prefabricated homes, she had confessed her love for a coworker at his going away party. And though he gave her his phone number, he never responded to any of the text messages she sent.

She never liked any of the men who approached her, but when she tried to approach a man, for some reason, she always wound up getting rejected. This pattern continued to repeat itself, and Kyoko was fed up with the unfairness of it all.

Mistress Koharu

In elementary school, Kyoko was enamored of the leader of the idol group SMAP, Nakai Masahiro, who in 1989 had made his debut in the TV drama *Jikan Desuyo! Heisei Gannen*. And, fifteen years later, in 2004, when Kyoko learned that Nakai would star in the TBS drama *Vessel of Sand*, she made a big move. After finding the application form on TBS's webpage to apply to be an extra, she waited for them to contact her. At the time, Kyoko was working for the temp agency while attending translation school.

Matsumoto Seicho's 1961 bestseller *Vessel of Sand* had first been adapted for the big screen by director Nomura Yoshitaro, with a screenplay by Hashimoto Shinobu and Yamada Yoji, and was later adapted for TV several times, but this new version was a modern revisioning that would span eleven episodes.

Kyoko was cast to appear as an audience member at a classical music concert, and filming was set for Omiya Sonic City.

She set off for Omiya on the day's first train and was stuck on set until the evening, and though they handed out bentos for lunch, she was not paid. Still, all would have been fine if she had been able to meet Nakai as she had hoped, but the only actor who made an appearance was Watanabe Ken. She also came to the shocking discovery that those extras assigned to places near the main characters all belonged to acting agencies.

Her next chance came in 2008. She had already begun working as a professional subtitle translator, but she was determined and applied again to be an extra so she could meet Nakai. The film was a Toho Production, *I Want to Become a Seashell*, and it was to be shot in TBS's Midoriyama Studio. She was assigned the roll of a passerby walking through the crowd in a black market.

This time she had to change into a costume and have her hair and makeup done, but of course Nakai did not show up yet again, and all she got to see was the face of the actress Nakama Yukie. On the train home she gazed at the caricature of Nakai printed on the commemorative shirt she received and thought to herself, I can't do this again.

But this shoot did bring her an unexpected reward. On a break, she and a woman about her age, who was cast to walk next to her as another passerby, introduced themselves to each other and started talking. Kyoko learned that this woman, Kamijo Aoi, was a freelance editor who worked directly with a large publisher, and she was also single.

"I'm in charge of the novelization of the *Shinshokoku Monogatari* series. It was on NHK forever ago. Have you heard of *The Flute Boy* or *The Crimson Peacock*?" Kamijo asked her.

Some days later, they met again at Café Du near Meguro Station—Kyoko's recommendation—and Kyoko learned that Kamijo was two years older than her, born in Iwata City in Shizuoka Prefecture, and currently lived in Yamabukicho in Shinjuku. She said she liked movies, and when Kyoko asked which directors she was fond of, she said Edward Yang from Taiwan, and if she were to name one more, it would be Jim Jarmusch. Kyoko, who at this point was living in Kitashinagawa in Shinagawa Ward, would go on to meet Kamijo in several of her favorite cafés around the city and discuss movies with her.

Kyoko and Aoi's womanly friendship would continue for quite some time, and Aoi, who was passionate about learning, was inspired by Kyoko's English ability and began to attend classes at an English school in Yotsuya. Once she asked Kyoko,

"I always struggle in the listening classes. What can I do to improve my listening?"

Kyoko wanted to know how those classes were conducted.

"An older Japanese-American woman plays a tape—there aren't many people still using cassette tapes these days, right?—anyway, she plays a tape of some listening practices and then asks us about the content. We do that about three times, and then she hands out a printout of the script and it's over. I always get about half. I just want to understand like seventy or eighty percent."

Kyoko said that the class was only testing listening ability, not training Aoi to be a better listener. She recommended Aoi start watching NHK E Television's English show, *English Conversation News*, and said the key was to record it and watch the recording, pausing the video and reading the text on the screen before listening to the presenters talk. She stressed that it was important to understand the content before listening. Then if she read the script aloud two to three times and then listened again, no matter how fast the newscaster was speaking, she would be able to catch most of it. If she kept doing that, eventually she'd start to develop something like "English receptors" in her mind.

Aoi did exactly what she was told and would come to discover just how right Kyoko was.

Once a week, Aoi would visit the publisher she worked for to deliver her edited drafts, have a meeting with her manager in the editorial department, and take her next drafts home.

In September 2013, after she had received her proofs and was preparing to leave, her manager offered her a ticket. It was for the annual Family Party held in a hotel in Mejirodai every October, and with that ticket, one employee and their family, up to two adults, could participate. Aoi's manager had been planning to go with her two children but suddenly had to visit her husband's family that day in north Kanto.

"Can I bring people who aren't family?"

"As long as you have the ticket, it should be fine."

Aoi suggested the idea to Kyoko, and the two decided to go together. They met at the ticket gate to Edogawabashi Station on the Yurakucho Line, then exited the station and climbed the steep road following the Kanda River up to the hotel. The Family Party started at one o'clock, but as the hotel was famous for its garden designed by Yamagata Aritomo, they arrived a little after twelve, planning to explore the grounds, and made a loop through the enormous kaiyu-shiki garden. The distribution of ponds and small hills throughout the grounds was complex yet well balanced; the garden was also adorned with a three-story pagoda, an arched bridge, a tearoom, and stone statues based on Ito Jakuchu's carvings of the five hundred arhats, and the entire grounds were encircled by enormous chinquapin trees.

At university, Aoi had majored in East Asian history, and she said wandering the garden caused her to recall *Dream Memories of Tao'an* by Ming dynasty essayist Zhang Dai.

"It's like a collection of essays. Of course I read it in Japanese translation. There was a garden in Shaoxing in Zhejiang called 'Kaien,' and that part started like this. 'The whole of the Kaien was crossed with water.' But because the water was distributed so carefully, and since they made such good use of it, no one could notice it anywhere at first glance."

Mistress Koharu

In the middle of climbing up one of the roads to Plaza Tower, where the Family Party was being held, Kyoko turned around and looked out at the garden from above, recalling that line of text that Aoi had shared.

Just a little before the one o'clock start time, they arrived at the Grand Hall Tsubaki on the fifth floor of Plaza Tower, and after checking in as the relatives of Aoi's boss from the editorial department, they entered. The spacious hall was already filled with employees and their families. Along three of the walls were food stalls serving sushi, soba, tempura, yakisoba, yakitori, and roast beef and also a few stalls for children serving cotton candy or letting them fish for goldfish.

The other wall was almost entirely glass, and right below them, Kyoko and Aoi could see the whole of the garden they had just walked.

To the side of the temporary stage in the front of the room, someone on the mic explained the space and what attractions they had, but there was no greeting from the president or managers, or any other overly formal ceremoniousness.

Eventually, the magician Shokyokusai Kotensho began his performance on the stage set to the song "Magician in the Park" by Frank Nagai. Next, a comedy duo hired from the entertainment company Yoshimoto Kogyo took the stage and stirred up a bout of laughter. Finally, three female idols who often appeared on the covers of the publishing house's magazines made an appearance and charmed the crowd with song and dance.

As she knew him from her weekly meetings at the editorial department, when Aoi spotted Yano Akira at the side of the stage, she ran over to him. Akira was on the organizing committee for this year's Family Party and was actually wearing a suit for once.

Akira greeted Aoi with surprise, and when he mentioned her boss, she said, "I'm here as her alternate. It's a huge party." Then she introduced Kyoko.

Akira gave a slight nod and offered her his card. Kyoko accepted it, admiring his long and graceful fingers, and felt a slight fluttering in her chest.

His gray suit came in at his waist, and Kyoko was stunned by his sharp silhouette. He had on a white button-down shirt and a skinny, dotted necktie. His hair was split in a 7:3 part, and his eyes had a strange glimmer to them, as though he was looking somewhere far off.

In fact, at that moment Akira was incredibly panicked. The idols were singing on the stage now, but this act ended at 2:45 p.m. and from 3 p.m. the Doraemon show for which he had booked an acting troupe from Kichijoji was supposed to begin.

The troupe had agreed that they would meet Akira at the entrance to the Plaza Tower on the first floor at 2:30 p.m., and though he waited past 2:30 p.m. they still had not appeared. He thought he might have passed them as he went down to get them at the first floor, that maybe they had already arrived on location, so he had returned to the Grand Hall to check, but they weren't here either. Just as he was about to return to the first floor, he had run into Kamijo Aoi and her friend.

Now was not the time to be talking with these women. Absentmindedly he handed over his business card, and as the friend tried to say something he said, "I'm sorry. Excuse me," cutting her off, and dashed back to the first-floor entrance.

Mistress Koharu

The four men and one woman of the troupe arrived at 2:50 p.m. The leader who played Nobita lowered his head in apology, saying their previous shoot just wouldn't end. They had rushed here in a cab from a studio somewhere in the middle of the city.

Backstage they raced frantically to prepare, and just five or six minutes late, a performance featuring actors in character costumes from Doraemon began.

Kyoko and Aoi had turned their backs to the stage and were eating soba at a stall.

"That man's name was Yano-san?" Kyoko asked plainly.

"He's single, and I haven't heard anything about a girlfriend or anything. I guess he's a bit of a bookish type."

Kyoko thought back to the way he carried himself and those bookish fingers and hoped that she would have another chance to meet him, though she did not voice this.

"Should we get going? There's a small museum nearby called Eisei Bunko. They've got sancai pottery from the Tang period."

Kyoko went along with Aoi's suggestion and they left the party together.

The Doraemon show ended without incident, and the actors wandered the Grand Hall in costume, shaking children's hands and taking pictures with them.

Akira, relieved, loosened his necktie backstage, removed his jacket, took a deep breath, and downed a paper cup of beer. With all this running about, he had completely forgotten the two women he had just met.

10

Kyoko's love for Yano Akira, whom she had met just that once, only grew more extreme and harder to control with the passage of time.

She could not have Kamijo Aoi relay to him how she felt, however. Kyoko did not know how Aoi felt about Akira, and even if Aoi was willing to pass her feelings along, she sensed that would cause some sort of bad blood between them. She felt that Aoi was not the sort of woman who would enjoy playing the role of cupid.

She decided that first she must find out as much about Akira as she could, and so she headed to a detective agency in Nihonbashi in Chuo Ward, requested them to do a background check, and as a starting point handed them the business card she received at the Family Party. One month later, she received their report along with an exorbitant bill. It was worth every penny; she now had in her hands far more detailed information about Akira than she had ever imagined.

In the report she found his address and phone number as listed in his university's alumni registry, a brief explanation of the company where he was employed and his current work patterns, a description of his role and his relationships with his coworkers, an estimate of his annual income and savings balance, and the types of insurance he was enrolled in, along with the names of the respective insurance companies.

As for his personal life, the report included the names of the bars and cafés he frequented, the type of car he owned, and then, most important of all, was the line, "He does not appear to be dating anyone, and we have confirmed that there are no rumors of ongoing relationships."

Kyoko read the report carefully, and while her desire to approach Akira had increased dramatically, she decided not to make any other moves for the time being. She had more than enough experience to know that forcing herself on him would not lead to a desirable result.

In March of the following year, 2014, Aoi invited Kyoko to a café in the Imperial Hotel Plaza. Kyoko was the one who had told Aoi about this café famous for its egg sandwiches, saying, "The rolled omelet in the egg sandwiches is unbelievably big, so you should get half egg and half tuna."

One wall of the café was covered with a photo of the giant balcony-style bookshelves of the Bibliothèque nationale de France, and above the tables hung over a dozen empty bamboo bird cages of a variety of intricate designs.

"If you ask, they'll toast the bread for you as well," Kyoko had added.

Since Kyoko had told Aoi about these egg sandwiches at the Imperial Hotel, Aoi had begun stopping by on her way back home whenever she watched performances of the Takarazuka Revue.

After eating her toasted sandwich and ordering another coffee, Aoi abruptly announced, "I'm going to get married."

She was to marry the second son of a sake brewer in her hometown of Iwata.

Aoi looked down, averting her eyes from Kyoko, but there was a smile on her face.

Kyoko said, "What?!" but "Congratulations!" never followed. She was really thinking, "How?" but of course she did not say that aloud.

Aoi explained bit by bit, her eyes moving between the photo of the bookshelves and the birdcages. It had been decided after two arranged meetings, the ceremony would be just their families, and they'd go on a honeymoon soon. She did not provide Kyoko much more information than that.

Aoi's engagement urged Kyoko on in her pursuits. She took out the report on Akira and put his address and mobile number into her phone. While searching for a map of Nishi-Kanda 2-chome on the internet, she whispered to herself, "I have to make a move."

The next month, she went to Nishi-Kanda and found his apartment and noticed that the balconies on the rear of the building faced a park. After confirming that his red Toyota from the report was parked in front of the building, she stopped by a café he was said to frequent, Espace Biblio in Surugadai. She had looked up this café in a guidebook so knew that it was a "book café" with a collection of over six thousand books specializing in graphic design and film, but it was her first time visiting. As it was a weekday afternoon, there was no chance that she would bump into Akira.

She crossed Hakusan-dori and walked past Kanda Catholic Church, before climbing the steep stone steps up the hill of Onnazaka and walking down Tochinoki-dori towards Meiji University. There, on her right, was the café.

The premises were larger than she had expected, and the interior was in an antique style, with the walls on both sides covered with floor to ceiling bookshelves. At the back of the café there was a glass door, through which was a terrace that opened out into a bamboo grove.

The customers both inside and on the terrace were sitting in groups of twos and threes on the corners of big wooden tables; they had coffee, tea, or wine beside them and quietly flipped the pages of art books they had taken from the shelves or read books they had brought with them.

Kyoko ordered a glass of white wine and took it out to the terrace. What had a moment ago looked to her like a bamboo grove turned out to actually be a mix of different trees including some bamboo. On the other side of the small wood was a cliff, and standing on the edge of the terrace, one could see through the trees glimpses of the districts of Sarugakucho and Jimbocho spreading out below. Kyoko had ascended that same cliff a moment ago when she climbed the stone steps of Onnazaka.

Hid amidst the trees was a single, small wild cherry blossom tree; a gentle breeze shook its branches and carried to Kyoko's shoulder a petal. Would there come a day when she would stand here with Akira?

In June, Kyoko visited a real estate agent on Hakusan-dori in Jimbocho and began searching for a new apartment; she wanted to live somewhere near Akira in order to sniff out hidden opportunities for them to begin dating. She didn't want to become acquainted with him at the park or at Espace Biblio—she didn't want that kind of hackneyed boy meets girl story. Wasn't there some other, different option?

In October she found a place, and at the end of the year she moved from Kitashinagawa to the fifth floor of the Leopalace apartment building. The unit she moved to was in the perfect location, directly across the park from Akira's apartment, and, sweetening the deal, she would be on the fifth floor, where she could look down on his third-floor room. For Kyoko, there could be no better feature for an apartment than this positioning.

Kyoko had acquired binoculars because she had several scenes from one of Alfred Hitchcock's masterpieces, *Rear Window*, on her mind.

The film's main character, the photojournalist Jeff played by James Stewart, had broken his leg in an accident while on assignment and was forced into a wheelchair. He uses binoculars and a telephoto lens to observe day and night the man living in the apartment across from his, whom he believes to have killed his wife.

The nurse Jeff has hired—Stella, played by Selma Ritter—knows that he is spying on the lives of those in the surrounding apartments and tells him straight, "New York State sentence for a Peeping Tom is six months in the workhouse," and fumes, "We've become a race of Peeping Toms." His girlfriend, the fashion model Lisa, played by Grace Kelly, also complains with a look of shock spread across her face that he's "diseased," but she begins to sense some truth to Jeff's story, and she and Stella both join in spying on the suspicious man's room.

Kyoko, however, felt no guilt about peeping on Akira with her high-spec binoculars. She ignored the dubious legality of her actions, thinking that if they ended up together in marital bliss, any spying would be forgiven, and in fact when they were both gray haired, she might even confess to it as a little teatime chatter.

Mistress Koharu

She had read an article in which a Japanese director said of the master of suspense Alfred Hitchcock, "If he was a handsome man and popular with women, he wouldn't have made movies." The director pointed out that behind the man's rotundity and humorous looks, he hid a deep insecurity about his appearance. Kyoko had also read accounts of his, one might even go so far as to say monomaniacal, obsession with blonde women. Whenever Kyoko watched one of Hitchcock's films on DVD, she always recalled these stories.

As a director, Hitchcock always prepared his most sadistic scenes for actresses of his type. Kyoko had felt that he was, within the fiction of his films, harassing these otherwise untouchable beauties. Joan Fontain, terrified her husband will kill her in *Suspicion*; Janet Lee, murdered in the shower in *Psycho*; Kim Novack jumping from a church bell tower in *Vertigo*; Tippi Hedren, attacked by a flock of birds in *The Birds*. The list went on and on.

However, there were exceptions. For example, the blonde Hitchcock most admired, Grace Kelly, never faced such a scene in any of her films with him. And in the case of *Rear Window*, the film is constructed such that she is never even shown the dead body. Because of that, Kyoko had always imagined that Hitchcock really wanted to cast Grace Kelly for some role other than Lisa. Oh, how Hitchcockian would it be if, on the other side of his long, telephoto lens, James Stewart peeped not a killer, but a nude Grace Kelly?

Of course, Hitchcock would never reveal his reason for such a casting choice, but—though she knew this wasn't quite the right word to describe the sensation—Kyoko felt his "pity" for

Grace Kelly in choosing to cast her as Lisa instead of a tortured beauty.

To better understand this pathos, Kyoko decided to search for clues in the short story on which the film was based and discovered that its author, Cornell Woolrich, had titled it not "Rear Window" but "It Had to Be Murder." Enchanted by the world of Woolrich's story, a world called noir, Kyoko went on to buy all of his essential works and began reading them in the original English. She also discovered *The Life of Cornell Woolrich,* published in two volumes in Japanese by Hayakawa Shobo, and while reading it was shocked to learn that Woolrich's hidden life, drawn onto the page by his biographer, was one that consisted of "fretting over his homosexuality, failing in marriage, failing as an author, living with his mother in a hotel, and eventually dying alone."

Martha Foley, editor of *Story* magazine, recollected that Woolrich was a "thin, shabby, shaking, hungry-looking man," and his editor at Simon and Schuster, Lee Wright, said, "It was difficult to like him … I felt sorry for him, but that doesn't constitute liking him," and even went so far as to say, "How those words came out of that skinny rat of a man!" In the Japanese translation, both editors used the word "hinsou" to describe Woolrich, denoting a look of impoverishment, of shabbiness. Kyoko was moved by the cruel, frank, and merciless assessment of his person.

Sections of the book based on statements from Marian, the half-sister of the wife Woolrich divorced after only three months, were raw and salacious and touched on a secret of his that remained unknown until this biography made its way into the world. She exposed the contents of a suitcase of Woolrich's, which he had conspicuously always kept locked.

"But one day he left his suitcase open by mistake, and she could see that there was a sailor suit in it. And he would don the sailor suit, get up in the night and leave her. In the dark he would put on the sailor suit and go down to the waterfront and find whatever experience he was looking for."

Kyoko did not have sympathy for men like Hitchcock and Woolrich who had these dark passions and perversions that they could not reveal to others, but she did have an intellectual interest in their strange sexual predilections and felt an urge to try and understand them. She felt she would be better off if she could understand the sexuality of men who, for example, were prone to perversions like getting aroused at the mere sight of women's underwear due to some association they made between undergarments and the eroticism of an actual flesh-and-blood person. Yet while Kyoko was in possession of the mental flexibility necessary for such dispassionate inquiry, she could not bring herself to imagine that Yano Akira might be inclined to similar bizarre actions and grotesque proclivities. She was convinced that he had a different sort of personality from Hitchcock or Woolrich and never once doubted that assumption.

When she was a student, Kyoko once read a novel called *A Simple Life*, which was recommended to her by a friend who read a lot of high-brow literary fiction. In the novel, the author depicted his daily life in plain terms, and Kyoko remembered reaching the end still unsure if what she had read was a novel, or an essay, or a diary. But now, observing his daily life through her binoculars, she thought that Akira's own story might be titled *A Monotonous Life*.

He had an office job, so it was inevitable that his life lacked variety and drama. Every day he would go to work in the morning and return home at night and have a nightcap while watching TV. When he would occasionally deviate from this pattern and come home early, he'd sit on the couch and read books or watch movies.

He spent every weekend in just about the same way; aside from cleaning and doing the laundry, he mostly read books or watched movies.

The author of *A Simple Life* occasionally revealed the goings on of his mind, but from where she was, Kyoko was not privy to Akira's thoughts.

What Kyoko found odd was that Akira never went for walks. She could not recall ever having seen him stroll through the nearby park or sit in the sun on the play equipment or benches there. And though Kyoko also became a regular at Espace Biblio, the café mentioned in the report, she never once saw him there.

He did not use his car to commute to work. He occasionally went for drives on the weekend, but on weekdays it just sat there in the parking lot in front of his apartment building.

But did this all mean that Akira was not a target worth staking out? No, that was not the case. Kyoko observed the unaffected behaviors and actions of his everyday life with much curiosity.

When he put on socks, he would stand on one leg and put on one sock, then switch legs to put on the other. His posture and movement made her think of the goofball pantomimes of Chaplin and silent-era films. When he would go out to his balcony and do shoulder rolls, she found his unique form entertaining. After spending a long time glued to her desk for work, she would copy him, rolling her shoulder blades about in exaggerated circles.

She had once observed him trimming his finger and toenails as well. As he brought the clipper to his nails, he bit his bottom lip and made the most serious face, and Kyoko felt she could hear the sound of those nails being clipped off as though he were right beside her.

When he took a nap one Sunday, she stared continuously at his face and could tell when he had progressed from non-REM to REM sleep. His eyelids had suddenly begun to twitch, and his hands started to tremble.

Moreover, one morning in the early summer, having just awoke, Akira walked out to the balcony with the front of his pajama shirt open. Kyoko was shocked. She stared at his fine chest hair and thick armpit hair and found her breathing growing heavy.

Generally, he seemed unconcerned with how he was dressed. He would simply wear knit sweaters in the winter, jersey sweaters in the spring, and T-shirts in the summer, and he never wore clothing with patterns or bold colors. Jeans were ever present— maybe he believed in making himself inconspicuous.

Just as Aoi had said, and confirmed by the report from the detective agency, there was no evidence of a girlfriend, but just once a large, middle-aged woman with glasses appeared in his living-dining room. The woman had placed some bags and a standing light she brought with her on the floor and, for some reason, closed the curtains, cutting off Kyoko's view.

Kyoko couldn't bear not knowing what was happening in that closed room and even felt pangs of jealousy. When the curtains opened again, Akira was sitting alone on the couch looking purposeless. Judging from the way she had dressed, the woman certainly wasn't a prostitute, but she also didn't seem to be someone particularly close to Akira, and Kyoko just could not piece together who she was.

Kyoko thought to herself that she'd better call it a day with her peeping on Akira. It was about time that she show herself to him. Once they became close, she'd move somewhere around Gotanda and cover up her history of having snuck into his neighborhood and spying on him.

She had long ago confirmed the location of the bar Rosebud in Jimbocho and would have to begin visiting on nights he wasn't there in order to blend in.

"Rosebud," the mysterious words muttered in the film modeled after the life of the newspaper magnate Hearst, *Citizen Kane*—but presumably he already knew that. If he doesn't, I'll tell him, she thought.

Well then, what do I wear to a good old-fashioned bar?

11.

After Akira had set out for work, Koharu, left alone in bed, began to dream. Fragments of memories fluttered before her eyes like a ribbon.

North of Budapest, a studio in the suburban town of Szentendre, the man lying face down on the work bench was her maker, Giuseppe.

His wife had passed away some years ago, and now, instead of returning to his home on the western side of the Danube River in the Buda district of Budapest, he often drank in his studio and would frequently get so drunk he'd sleep there till sunrise. He was snoring, his balding head resting on his arms, and an empty bottle of botrytized wine rolled about the workshop floor.

Koharu sat in a rocking chair, completely naked and bald, a hole cap inserted between her legs, her newly installed eyes fixed on the bald spot on Giuseppe's head.

A single fly settled near his hair whorl. A neighborhood dog howled, and when Giuseppe lifted up his head, the fly took off. He went back to sleep, and Koharu continued staring at his head until the eastern sky grew bright.

The St. Petersburg love doll exhibition was located in the basement of a shabby community center on Pereulok Brin'ko, near Sennaya Ploschad. Koharu was placed in the corner of a section of Russian-made dolls, exposed to the unceasing and curious gazes of middle-aged and elderly men, but not a single one stopped before her. The dealer called her "leftovers," and she assumed she would soon be discarded. That is, until one day, a rich Japanese buyer appeared.

In the exhibition space, someone had put on a dance number by Dmitri Shostakovich, "Jazz Suite No. 2 Waltz II", and the ambience produced by those exotic and lonesome strains resembled that of a circus.

Koharu gradually awoke.

A slight trembling arose in the tips of her fingers and toes, her eyelids opened and closed and opened again.

She sat up slowly and then stood, planting both her feet on

the ground. She was wearing an ivory white dress of chiffon, and her feet were bare.

When she awoke, she would always head straight for the bathroom, looking for the mirror.

After turning on the lights, like the young queen from Snow White, she would say to her reflection, "Mirror, mirror on the wall," and she never failed to be enchanted by her beautiful features, produced by the most advanced doll-making technology, and would stand there, absorbed.

The makeup artist had crafted a beautiful face, one that no living person could ever possess, one with a bewitching quality only a doll could manifest. The artist had sensed something inauspicious within that look, but she could not have foreseen what kind of future awaited this love doll.

Koharu, finally removing herself from in front of the mirror, headed to the living-dining-kitchen. Despite having heard Akira describe time after time before he fell asleep how charming, how cute his pet red ranchu was, she had still never seen that goldfish.

She walked straight to the fish tank on the left of the closet and looked down at the water illuminated from above by fluorescent lights, but there swimming were just the two red and white sarasa comets. The ranchu was nowhere to be seen.

As it turned out, the ranchu was hiding itself in a crevice between the corner of the tank and the heater cord, seemingly rejecting her with his whole being. Koharu could detect this slight enmity precisely, and her beautiful face twisted in displeasure, but then she lifted her head up and, making as though nothing had happened, went to the closet and opened a dresser drawer.

Koharu had inspected every object in the apartment several

times over and memorized each of their locations—if anyone were to have asked after anything, from the spare keys to Akira's bank book, to his condoms, she would have been able to instantly tell them where it was.

In that drawer, along with cellophane tape, calculator, and corkscrew, was a strange item, the use of which Akira didn't understand. Koharu had grown fond of this bizarre object, and each time she came to the living-dining room she would take it out and play with it for a moment before returning it to its place.

The item was a gift Akira had received from one of his female coworkers, a souvenir from the Izumo Taisha Shrine. It was oval in shape, about three centimeters across, two centimeters tall, and eight millimeters thick, and was made of metal. In the middle of the oval was a button about one centimeter in diameter, and if you pressed on it, a spring would push it back to its original place. Flipping it over, one could see "Happy Izumo" engraved on the back of it in hiragana. Akira had not understood what purpose this item was made for. Was he just supposed to press the button? And not understanding what to do with the thing, he had just left it in that drawer.

Koharu felt an inexplicable admiration for the simple way this object displayed its power, the way that when pressing on the button with one's fingertip, there would always be a certain degree of resistance, and never tiring of this, she would press on it again and again.

Satisfied after completing her usual course around the apartment, Koharu returned to the bed, placed herself just as she was before getting up, and began once again to wind back the ribbon of her dreams.

Part Two

<u>1.</u>

The call came in the middle of April, sometime after 7 p.m. while Chikako had been listening to a self-proclaimed "fan" of hers, a man in his thirties who worked at a trading company, complain about his job.

The caller was a young woman who introduced herself as the editor of a magazine, and, presuming that it was going to be an interview request, Chikako was about to ask her to come before the bar opened when the woman explained that she was planning a small gathering, and she wondered if it would be possible to use Rosebud for such a get together.

Rosebud had an alcove space where a party of five or six people could sit at a mahogany table and drink in private. For larger groups, she had three folding chairs at the ready.

The following evening, the woman visited to see the space, handed Chikako a business card that identified her as the assistant editor of the monthly magazine *Atlantis*, and explained that she was planning to gather four enthusiastic readers of the magazine who post regularly to their website, giving them a chance to "share their knowledge and experience" and discuss the magazine together, and two or three additional readers might participate as "observers" and listen in on the discussion as well.

Chikako had never heard of the magazine, and when she asked what sort of publication it was, the assistant editor answered, "A magazine about the occult."

While Chikako gave the okay, she imagined a group of young cult members gathering late at night on the roof of an abandoned building, whispering to each other, "It's a UFO," each time they saw a shooting star, and she questioned whether she should really have a group of megalomaniacs using her bar as a space to elaborate on their conspiracy theories in hushed tones. In truth, she wished she had turned them down.

But come the day of their meeting, the participants all arrived in jackets and ties and turned out to be earnest salaryman types. Only the man who introduced himself as the editor stood out with his long hair and sunglasses, dressed in what looked like US military surplus clothing.

Atlantis was a monthly magazine, printed in B5 format, that was established in 1983. It was a specialty publication for occult maniacs and claimed it would "reveal the truth of the world's mysteries and secrets." The magazine covered a wide range of topics including UFOs, cryptids, psychic powers, paranormal activities, reincarnation, and conspiracy theories. What most distinguished them from other similar magazines was that they included as much scientific explanation as possible, trying their hardest to build credibility rather than simply publishing whatever preposterous stories they could find.

Kicking things off, the editor said that he wanted to name this gathering the "Paranormal Activity Research Committee" and begin convening regularly, once every two months. He intended to take what he learned from their discussions and apply it to the pages of the magazine. The assistant editor added that today's plan was to discuss occult activities that had been on

TV, and she explained that they would be recording their entire conversation. Then the discussion began.

Aside from the six members of the group sitting around the table, two additional men joined as "observers," and Chikako prepared an additional small table for them.

The first man to speak was an older accountant who had a firm in Suginami Ward. He began by mentioning his hobby of diving and his interest in aquatic life, then asked if any of them had happened to have heard of the megalodon before, before launching into an explanation of the giant shark species and the rumors that it still exists.

A species of shark said to have lived approximately 1.5 million years ago, megalodons were about ten to fifteen meters long. A monster shark close in size to a whale.

Throughout the twentieth century, theories that various cryptids were actually surviving megalodons circulated from time to time, such as in 1918, when something resembling a giant shark was spotted in Australia, and again in 1954, when a tooth ten centimeters long was found piercing the hull of a ship. However, definitive evidence that the species still roamed the oceans was yet to be discovered.

"I used to watch Animal Planet on satellite TV quite frequently, and in November of 2013 they aired a program called *Megalodon: The Monster Shark Lives*. I'm not really a fan of documentaries, but I thought this one was deeply fascinating, not the kind you see every day …"

At the beginning of this documentary ran a sensational warning bound to raise the hopes of any viewers: "The following program contains graphic images. Viewer discretion is advised." The story begins with footage recorded on April 5, 2013, of the sinking of a charter ship.

The ship was lost in the deeps off the coast of Cape Town, South Africa, and not a single body of those who had chartered the fishing boat was found. In the footage recovered from the accident, one of the female passengers can be heard screaming, "Oh my God! A shark!"

Marine biologist Colin Drake was invited to survey the area in hopes of finding the truth behind this tragedy, and the Discovery Channel film crew were allowed exclusive access to film his expedition.

Ten days after the incident, on April 15, a shark lookout watching the sea with binoculars witnessed movement on the surface of the water off the cape, seemingly waves produced by the thrashing of a whale. She photographed and recorded the scene with her telephoto lens, and later, when she checked the video, she noticed behind the thrashing whale a dorsal fin of approximately 1.8 meters in height breeching the water.

In the show, Drake discovers a black and white photograph of a very similar dorsal fin, said to be taken seventy years earlier by a crewman on a German U-boat as it was leaving the Cape of Good Hope, and he compares these two images to videos and photographs of a whale carcass in Hawaii taken January 21, 2009. He raises the question of whether a megalodon could have been the culprit in all these incidents.

One after the other come clips that had to have been real, such as footage captured on November 20, 2012, by the Brazilian Coast Guard, when, attempting a rescue by helicopter on stormy seas, the shadow of a fish more than eighteen meters in length appears in the water beneath them. Then, the documentary reaches its climax with Drake, attempting to capture this elusive monster, boarding a research vessel and heading out to where the charter ship had met its end.

"However, after *The Monster Shark Lives* aired in America, doubts were raised about whether it was or was not a documentary, and ultimately it was revealed to be fiction. Drake and all the rest were actually actors, but since it was done so skillfully and put together like a documentary, even I bought it completely.

"The public's faith in Animal Planet was shaken, and people started doubting everything. They'd see polar bear families suffering from global warming and wonder if it wasn't fake news."

The middle-aged man sitting next to the accountant, who had introduced himself as a high school teacher, then said, "I once watched a documentary on the Discovery Channel about levitation, and I'm still not sure if I should trust it."

The Supernaturalist was an adventure documentary which followed Dan White, an American with a twenty-year career as a magician, to Kathmandu, the capital of Nepal, where he went to investigate rumors of monks with supernatural powers who live in the Himalayan Mountains.

Led by a shaman named Hizbaba, they head east by plane to an "unnamed mountain village." From there they travel by foot into unexplored regions of the mountains, but White is abandoned by Hizbaba after the shaman receives a message in his dreams telling him to turn back. White is left with no choice but to travel alone to the "orange monastery" he is told of by a sadhu, a Hindu holy man.

Upon finally arriving at the monastery, White tells an old

monk that he heard the monk could levitate, and the monk initially refuses to cooperate, saying, "Your magic is fantastic, but we are not the same. This is Buddhist meditation." Impressed by White's stubborn passion, however, the monk eventually agrees. "I will try one time. I need you to move back. If you stay close to me then my energy doesn't work."

The monk sits in a semicircle of candles, the wall behind him checkered with prayer flags, and begins chanting a mantra.

Being a magician, White questions the monk's request for them to step away, later commenting that there must have been something behind him he didn't want them to see, but still he backs up four or five meters away from the monk. He then witnesses the monk rise from the ground and levitate at a height of about two to three centimeters.

"There's no wires. I don't see anything. Isn't that crazy," he said, and then, turning to the cameraman who was filming the monk, "Can you believe this?" It seemed he still could not dismiss the possibility that this was all a trick.

After completing his performance, the monk says to White, "And remember this. Keep your mind open and always continue to learn."

His eyes staring off somewhere in the distance, the high school teacher said, "I wonder if his levitation looked more real than that famous photo of Asahara Shoko's. The monk looked a bit like the Dalai Lama."

A department manager of a life insurance company, who up until that point had simply been nodding along, listening, then spoke up. "It folded quite some time ago, but do you all remember the magazine *Sharaku*?" He looked around the group.

Mistress Koharu

"It was published by Shogakukan, and I'm pretty sure Shinoyama Kishin supervised editing. They ran color photos there of levitation, maybe in the mid-eighties? They hired expert trick photographers and had them investigate everything thoroughly. I remember there was a caption from the editor, a comment saying that this is no scam, they're really floating. There was a bearded man in lotus position, pretty high up, at least a meter off the ground, floating there in that picture."

And then, one of the observers, a skinny older man, covered his mouth with his hand and began speaking.

"That must have been Naruse Masaharu. I've still got a copy of his book, *Levitation*. It had quite a reputation at the time. 'He's not jumping, humans have finally overcome gravity,' they all said. There were eight frames of photos showing the process of his levitating, and I think they even ran in *Shukan Bunshun*. After Asahara's cult's Tokyo subway sarin attack, the media couldn't cover these kinds of topics anymore, but Naruse's still running a yoga studio in Gotanda."

By now, the atmosphere had grown more relaxed, and a man who said he had worked as a piano tuner at the Kawai instrument production facility for thirty years shared his story of visiting Café Anderson in the small town of Kawatana-cho in Higashisonogi-gun, Nagasaki Prefecture. This shop, known for its "Four-Dimensional Parlor," got its popularity from the owner who performs feats of psychic ability, and because the place is such a hot spot and can seat only thirty people, reservations need to be made at least two months in advance.

The piano tuner had seen the owner on TV startling customers by guessing their birthdays, so he made a reservation and took his wife and kids. The man explained that he was also a magic researcher, and after going into great detail about what kinds of tricks the owner had arranged around the restaurant, he said, "You can watch the psychic performance for free—the shop doesn't charge for anything but what you order off the menu, so it feels like a real good deal. And the beef curry was only 788 yen anyway. When customers go home, they want some sort of memorabilia from the place. That's probably where he makes his money. A signed spoon bent with his telekinesis costs three hundred yen. And based on what I saw, each person bought three on average."

Since there were no other customers, Chikako listened in and enjoyed these otherworldly conversations. She began to take notice of one of the observers, a young man who had not spoken and simply sat there, looking up at the others when they spoke and drinking his shochu with water.

He had showed up with a heavy-looking camera bag hanging from his right shoulder and a tripod in his left hand, and though he was surely not even 170 centimeters tall, he must have weighed over one hundred kilos. Chikako worried that her folding chair would meet its end in agony, crushed under his weight.

Giving a slight bow to the assistant editor when he arrived, he spent the rest of the event in complete silence, then after the meeting was over, he moved to one of the circular counter seats and began drinking bourbon on the rocks.

When Chikako tried speaking to him, he initially seemed shy, but she soon discovered that once he got drunk, he suddenly became arrogant and naively talked about the profits of his family business with stupid directness, giving concrete numbers.

Mistress Koharu

He introduced himself as Kondo Tatsuya. He was thirty-one, single, and the heir to a Chinese restaurant chain that had its original store in front of Kiyosumi-shirakawa Station on the Hanzomon Line. Despite graduating from a photography school, he hadn't gone into the industry. Instead, he worked at his father's shop and was a "toritetsu," one of those train geeks always taking photos in and around train stations. He bragged that he owned every issue of *Atlantis* from the time its publication had begun.

Thereafter, he began coming to see Chikako every Wednesday, the day of the week his family restaurant was closed, and he intended to join the next Paranormal Activity Research Committee meeting in June as well.

There were at least four or five other men who visited the bar just to see Chikako, but no matter how many times Tatsuya visited, he never once tried to seduce her. He had a habit of staring up at her face or neck whenever Chikako was not paying attention to him. She was used to those sorts of stares from her time training as a bartender in Ueno-Hirokoji, but occasionally she felt the forcefulness and persistence of his gaze to be threatening.

What was more, his eyes were a bit too far apart and the outer corners sloped downwards, which made her associate his gaze with that of an amphibian or reptile, both of which she hated. Occasionally he would send a small shiver down her spine.

2.

Akira wanted to show Koharu the sea.

They would go by his trusty Land Cruiser, and he figured

when he had to step away from the car, he could hide her in a sleeping bag, so he purchased one with a center zip at a camping goods store called Kandahar in Ogawamachi. Since the zipper in the middle went all the way down to the bottom of the bag and could be opened in either direction, it would be easy to take her in and out of the bag. It was perfect for hiding her full body.

One Sunday in June, Akira woke up early and went out to the balcony with the front of his pajama shirt open. The early summer sun had just come up and was beginning to shine from beyond the roof of the Leopalace across the park. After stretching as he squinted into the sun, he put on some coffee, ate a breakfast of a single piece of toast and yogurt, returned to his bedroom, and began preparing Koharu.

This would be her first outing. He dressed her in the French tricolor—a red cache-coeur blouse of a cotton-linen blend over a white, sleeveless cotton shirt, with white suede wide-leg pants, and a bright blue raincoat. He fastened a simple platinum choker around her neck and a platinum bracelet on her left wrist. On her feet, he put white lace-up Nike Air Zoom Pegasus sneakers.

And as though it was made just for her, Koharu fit perfectly in the sleeping bag. Akira pulled up the zipper over her head, picked her up like he was lifting a surfboard, and carried her through the hallway, down the elevator, and through the building's entrance; he managed to get her all the way to the car without meeting anyone. He sat her down in the rear left car seat, unzipped the sleeping bag down to her waist, and placed round sunglasses on her. If he needed to shield her from view, he would just have to close the zipper.

At the Kandabashi Interchange, he entered the Inner Circular

Mistress Koharu

Loop Expressway, and after passing through Shiodome, merged onto Expressway Route 1 Haneda Line at Hamazakibashi Junction. Morning light still drifted over the Tokyo Bay, flowing as smoothly as the traffic.

"Look. That suspension bridge, that's Rainbow Bridge," he said to Koharu, glancing at her in the rearview mirror.

The car ran parallel to the monorail heading to Haneda, and then, at Oi Junction, Akira merged onto the Bayshore Route. They passed through the Haneda Airport North Tunnel, the South Tunnel, the Tamagawa Tunnel, and the Kawasaki Fairway Tunnel, before speeding across the manmade islands of the Keihin Refinery, Higashi Ogishima, and central Ogishima at one hundred kilometers per hour.

White smoke rose from the smokestacks of the thermal power plants and the distillery tower at the oil terminal. The dark mountains of the materials yard of JFE Steel closed in on them, and on both sides of the road, multilayered chains of belt conveyers connected the blast furnaces with the steel rolling, sintering, and pressing factories.

"It's like a giant fortress, isn't it? We've still got to cross Tsurumi Tsubasa Bridge and Yokohama Bay Bridge. There, at the edge of the container yard are those tall skinny gantry cranes, right? People call them giraffes."

Koharu whispered, "Giraffes."

Once they started on Yokohama-Yokosuka Road at the Namiki Interchange, all that was left was to head south down the spine of the Miura Peninsula.

About an hour and a half after leaving Nishi-Kanda, Akira's Toyota Land Cruiser arrived at the Uraga Interchange. They exited the highway, and Akira took them all the way to Cape Tomyozaki in search of a spot where they could look out over the Uraga Channel. However, all the good parking spots were claimed by the marina, and not only were the parking lots full, they were all members only. After travelling further up the cape, they found an abandoned lot where they could see out over everything. There was a sign reading CITY MARINA VERASIS PARKING LOT 2 (FREE), and it was quiet, not a person in sight.

Akira drove to the edge of the lot, parked facing the ocean, and rolled the backseat windows all the way down. The pleasant breeze played with Koharu's hair, and she blinked two or three times.

Placing his hands on the fence, Akira looked out over the Uraga Channel. His gaze took in the enormity of a passenger ship weaving among the other boats. Leisurely, it departed the Tokyo Bay and headed out to sea. A cabin cruiser then appeared from its shadow and approached the marina. The body of the boat was off white, her hull was deep blue, and on her side was written VIKING 48 CONVERTIBLE. Before docking at the berth in the marina, she turned 180 degrees, and when she showed her back to Akira, he could make out her name. Anastasia.

Two men appeared on the deck. The short and stout one picked up the moorings, and the other, average in height and skinny, held his smartphone to his ear. Someone from the marina staff jumped onboard and shook both their hands.

Akira closed the windows and set off towards Yokosuka. In about fifteen minutes they arrived at Yokosuka Harbor Shioiri Pier; Akira closed the zipper of the sleeping bag and laid Koharu down on the back seat. He entered the boat terminal and bought a 1 p.m. ticket for the "Cruise of YOKOSUKA Naval Port."

It was Sunday so virtually all of the boat tours were full. This cruise offered a deck-top view of the various battleships docked at the American Yokosuka Base and the Maritime Self-Defense Force base.

As they passed by the escort ships Murasame and Ikazuchi, which Akira was told had just returned from a mop-up operation involving pirates in the Somalian seas, the naval men on the decks stopped their work to wave at the passengers on the tour. The guide pointed front starboard and told them they could see Berth 12, serving the US Navy. It was 410 meters long, the longest of any military berth, able to fit an aircraft carrier. Nuclear aircraft carrier USS Ronald Reagan was expected to dock there in early October.

The tour boat weaved between sportsboats, aegis cruisers, and submarines for forty-five minutes before completing its journey by returning to Shioiri Pier.

After disembarking, Akira headed to the main drag, Dobuita-dori, and at a restaurant called Tsunami ordered their famous 227-gram Navy Burger with a drink and fries, which he took back to his car.

"Sorry for keeping you," he called out to Koharu, wrapped in her sleeping bag, before lifting her up, unzipping her, and leaning her against the right rear window. He started the car, headed east down Kaigan-dori, and pulled into the parking lot of Maborikaigan Park. Right before their eyes was a white sand beach and the sea, illuminated by the full force of the afternoon sun.

As Akira unwrapped his hamburger, he talked to Koharu.

"Before, when I worked on the monthly magazine, I edited this nonfiction piece called 'The Dowager Killer.'

"In 1989, Okashita Kaoru tricked a rich old woman who lived in Suginami Ward out of her land and got more than two hundred million yen. After that, he killed the old woman and his accomplice. Six years later, in 1995, he was arrested.

"He had priors. In the 1970s some land deal in Hiroshima wasn't going the way he wanted, and he locked his rival's daughter in a freezer for twenty-five hours. He got seven years for that. The girl lost both her hands and feet to frostbite.

"Then after being sentenced to death in 2005, Okashita started writing free-verse vernacular tanka in prison. I only remember one.

"'I love the ocean in the shadow of the mountains at twilight / Youth is driving two hours from Miyoshi.'"

Koharu repeated, "I love the ocean in the shadow of the mountains."

"Skill aside, isn't it so unnatural to imagine a villain like that going to see the ocean? And then writing this sort of lyrical poem? I don't think he could write something so self-absorbed yet so desperate to appeal to the reader like this in prose. I guess it's a genre problem."

After a visit to the bathroom, Akira ignited the car engine, set out on the Yokohama-Yokosuka Road from the Maborikaigan Interchange, and headed home.

A short while after passing the Uraga Interchange, a black Jeep Wrangler appeared behind him. Akira's Toyota was following the speed limit of eighty kilometers an hour, but the jeep approached at close to ninety. When it got close, the Jeep changed to the right lane, and quickly passed. However, forty or fifty meters later, the Jeep suddenly slowed down until it was beside Akira, and after driving alongside him for a moment, it slowed a little more so it was in line with the back half of Akira's car and maintained that position.

Thinking this suspicious, Akira checked his back and side mirrors. Behind the Jeep's left-side steering wheel was a middle-aged white man. He resembled Jack Palance, who had once made a name for himself in Hollywood playing singular villains. The license plate number began with a "T"—indicating a private vehicle of American military personnel, brought over from America.

The man seemed as though he was peering at the back seat, trying to make out Koharu's features. Though they were in different cars, the American and Koharu were virtually sitting next to each other, just like a couple.

Akira noticed an expression appear on the man's face of surprise intermingled with curiosity. He must have realized Koharu was not a human.

When Akira had returned to the car after getting a hamburger at Dobuita-dori and unzipped Koharu's sleeping bag, her glasses had fallen off somewhere inside. He was wrong to have left them there like that instead of making the effort to pick them up. That was the start of all this trouble.

Akira searched the road ahead for any indication of a rest area. For some reason, one just wouldn't show up. Could it be? Could there be no rest area on the Yokohama-Yokosuka Road?

After driving alongside the Jeep for over five minutes, he

finally found one. A sign stating REST AREA 1 KM, followed by REST AREA 200 M. But Akira did not slow down. He pressed down further on the accelerator. The Jeep sped up as well.

Akira did not turn on his left blinker; he made a sudden turn onto the ramp for the rest area. The Jeep sped off regretfully.

After parking on the far-left side of the rest area, Akira quickly zipped up the sleeping bag, laid Koharu down on the backseat, and drank a coffee at the terrace of a café to kill time. Afterwards, he drove paying careful attention just in case the Jeep was waiting for him somewhere.

"You shouldn't let anyone else see her, man or woman. I think something bad might happen if you do."

The makeup artist had been right. Akira had just learned exactly what kinds of danger awaited if anyone else were to see Koharu. Jack Palance couldn't take out his phone because he was driving. But if there had been someone else in that car with him, they could have taken a video of her. And not just of the beautiful face of the love doll but the profile of her owner as well. If such a queer video were to appear online, gain traction, and spread endlessly, well then … there was a chance it would spread around the entire world.

After that experience, Akira never again made plans to take Koharu outside.

<u>3.</u>

Ten minutes to six, Chikako had finished preparing to open her bar. She took out a Sony CD Walkman from a small cabinet on the shelf lined with bottles of alcohol and put in the earphones.

She had used the media player on her computer at home to make a mix of Chiaki Naomi songs from three of her albums, and she was in the routine of listening to one or two songs before opening for the night, just as a fighter might listen to Queen's "We Are the Champions" to pump themself up before getting into the ring.

There was no image on the CD jacket, just the words "Chiaki Naomi Best 8." The eight songs Chikako had chosen were "Seagull's Town," "Red Dragonfly," "Yagiri Passage," "Actor," "Twilight Begin," "Starlight Path," "Harbor View Hill," and "Riru Coming Home from Shanghai"—the last three songs being covers. She did not include any of the big Chiaki Naomi hits like "Kassai" or "Four Wishes," and she preferred the Chiaki version of "Yagiri Passage" even though the version sung by Hosokawa Takashi later won the Japan Record Award. She always sang "Red Dragonfly" at karaoke, although she thought the best of all those songs was "Twilight Begin."

Today she would first listen to "Seagull's Town."

Oh, Seagull,
Oh, Seagull,
Aren't you lonely?
Nowhere to go home to
Your whole life too
On the waves
Just like mine
On the waves
Ohhhh
Splash

This was when the door opened and a customer came in, so Chikako rushed to remove her earphones and say, "Irasshai." When she checked her watch, it was five till six.

The customer was a woman about her own age. She was dressed in high-end brands, and on her shoulder was a large Genten brand shoulder bag, maybe with documents in it. Her face was plain, but Chikako saw in the look in her eyes and the area around her mouth a strong will and a sense of individuality. Chikako sensed she wasn't the type you usually saw in a bar like hers.

While she was aware that, Akira aside, she had no ability to judge the quality of men, Chikako was quite confident in her ability to see the truth in a woman

The woman ordered a Moscow Mule, then opened the menu and stared at the food for a moment. After Chikako served her granola she asked, "Would you like some cheese? We have camembert, cheddar, and gorgonzola."

The woman chose the blue mold gorgonzola.

As she prepared it Chikako asked, "Do you like cheese?"

The woman began talking about a specialty shop she had recently found at Kagurazakaue.

At that shop she had found goat cheese from Denmark, and when she tried it at home it had something distinctive about it, and she thought there was no way she could eat it, but as she shaved off and ate little bits, she got used to it and was now fine with stinky cheeses.

After her cocktail, the woman ordered the Polish vodka Żubrówka with soda, and then got another, so it was clear she could handle even strong spirits.

Mistress Koharu

Since no other customers showed, Chikako kept the conversation going, asking, "Do you live nearby?"

The woman shook her head, looked down, and said, "Kitashinagawa." Chikako thought immediately, You couldn't tell a lie to save your life—what are you trying to hide? but she nodded along as though she hadn't noticed anything.

The woman stayed for about an hour total and said on her way out, "This place has a lovely atmosphere. I'll come back again next week." Chikako made a mental note of the single woman who liked cheese and strong alcohol.

Just as she left, Chikako's second customer for the night appeared. He was a regular, a university professor who would go to the beer hall Rancon after his English literature lecture, then stop by Rosebud before heading home.

As always, he placed his elbows on the counter, interlaced his fingers, looked around the bar, and said, "Good evening," in English.

On the third Wednesday of June, the second meeting of the Paranormal Activity Research Committee was held at Rosebud. Again, four members gathered, this time to discuss, as proposed by the editor, books about paranormal phenomena. Not, of course, the nonsense books most people associate with such topics but respectable ones with serious content. The only observer this time was Kondo Tatsuya, and in the place of the manager at the life insurance company was a middle-aged woman who worked as a local government employee.

First the piano tuner took out from his bag *On the Track of Unknown Animals* by the French zoologist Bernard Heuvelmans.

Published in Japanese by Kodansha in 1981, it was a book primarily about cryptids, and he explained briefly the content of chapter six, "The South American Monkey Man Ameranthropoides."

When he had first picked up this book, he had been drawn in by the strange appearance of De Loys's Ape in a photo at the beginning of the chapter, and he became fascinated by this unusual looking animal. The events that led to this photograph and the discovery of the monkey there pictured happened as follows.

Swiss geologist Francois de Loys spent three years exploring the mountains on the border of Columbia and Venezuela, and in 1920, in the middle of the jungle, he discovered two "apes of great height," a male and a female. His crew were attacked by these apes, and in order to rescue them, de Loys shot and killed the female, the body of which they carried to the riverside, where they sat it down on a fuel crate, propped up its chin with a stick, and then photographed it.

The creature's face shared the features of a spider monkey, but the size of the animal amazed de Loys. The height of the ape could be estimated quite accurately by using the fuel crate in the photograph, and the primate was determined to be "between 150 and 157 centimeters." It had been generally accepted that there were no monkeys over a meter tall in South America, and thus no wonder de Loys was surprised to encounter such a creature.

On March 11, 1929, at a conference in Paris, the "seemingly anthropoid ape" was presented and officially named *Ameranthropoides loysi*, though there is no record of the enormous monkey ever being spotted again after this encounter.

The piano tuner said that the famous director at NHK

broadcasting corporation Kokubun Hiromu had gone to South America three times over the past year to work on a forthcoming documentary, *The Great Amazon, The Last Frontier*, and that he's supposed to be working with a tribe called the Isolados to track a "mysterious giant monkey." The piano tuner was looking forward to next year's broadcast of this "series exploring the yet unseen world of the Amazon River."

Next, the middle-aged high school physics teacher took out both the 1974 hardcover and paperback versions of Arthur Koestler's *The Roots of Coincidence*, translated by Murakami Yoichiro, and laid them on the table. He began his introduction to the book by saying that the fact the translator of this book was Professor Murakami, an emeritus professor at Tokyo University specializing in the history of science, was the best evidence of this book's value, and then he explained that the book attempted to prove that extrasensory perception and psychokinesis were not scams but valuable fields for potential academic research.

In the book, Koestler writes in detail about successful experiments using Zener cards to send messages telepathically and controlling the results of dice throws with telekinesis. He describes how experts in particle physics interpret those amazing results and then attempts to explain them through Pauli and Jung's theory of synchronicity.

After touching specifically on Cambridge Professor, physicist, and mathematician Adrian Dobbs's hypothesis, the high school teacher shared that there were many parts of the book that he was still not confident he fully understood.

After the high school teacher had finished, the accountant who had talked about the megalodon in the previous session took out a copy of University of Chicago professor, zoologist, and biochemist Roy P. Mackal's *A Living Dinosaur?: In Search of Mokele-Mbembe*, stressing that the book could be read as an adventure novel based on fact. "In the Likouala region of the Democratic Republic of the Congo is an expanse of fourteen thousand square kilometers of untouched swampland and rainforest. The depictions of the party on the search for the legendary dinosaur Mokele-Mbembe, advancing through the jungle, dark even at midday, on the hunt for clues, reminded me so much of the adventures of the times of Stanley and Livingstone. There's really nothing more thrilling."

Mackal had served for ten years as the director of the Loch Ness Phenomena Investigation Bureau that had been established by the British Parliament, and in September of 1970, along with two assistants, he had actually spotted Nessie at Urquhart Bay. In his book, he said it was this experience that sent him on his journey to find Mokele-Mbembe.

The accountant said he saw on some Japanese TV channel a shot of Lake Tele, the location where the professor searched for Mokele-Mbembe, taken from a helicopter or Cessna flying low over the lake, and captured in that footage were the waves left in the wake of a giant creature as it made its way toward the shore, but the accountant added that as the water was too cloudy, one could not judge whether it was a hippopotamus, or a crocodile, or Mokele-Mbembe.

The middle-aged woman who was participating for the first time then introduced herself as an employee of a ward office and also said she was an acting guide and member of the Japan Mountain Guide Association.

Mistress Koharu

The book she wanted to recommend was Kakuhata Yusuke's *The Yeti Came from Across the Way*, a work of nonfiction that won the thirty-first Nitta Jiro Literary Prize.

"I was surprised to find that famous Japanese mountaineers like Konishi Hirofumi-san, Tabei Junko-san, and Imai Michiko-san claim to have seen the abominable snowman, but Yoshino Mitsuhiko's report—he was the first Japanese person to scale the north face of the Matterhorn—was so shocking, it totally changed my image of the abominable snowman."

From a page she had marked with a sticky note, and adding her own simple explanations as she went along, she read aloud how Yoshino had spotted the yeti while heading for Dhaulagiri IV in the Himalayan Mountains on May 7, 1971.

"Yoshino arrived at Camp Two and entered a sherpa tent. After drinking tea and having a quick rest, he headed back out … Wanting to urinate, he took five or six steps towards Camp One and stared off into the distance as he did his business. And then, about eighty meters down the slope, he saw someone making their way up on all fours in knee-deep snow. Yoshino presumed it must have been a sherpa, so he called out five or six times but got no response. The figure climbed up the wall of snow and eventually reached the mountain ridge. And then, just as Yoshino saw the figure rise up suddenly onto his rear legs, he turned back down towards him and stared."

Yoshino himself described that scene in a report for Yamakei Publishing Group's magazine *Modern Adventure* as follows: "I had thought until then he was a sherpa, so for a moment I was surprised to see it was an animal. He, too, looked at me a bit startled and confused, his head bent in puzzlement. His eyes were

large, round, and clear. We looked at each other for a moment ...
I had thought it was not a human but an animal at first because
his ears stood up like those of a bear, dog, or fox, but actually
what had appeared to be ears was just his hair blown up by the
strong winds rising from the valley below."

Yoshino rushed back to the tent to retrieve his camera and
managed to get three shots of the yeti making his way towards
the Tareja Valley side.

However, he later discovered that all three photos were over-
exposed, leaving no image, and his scoop of the century had
vanished forever. The woman ended the story by saying, "I'm so
jealous of Yoshino-san being chosen to see the yeti up close like
that. Ever since Eric Shipton photographed its footprints, the
image of the yeti as a large, bipedal creature has spread far and
wide, but Yoshino-san claimed that it was a little bit shorter than
the one-and-a-half-meter tall bamboo poles they had erected
near the hiker's camp."

After the meeting ended, Kondo Tatsuya took a seat at the
counter and drank a bourbon as always.

He asked Chikako, "According to that yeti story, he climbed
an impossibly steep cliff face covered in snow. Doesn't that
make you think that rather than an ancestor of the humans, it's
a new breed of monkey?"

As Chikako went through the motions of engaging in conversation with him, he steadily got drunk. Then he whispered, almost
as if to himself, "Hey, there's something I've been wondering."

"What is it? What are you holding back here for? If you're
worried about something, I'll find a way to fix it. Tell me whatever's on your mind."

Mistress Koharu

Tatsuya looked up at her and licked his upper lip with the tip of his tongue.

"You're Mayumi-san, right? Steamy Mayumi."

4.

From the middle of June to the end of July, the Kanagawa Museum of Modern Literature held an exhibition, "Poet and Ambassador: Paul Claudel and Japan," celebrating the sixtieth anniversary of Claudel's passing. One of Akira's friends from his college days, Higa Katsuyuki, was set to appear as a panelist at one of the related events, a symposium titled "The Mystery of Claudel's *Cent phrases pour eventails*," which brought him from Kyoto. So on the first Sunday of July, Akira headed to the museum in Harbor View Park in Yamate, Yokohama.

Higa was originally from Naha, and back when they were students, he once led Akira around Okinawa Island for a full week. They saw the sights of Gusuku, Himeyuri Tower, Sefa Utaki, even making it to Kudaka Island. In his third year of university, Higa switched his major from Japanese literature to comparative literature with a focus in comparative culture. And after going on to graduate school, he received a scholarship from the French government to study at the Sorbonne, where he received his doctorate. Upon returning to Japan, after stints lecturing at the Humanities Department of Mie University and the Literature Department of Nagoya University, a few years ago he was invited to serve as an assistant professor at the International Research Center for Japanese Culture in Kyoto. In the New Year's card he sent to Akira last year, he said not having to teach was a huge relief. He had published two books, *Renaissance Painting and Perspective* and *Emile Guimet and Japonisme*.

Akira decided to take Higa out to the Noge nightlife district after the symposium. Akira wasn't particularly familiar with the area, but he felt that for catching up on the years he and his old friend had spent out of contact, a new place in Noge would be far more fun than a standard old restaurant in the nearby Chinatown. So he made a reservation at the wine bar SimonS on Noge Nakamichi. Their popular items included home-made roast ham, young chicken and maitake mushrooms in salt and lemon sauce, and green apple pizza, and their wine list included renowned vintages of the red wine Barolo. Akira, however, also had another motive. Among the many bars on Noge Nakamichi, SimonS was located particularly close to Gallery Hitogata, where Akira had just happened to have recently received an invitation to an event titled "Falling in Love with a Doll: A Retrospective and Overview."

Just over half a year had passed since Koharu had joined him at his home, but Akira had no interest in any other dolls. He was about to throw the invitation unopened into the garbage when he found himself considering taking Higa to the exhibition at Gallery Hitogata. He was curious what kind of reaction he would get out of this man from Okinawa, the superstitious land of mabui and noro, and educated in comparative literature at a Parisian university.

When they were students, Akira and Higa had once debated in class whether or not objects exist independently of people's observations. Akira still remembered clearly that it was a rainy afternoon. Taking the orthodox side of the debate, Higa was a fearsome debater who would repeatedly throw out tricky questions.

Akira messaged him saying, "There's a love doll gallery in this spot under the Keikyu Main Line that's got a bit of a reputation recently for being artsy. It seems interesting. Want to take a look?"

After the symposium Higa was attending ended, while Akira waited in the ground floor foyer, he placed a call to Gallery Hitogata, checked with the manager that they were still open, and explained that he would be coming with a friend but would like the manager to approach him as though he were a first-time visitor.

They got into the cab they'd called to the museum.

Akira gave himself over to the shaking of the car as it descended from Harbor View Hill Park, as he intoned a part of one of the short phrases from *Cent phrases pour eventails*.

"'From the edges of this earth / passing all the distance / the white peonies of Hasedera.' Was that how it went?"

Cent phrases pour eventails, or *A Hundred Movements for a Fan*, was a collection of poetry by Paul Claudel, who had served as the French Ambassador to Japan for five years, during which time he experienced the Great Kanto Earthquake. The work was published in Tokyo in Showa 2 (1927), just before Claudel was to leave Japan to take up the position of French Ambassador to the US; it was composed in three volumes containing 172 parts, and designed to fold out like a book of sutras. The original poems were written by Claudel's own hand in ink. The third volume ended with, "If they try to sever me from Japan / Please let it be with grains of golden sand."

Higa took over and recited, "'Amongst them one / showing faint crimson / The center of a peony / Memory of a color of no color / Memory of a scent of no scent.'"

"It was great how that poet guy quoted Kyoshi after you got on stage and read that. 'White peonies / Still we call them though / crimson faintly,'" Akira said, and then added, "And by the entrance, the bust of him made by his sister Camille, did you notice the single red rose they put there? That was a nice touch."

"The bust was at Maison franco-japonaise in Kyoto. I had asked them if we could display it for the symposium, but they really didn't want to approve it. It was hard to ship over. But we made it work somehow." Higa added bashfully, "The rose was my idea. I asked the museum to do that. I'm having them change it every couple of days. A small homage to Camille Claudel."

"I watched the biopic about her starring Isabelle Adjani. She was betrayed by Rodin and wound up spending her last days in a sanitorium, right? A female sculptor praised for her beauty meets a tragic end."

The pair got out of the taxi at an intersection near Keikyu Hinodecho Station and walked along the path on the left bank of Ooka River, heading to Konagecho New Studio Beneath the Rails. When they peeked inside the used artbook shop on the way, Artbook Bazaar, they found both of Higa's books lined up on a shelf. The fact that they were priced above the list price pleased Higa.

They climbed the wooden stairs of Gallery Hitogata and made their way through the door. The gallery manager was talking to a few customers and upon noticing Akira and Higa, gave a slight nod.

Mistress Koharu

In the gallery, love dolls from Japanese makers—primarily Orient Industry, but also 4woods and Level-D, among others—were on display, arranged by year from 1977 to 2015. The earliest doll on display was named Hohoemi, produced by Orient Industry in 1977. This first model was made of polyurethane and was what was called a "torso type" doll. It had only a head, breasts, and crotch. From 1982, they began using a new material, latex, and their new, full-body model, Omokage, was released, but one would have to wait for the debut of Orient Industry's Candy Girl Jewel in 2001 to see a doll with a full-body frame that also used silicone, the material closest to the feeling of human skin. This was the start of a full Candy Girl series, and the exhibition followed their yearly model changes and updates to the present day.

In the final exhibition space, where Koharu had sat half a year ago, five "cutting edge" dolls by the three major Japanese makers were displayed, each in a different costume, striking a different pose.

After seeing off his previous customers, the manager rushed over to Akira and Higa and greeted them. Higa rained down questions one might have expected from an engineer about the range of motion of the dolls' joints, the proportion of silicone in the skin, the melting and combustion points of the materials, and their internal structure.

"Silicone is quite resistant to heat and can withstand temperatures of up to 300 degrees. The combustion point is said to be 450 degrees, and, what's more, burning silicone does not release any toxic fumes. It's the perfect material for a love doll," the manager answered politely. "Shall I bring you some coffee?" he added, before vanishing behind a partition.

"I believe the furnaces in crematoriums reach between eight hundred and one thousand degrees. Also, doesn't he look like Sartre?" Akira whispered.

Higa nodded in agreement and said, "He also looks like Peter Lorre playing that Soviet Party spy in the musical *Silk Stockings*."

The manager returned carrying two mugs. Higa took a sip of coffee and asked, "These 'cutting edge' dolls are quite different from the older models, aren't they?"

"That's right. These girls represent idealized proportions you won't see on any real woman. Just striving for realism will leave you falling behind these days. If we were to compare them to cars, these are not the Toyotas and Nissans, but the Porsches and Ferraris, high-class sports cars."

"I heard prices range from seven hundred thousand to a million, and that there are even more expensive models. What is it that draws your customers to buy something so expensive?"

The manager blinked his asymmetrically placed eyes for a moment before saying, "Of course, there is obviously the desire to have sex with a beautiful woman, to satisfy, or realize that desire. And we do our best to maintain a wide selection of types so as to meet the various preferences of our customers, whether that be for older women, innocent types, or anime characters."

The manager paused for the length of one breath.

"However, I believe that many of our customers actually have another reason, one that, surprisingly, they are not consciously aware of."

"They're not consciously aware of?"

"Yes. I think in their unconscious, many men actually desire something different from normal sexual activity—they crave

Mistress Koharu

something obscene or indecent, or shall we say, erotic, that they cannot get from a flesh-and-blood woman."

"Obscene or indecent?" Higa repeated without missing a beat.

"One moment please."

The manager unfolded a steel folding chair that had been leaning against the wall, offered it to Higa, and told him to sit; he then carried over a love doll in navy lingerie with white lace flowers on it. It was a Level-D product named Ayana. He stood the doll up on her special stand, faced her directly at Higa, and leaned her forward. "You can move these," he said before adjusting the direction of her eyes with his fingertips, sheathed in white gloves. He set her gaze on Higa.

"Do you feel her staring at your face?"

Higa nodded.

"The relationship between man and woman is a sort of relationship between self and other. When a man feels a woman, an other, looking at him like this, he cannot help but feel that they are an agent with a will of their own. And this means that there will never be a feeling of eroticism. You'll see what I mean when we do this."

With a slight flutter, his gloved hands turned Ayana's neck slightly, making her face down to the left.

"Now the doll's gaze is not on you. And now your gaze can capture the doll's profile, you have complete control. One fully enjoys the feeling of eroticism when the woman is in a state such that her will has been deprived, when she has fallen into a position unable to take action on her own. There was an author who said that the most obscene thing in this world is the body of a bound woman.

"A doll is the single best item for satisfying this particular proclivity. The people who purchase them are, surprisingly, often unaware of that. However, I wonder if after their purchase, when they try a few things out, they don't discover it later."

Higa smiled softly and whispered, "So men, deep down, are hoping for women as others to become a sort of object that they can control however they please."

He turned to Akira and added, half in jest, "I never imagined I'd meet someone who could explain Sartre's twisted logic in *Being and Nothingness* quite like that. I should invite this guy to Kyoto as a visiting professor."

After being seated at a back table at SimonS, the pair ordered a few things off a blackboard menu that a young waitress carried—home-made roast ham, summer pickles, liver mousse—and toasted with small mugs of draft black beer.

"When you texted to say you were going to take me to a love doll gallery, I went back and reread Freud's essay 'The Uncanny.'"

By the time the Barolo was uncorked, the seven-seat counter and the four-person table next to Akira and Higa were all full. Behind the counter in the small kitchen space, a single man was fighting for his life; the chef, who appeared to be about the same age as Akira, never stopped bantering with the customers, though his hands also never slowed as he prepared the food.

Higa took a sip of wine and calmly continued his story.

"Freud begins by examining the definitions of 'heimlich,' or familiar things, and then their opposite, uncanny things, the 'unheimlich.' And he says the reason we find wax dolls and automata to be unheimlich is because we get confused and feel a sort of fear when we see things that we can't determine are living or not."

Next, Higa began speaking about E. T. A. Hoffmann's short story "The Sandman."

"This was the story Freud picks as an example in his research on the unheimlich. Offenbach's opera *The Tales of Hoffmann* also references it, but the narratives are quite different. One day, a college student, Nathaniel, the main character of 'The Sandman,' purchases a small telescope at the insistence of an Italian glasses salesman named Giuseppe Coppola."

When Akira heard the name Giuseppe, his back straightened in his seat.

"Nathaniel peeks into the home of the university professor who lives across the street with that telescope, and there he finds the professor's beautiful and mysterious daughter, Olympia, and he falls for her immediately, head over heels. Olympia, however, is not a person but an automaton. The professor created a gear system that moves her body, and Giuseppe gave her eyes. But since dolls are not alive in the first place, they're a symbol of death. And Nathaniel, who's mistaken this doll for a girl with a soul, is in for a tragic end. He jumps to his death from a tower. This is a work of fiction, but this really happens. There are real examples of men who fell in love with dolls."

This was just the prologue for Higa to begin discussing Oskar Kokoschka, one of the men who, along with Klimt and Schiele, made up the driving force behind the Austrian branch of German Expressionism.

Kokoschka had a passionate relationship with Alma Mahler, the widow of Gustav Mahler, and two of his paintings depicting her are his best known works—"Portrait of Alma Mahler," said to be his Mona Lisa and housed in the Tokyo National Museum of Modern Art, and "The Bride of the Wind." However, while away serving in World War I, he received a serious head injury and returned to discover that Alma had married another man. Depressed, Kokoschka enlisted the help of the painter Hermine Moos to create a life-sized replica of Alma, which he then lived with and even took out to visit restaurants and attend parties.

Kokoschka's life with his Alma doll continued for just over three years. Then, one night in 1922, he held a party and invited his friends. After enjoying drinks, music, and dancing, he suddenly, and without clear reason, cut the head off the doll that was dressed in a dazzling gown and threw her out of a window into his garden.

His motive was unknown, but some said that the doll was possessed by the spirit of his lost love, Alma, and that after he destroyed the doll, he was freed from its curse.

After listening patiently to Higa's long story, Akira put in his two cents. "So we have a story of the dangers of falling in love with something that's not human, and another about living with something possessed by the spirit of an ex-lover. That reminds me of that very unheimlich movie, also starring Isabelle Adjani, *Possession*. But aren't things a bit different now in the twenty-first century? I mean, you just saw in that gallery, love dolls are a mass-produced commodity here in Japan. Not every doll can have that kind of bone-chilling story behind it. Is it still impossible for people to see dolls as equal to humans, and build a loving relationship with them?"

"Are you suggesting that you could purchase a love doll and live with it?"

Mistress Koharu

Akira sneered and went silent.

"In our everyday lives we can rarely appreciate the fullness of reality, the sense of living through unmediated presence. But can one salvage a sense of unmediated reality by living with a love doll, something dead pretending to be alive? There is always the option of buying Ayana from that Sartre lookalike and testing it out."

"Your wifey'd never allow that." Akira slipped into Osaka dialect, then changed the subject. "Should we get a green apple pizza to finish up?"

Koharu locked the door behind her with the spare key and, careful not to run into any of the other tenants, made her way slowly down the stairs. She dressed herself in the same clothes she had worn when they went to see the ocean and planned to return home after strolling around the vicinity of the apartment.

She stood next to Akira's car, parked in front of the entrance, and after identifying the placement of the sun in the sky, she took her first step into the labyrinth of the city.

Kyoko watched Akira leave in the morning, and then she sank fully into her subtitle translation work, leaving the window open. When she lifted her eyes from the computer on her work desk, she happened to see a young woman standing in the middle of the park. She sensed something odd about this woman. Kyoko stood up and began observing her carefully.

The cause of Kyoko's odd feeling was the woman's bright blue raincoat. The woman was beautiful, with a body like a model, and wore glasses. It was quite the uncanny scene to watch this woman stand in the center of the park in the middle of the afternoon and simply study her surroundings.

There was no one else in the park, so what could she be looking at? The way she continued to just stand there, aimlessly, sparked further interest in Kyoko.

The word "flaneur"—one who walks around a city purposelessly, observing—scraped around at the bottom of her mind. And as she then thought of the wandering character in Edgar Allen Poe's "The Man of the Crowd," the beautiful woman turned her body, stared for a moment at the balcony on the third floor of the building across from Kyoko's, and suddenly began walking towards the road. The woman quickly vanished from Kyoko's line of sight.

Kyoko returned to her computer and tried to get back to work, but she couldn't focus. She took Walter Benjamin's *Berlin Childhood around 1900* from her bookshelf and flipped through it.

Koharu followed the foot traffic, crossed Hakusan-dori at an intersection, and continuing straight, wound up walking down a smaller road until she arrived in front of Kanda Catholic Church. The large windows of the brick church, rectangular panes of stained glass that reached up towards the eaves of the building, were bathed in the afternoon light and gave off a colorful shine. It was almost time for the Sunday Mass to begin, and the faithful were streaming inside. Koharu paused at the entrance, and as she stared at the statues of the Holy Virgin Mary on either side of the entrance, an old woman approached her and said, "Please, come in. You don't have to be a believer to join the Mass."

Mistress Koharu

Koharu pulled back, turned around, and sped off down a nearby narrow road. Before her was now a tall and steep set of stone steps. After staring up the steps for a few seconds, she sprinted up them in one go, without losing her breath, and found herself on a sidewalk in the district of Surugadaiue. The rows of horse chestnut trees had deep green leaves, and from between them peeked countless small white flowers.

As she walked along in the shadow of the trees, she almost bumped into a woman rushing up the stairs from a basement café. Koharu quickly dodged her and continued on her way as though nothing had happened. The other woman froze where she was, stunned. She adjusted her shoulder bag, moving it from her right shoulder to her left, as she watched the young woman race away with all the speed of a power walker.

From the street lined with rows of horse chestnut trees, Koharu crossed over to Meidai-dori and climbed the gentle slope of Gangizaka until she arrived in front of Nikolai Orthodox Cathedral. As she stared up at the green dome and arched windows of the main hall, a bell suddenly rang out loudly. Koharu saw a priest dressed in all black at the very top of the bell tower standing next to the dome. He used an array of ropes and pedals to ring bells of various sizes, putting on a performance of a rich variety of sounds.

There were several worshippers in the church courtyard. Here too services were about to begin. Koharu, placing both arms on the half-opened iron front gate, leaned over and focused on the sound of the bells. Her body completely still, she closed her eyes softly, and a look of ecstasy spread across her face. She felt as if she was in a dream. Just once, Giuseppe had taken her to visit Matthias Church, with its towering steeples located atop Buda Castle Hill. She wasn't allowed to enter the building itself, but she could not forget the sounds of the pipe organ escaping from the church.

The bells stopped ringing.

"I'm going to close the gate. Please step away from the fence."

A security guard had come over, his voice cold and intimidating.

Koharu began walking again. She travelled down Hongo-dori, turned left at the Ogawamachi intersection, and then headed east on Yasukuni-dori. She crossed the Sudacho intersection, and as she was about to pass under the elevated rail of the JR Chuo Line, a dog being walked by an old man started barking at her.

Beside the gently curving red brick wall which supported the overhead train tracks was an alleyway one could use to cross to the other side of the tracks. At the entrance of the alley were eight steel pipe arches arranged to prevent cars from passing through.

From the other end of the alley, the shiba inu that had barked at her glared at Koharu and growled. It had noticed that she did not smell human. She stepped back and let them pass, and after they had moved along and Koharu had checked that no one was looking, she stretched her back and jumped over the steel pipe arches.

Originally, the elevated rail of the JR Chuo Line was supported by a series of arches made of brick, but these archways had all been filled in with concrete. Koharu pressed the palm of her hand up against the old, blackened brick, feeling the vibrations of the trains overhead pass through her body.

Mistress Koharu

The alleyway let out near Mansei Bridge, but just before crossing she turned right onto Yanagihara-dori and passed under the Yamanote Line, Keihin Tohoku Line, and Tohoku and Joetsu bullet train tracks. Then, on her left, appeared a stone torii gate.

A middle-aged woman holding a parasol walked briskly in Koharu's direction, and when there were just a few meters separating them, the woman turned to the right and passed under the torii, climbing down the set of stone steps into the grounds of a shrine. Koharu crouched behind the torii and observed the woman's movement.

Yanagimori Inari Shrine was on the edge of the Kanda River. The main shrine being below the torii, it was a so-called "descending pilgrimage," and there were several smaller shrines on the way from the entrance. On either side of each shrine sat foxes, tanuki, komainu, or heavenly dragons. The woman with the parasol visited every shrine without exception, and paused by the small, red torii at the entrance. There, right before the woman, was a bronze statue of a tanuki, its enormous belly jutting out. The woman brought her hands together, rubbed the lower belly of the tanuki gently with her fingertips, and then, twirling her parasol at her shoulders, rushed back the way she had come. Koharu descended the stone steps and stood in front of the tanuki statue; she copied the woman and rubbed its shining belly.

Realizing that she had come too far, Koharu left the shrine and took the fastest route she could home.

As she crossed Hakusan-dori again, Koharu recalled that she had still yet to see the ranchu goldfish that Akira had repeatedly called "painfully cute." If when she went home, she slipped into the living-dining-kitchen without making a noise, and rushed to peak into the tank, would she be able to see the little fish swimming about? No matter what, she would have disliked that ranchu because Akira held it in his favor, but on top of that the fish had this groundless resentment towards her. Maybe it deserved a little shock.

Koharu opened the door with the spare key and quietly entered the apartment. She could make out the faint whirring of the filtration system and bubbling of the oxygenator from the living-dining-kitchen. Stepping softly, she slipped past the bedroom.

Sitting in the train on the Keihin Tohoku Line after seeing Higa off at his hotel in Sakuragicho, Akira thought about Freud's essay and the Hoffmann short story. Would he, living with Koharu, reach an end like the college student Nathaniel of "The Sandman"? Would he become mad like the painter Kokoschka?

Akira's fascination with love dolls had been instigated by the article he happened to find in a magazine, and through actually living with Koharu, many of the problems and anxieties that had plagued him had been resolved. He now slept deeply at night, something that for a time had felt impossible for him.

Akira considered this the result of him choosing Koharu of his own free will. If that were the case, it would be impossible for him to be possessed or otherwise the victim of his situation.

He had never felt Koharu to be unheimlich in the Freudian sense. He had grown convinced that the very purpose of her existence was to serve as his lifeline, so to speak. Not only did Koharu make love to him, but eventually she even began speaking with him. At that moment, she had broken free from the role of mere sex doll and had become something no less than a human woman; she had assumed the role of a dutiful wife.

Higa would have probably smugly pointed out that that in itself was proof Akira was possessed by the doll. And if that was the case, the fact that he still had a real-life mistress in Chikako, while it would differentiate him from Nathaniel and Kokoschka, might not preclude the possibility that his life was in jeopardy. So then, what sorts of dangers, what pitfalls awaited him?

Akira changed trains for the Sobu Line at Akihabara and then got off at Suidobashi.

He opened his bedroom door just a crack.

"I'm home," he said to Koharu before heading to the living-dining-kitchen. He walked up to the fish tank, and as he was about to ask as always, "And how are you doing today?" he was shocked to see his ranchu floating. What could have happened? He checked the aerator and filtration system, but there was nothing out of place. The two comets were swimming about happily as ever. Why, why was just the ranchu dead?

Though upset, he did his best to control his emotions, carefully wrapping up the ranchu's body in a wet tissue. After disposing of it in the garbage, he took a shower.

Akira laid down in bed, imagining the ranchu swimming joyfully, fluttering through the water, and as Koharu brought her body up to his, he said to her, "He's dead. Why? I wonder what could have caused it. I never imagined it would be so soon. This is such a shock."

Koharu wrapped her arms around Akira's head to comfort him and brought his cheek towards her. Between the index and middle fingers of her right hand, there was a single, tiny fish scale.

5.

Chikako carried her laundry basket out to the veranda. The rainy season ended yesterday. The morning's clear, blue sky foretold the coming of a summer day.

Although Chikako's apartment address was in Kaminarimon 1-chome, her veranda unfortunately faced west, meaning she had no view of the famous Kaminarimon Gate itself, nor of Sensoji Temple or the Tokyo Skytree.

Directly across from her apartment, on the other side of Kokusai-dori, was Sanzendo, a shop where they built and sold Buddhist alters and other Buddhist wares, and as soon as she stepped out on her veranda, the first thing that caught her eye was the enormous billboard standing on their roof. On the left half of it was an image of Miroku Boddhisatva in subdued colors bringing his right fingers up to his cheek, and on the right was written, in a font which looked like brush strokes, SPIRIT SEEKS FORM, FORM CHEERS THE SPIRIT. She had not once considered the meaning of those mysterious words. Beyond the sign, she could see the tiled roof of the central hall of the Higashi Honganji Temple.

Wind blew overhead, bringing with it white fragments of cloud which gathered together, forming a large lenticular cloud and blocking out the sun. Chikako stopped hanging up her clothes. She recalled the details of the threat she had received from Kondo Tatsuya and stood there for a moment lost in thought.

Mistress Koharu

On that third Wednesday of June, after the second Paranormal Activity Research Committee meeting had ended and the other members had left, Kondo Tatsuya had moved to a counter seat and drank bourbon. When he got a little drunk, he had whispered something, and then he had looked up at Chikako and unexpectedly asked that bizarre question.

She decided not to answer that question and had remained silent, but waiting for an answer, he had continued to stare at her face with deep suspicion. Thankfully, one of her regulars, the university professor, appeared at an uncharacteristically late hour and saved her from the tenseness of the moment.

Tatsuya stood up, placed a ten thousand yen note in front of the register, said he didn't need any change, and left.

With his question, Tatsuya had finally given voice to a suspicion that he had been mulling over for two months. Chikako had refused to answer, but he presumed her inability to respond was proof that it was the truth, and thus there was now no doubt in his mind that Mayumi and Chikako were the same person.

After Chikako saw off the professor, she closed the bar earlier than usual, and instead of taking the subway home like always, she caught a cab. Once home, she hurried to the shower and then wrapped herself in her bathrobe, sunk her whole body into her sofa, and downed a glass of Black Amami brown sugar shochu on the rocks. Dribbles of condensation had slid down the sides of her ice pail and pooled on her teak table, and she angrily slid the bottom of her glass around through them. Chikako crossed her legs by placing her right foot on top of her left knee and, noticing that she was mimicking the half lotus pose with one raised hand in which Miroku Bodhisattva was often depicted, laughed at herself. She ran her fingers through her hair, lifting it away from her forehead.

When Chikako had worked at the bar Kohaku in Ueno-Hirokoji, one of her regulars was a woman who wore clothes too flashy and makeup too heavy for someone her age. She used to work under the name "Kazama Hitomi" when she was a popular adult video star and was even called by some the Queen of the Adult Entertainment World. After retiring, she started up her own adult video production company called Deep Throat and hit a streak of good luck.

She came to Kohaku once or twice a week and ordered cocktails like Bacardis and gimlets, would stay for about an hour each time, and then her driver would take her home.

One night, when the couple who owned Kohaku were deep in conversation with the owner of a nearby soba shop, that woman approached Chikako and said she had something she wanted to talk about, and they agreed to meet a few days later at Café Renoir, near the Shinobazu exit of Ueno Station.

"How would you feel about becoming an actress? I have a great hair and makeup artist at my company," she began. "I'll take her next time I visit the bar. You hardly wear any makeup, so it'll be easy to change your looks so no one will ever recognize you. She does makeup for the love dolls at Orient Industry. She's really amazing."

There was flattery in her gaze as she stared into Chikako's eyes.

"We are committed to taking care of our actresses, and we won't force you to do anything you don't want to," she said as she told Chikako about the director-actor. "You know the soccer player Nakazawa Yuji, right? He's a big guy who looks kind of like him. All the actresses say he takes the lead but very gently—he's got a good reputation among them. And it's great, his thing. It looks good on film, and he lasts a long time."

And she added that Deep Throat had the best of the best video editing technology to blur out the "most important" parts. They were second to none in the industry. They were extremely careful about data management—not once had an unedited video ever leaked, et cetera. After listing all these points, she concluded by discussing the rates for performers.

This was the fall of 2008, and Chikako was thinking about opening her own bar in the spring of the following year. She had planned to use the Japan Finance Corporation loan program for female entrepreneurs, but that alone would not provide her with enough money to open her own bar. When she heard how much she'd make performing, her heart leapt. If she appeared in just one film …

The director-cum-actor Takahashi Kenkichi was a quiet type with a relaxed way of talking. He was in his mid-forties and both his looks and build were in fact not that far off from Nakazawa Yuji's.

Deep Throat's *Hot Spring* series garnered enduring popularity due to the films' distinctive structure and content. There were a few important aspects which distinguished them from standard adult videos.

Steamy Journey of an Unfaithful Wife: The Case of Mayumi (36 years old) begins with Takahashi waiting to meet Mayumi, the married woman he got to know on a community web forum, at 9 a.m. at Shinjuku Station. An unusual opening, as the time of this rendezvous is virtually unheard of in pornographic works. Nine in the morning is less a time for a married woman to go on an adulterous tryst than for a family to head out for some wholesome fun.

Nonetheless, the pair get on the express luxury train, the Odakyu Romancecar, and Takahashi immediately begins digging into Mayumi's personal history.

Mayumi says she is thirty-six years old, four years younger than her husband, and then goes on to describe her daily life in great detail—from the episode of meeting her husband, a cram school teacher, at their shared workplace to how they have been married five years but still have no children. Every day she returns home before him to prepare dinner, they eat late while she listens to his complaints, and they sleep until past ten each morning. They discuss the meaning she finds in her work and the intimate aspects of their marriage, and just as things are starting to feel a bit like a normal pornographic video, the train arrives at Odawara Station.

Many viewers would get impatient at this point and press the fast-forward button, but the film proceeds coolly, giving time for a mood of artificial romance to arise between the two performers.

They change trains to the Tokaido Main Line and head to Atami, and from Atami Station they take a car to a restaurant with a view of the ocean. There they have lunch—pasta pescatore— and herb tea. To show such a scene of an actress actually eating is certainly very uncommon in adult videos.

That whole time, small confessions are being dragged out of Mayumi: "My first time was when I was fifteen," "I did it with four men before I met my husband."

Mistress Koharu

Before they finally arrive at their lodgings, they stop by a park and take a stroll on a nature trail full of red dragonflies. They kiss and hold hands while they walk, raising the viewers' anticipation for the next scene.

Occasionally they make mysterious comments as well, such as when Mayumi says, "The scent of roses stimulates women's hormone production."

What is also worthy of special note is that after they arrive at a traditional inn for the night, the menu for their 6 p.m. dinner is explained on the screen with pictures and on-screen captions describing each dish. The overwhelming impact of this multicourse dinner, including items such as spiny lobster sashimi and wagyu teppanyaki, is sure to demolish any expectations of an imminent sex scene in the inn's outdoor bath.

After dinner, the two head to the recreation room, where they tie back the sleeves of their yukata and play a game of table tennis to help with their digestion. The score is displayed on the upper left corner of the screen. Of course, this scene was often fast-forwarded.

After this, the sexy parts that viewers had all been waiting for come in ample measure, followed by a breakfast scene the following morning and more conversations in the train home. And then, when they go their separate ways at Shinjuku Station, perfunctory closing text reading, "To the woman who travelled with me, I hope you find happiness," runs across the screen, and the two-and-a-half-hour long masterpiece finally comes to an end.

While lengthy and ridiculous, this adult video also exuded a strange charm, and its star, Mayumi a.k.a. Chikako, was not left with a negative impression of her brief stint as an actress nor did she at all regret the experience. She simply blocked it out.

Steamy Journey of an Unfaithful Wife was a hit, and a sequel was planned to be a special commemorative release celebrating the tenth anniversary of the founding of Deep Throat, but Chikako rejected the offer and cut all ties with the adult entertainment industry.

The first time Kondo Tatsuya showed up at Rosebud and saw Chikako's face, he felt he had seen a jawline shaped like hers somewhere before, and as he searched his memory for where he could have met her, an image from his collection of adult video DVDs flickered in the back of his mind.

As he watched and rewatched his treasured *Steamy Journey of an Unfaithful Wife*, he found himself thinking that while she was surely using the magic of hair and makeup to pretend to be someone else, Mayumi's build and voice very much resembled Chikako's. Was it possible to find some definitive evidence? He set his sights on the first half of the DVD, the unending conversations.

He watched frame by frame Mayumi describe how she started working at the cram school, and he noticed she said, "I helb my husband with his classes." He confirmed that she did not say "help" or "helped" but "helb," and while he wasn't sure if that was just an odd feature of her own pronunciation or a local quirk from the area she was born, he kept that expression in the back of his head whenever he spoke with her and waited patiently for his chance.

Then when she had said, "When you helb your dad with his

shop," his eyes spread wide for a moment, and Chikako had no way of figuring out why.

Not once since Tatsuya had asked her if she was Mayumi did Chikako pay any mind to how he had found out; instead she thought only, desperately, about what he planned to do now. However, she could not find an opportunity to broach the subject, and as her frustration built, Tatsuya, who must have considered this mystery solved, changed his bearing, reaching out to try and touch her whenever the opportunity presented itself. He was still wary of the eyes of other customers, but he would, for example, grab her hand while pretending to take his change, and when they were alone, he'd act even more boldly, once even stroking her butt when she turned around.

At that time Chikako hid her anger and smiled softly, saying, "Wow, it's been a while since someone tried that."

Tatsuya took her seriously. "Has it been that long? Your dry spell?" he said and then laughed under his breath, happily. Seeing the red tip of his tongue dancing in his mouth, that was the first time in her whole life Chikako felt hatred for a man.

On a Wednesday in mid-July, just as eleven o'clock was rolling around, Chikako faced him from the other side of the bar and judging him to be drunk said, "Hey, don't you have something you want to ask me? Don't you have a proposition?" She made her voice soft as she led him on.

He stared at her with stunned eyes, and after thinking for just a moment he asked, "Don't you want to make something even more exciting? Better than your last video. The two of us. I've got film equipment and lights. We can do it in the Imperial Hotel, or at the Okura. You pick the hotel and I'll get us a suite."

And then he added, raising three figures, "And how's this for your fee? Three million."

He was drunk, but Chikako could also see he was serious.

"No way. Absolutely not," she said forcefully, and then turned away from him.

Tatsuya took a breath and then said, "Some of my classmates from photography school work as cameramen at evening editions and sports papers. I could get them to run an article about you, have them ask their editors. A pretty bartender's dirty secret. You'll get lots of new customers, I bet. Mayumi probably still has a bunch of fans."

The lenticular cloud passed from its position below the sun, and the rays of sunlight returned to the veranda with renewed strength.

Chikako wiped the sweat from her brow, pulled a slip from her laundry basket, and spread it out, but her thoughts continued to spiral.

Tatsuya was not the type of man to hesitate in seeking revenge on Chikako if his desires went unfulfilled. Her sales were up and business was as smooth as could be. Did she make it this far just for some worthless article to come out and draw rabbles of men to the bar, day after day, just after her body? Some time ago she had read a news article about the terrible trouble that occurred when a stripper named Ichijo Sayuri opened a bar. She had to do something to keep Tatsuya's mouth shut.

There was no way she would be able to solve this problem with money, even if she hired a lawyer to negotiate. Tatsuya was getting an ample allowance.

Mistress Koharu

Did Tatsuya have some weakness, something that would force him to change his mind? Probably not.

She could go to the police, but if nothing had happened to her, they would be unlikely to get involved, and if she went to the yakuza or some sort of fixer, she'd just be asking for even more trouble.

Akira. No, there was no one she wanted less to know about this situation.

There was no one she could go to for helb. Chikako had to face Tatsuya herself, pull off some amazing feat that would both shut him up and make him never come back. She knew there was no other choice.

He was surprisingly trusting, and she had the feeling he was not particularly guarded, given his combination of youthful naiveté and being a spoiled brat. Would there be an opportunity to take advantage of that and end things once and for all?

Chikako let out a tremendous sigh and looked down at the street. Once again, the billboard for Sanzendo, the Buddhist alter makers, caught her eye.

SPIRIT SEEKS FORM, FORM ...

Suddenly she recalled an expression she had read in her high school English textbook.

"Fight smarter."

She had forgot the context, but that was definitely it. So if she was going to fight this dude, what should she do to be smart?

She wondered to herself what would happen if she went along, if she got close to him, if then she might just have a chance. What if she accepted his proposition? Then the black tea can of sleeping pills she had received from Akira several months ago came to mind.

Fight smarter.

Would 0.25 milligrams of triazolam serve as an effective weapon?

One Friday evening at the end of July, after finishing up her translation work for the day, Kyoko turned off the AC and opened the window. The sky had been clear that morning, but at some point, black clouds must have gathered without her noticing, and now in the distance she could hear the rumbling of thunder. Wind, pregnant with foreboding of evening showers, rattled the trees as it whirled around the park, trapped by the surrounding buildings, and blew her white lace curtains back into her room.

When the rain finally came, it caused the smell of dirt and grass to waft up through the air and quickly transformed into a downpour. The apartment across the park was hidden behind a curtain of rain, and she could not make out Akira's balcony with her naked eye.

Kyoko picked up her binoculars from her desk and focused them not on the window of Akira's room but on a distance about halfway between their respective homes. The enlarged drops of rain reminded her of the "Cave of the Winds Tour" she took at Niagara Falls while studying abroad in America, the scene she saw looking up while standing basically right beneath the falls.

The shower did not last long; as she watched the rain through her binoculars, a crack formed in the clouds and light began to pour through.

A girl at the edge of the park shouted, "Look! A rainbow," but Kyoko could not see it from her room.

Mistress Koharu

Dressed in a mint-green cotton blouse and beige straight pants, Kyoko threw her tote bag over her shoulder and headed out. Cast in the slanting light, the gingko trees lining Hakusan-dori dripped a rich, lustrous green after their tussle with the rain.

At the ATM on the corner of the Jimbocho intersection, Kyoko checked that she had received her payments for the month. It was just after five, so she still had quite some time before Rosebud opened. She decided to visit the used bookshops, which she hadn't done in a while, so she headed toward Kudanshita down Yasukuni-dori. The shelves and carts of old books out in front of the shops were still covered in vinyl sheets, and the large droplets of rain coating them reflected the evening light.

Kyoko had so far only gone to Rosebud in the first half of the week and had avoided Fridays, when Akira showed up. She had planned to first get friendly with Chikako and to get used to the atmosphere of the bar and only then make direct contact with the object of her affection, so for just over a month she visited once or twice a week, made herself into one of the regulars, and now she was on such friendly terms with Chikako that the two could even engage in casual conversation.

While the restraint she had shown these past weeks getting to know Chikako stood in stark contrast to her relocating to the apartment building across from Akira's, Kyoko believed herself to be proceeding in a cool and collected manner, and she had a feeling resembling confidence that this time she would achieve her goal.

However, she also had a careless streak—she had taken at face value the claim in the report from the detective agency that Akira "does not appear to be dating anyone" and that there were "no rumors of ongoing relationships." She didn't see women entering his apartment, and she had believed he was a shy, bookish type, so she would have never predicted his relationship with Chikako. To have never so much as considered a possibility such as that one was very much like Kyoko.

On Tuesday three days prior, she had visited Rosebud soon after it had opened and drank a Żubrówka and soda. At that time, Chikako had asked her the following question.

"When I was listening to the radio a second ago, getting ready to open, there was this woman DJing, and she was talking about the Equal Employment Opportunity Law. It was amended eight years ago, and she said they added something about preventing sexual harassment to men. But how can a woman sexually harass a man?"

Kyoko tilted her head quizzically and after pausing for a couple of seconds said, "Before the amendment, office ladies would say all sorts of discriminatory things to badmouth their male bosses, like shrimp, fatso, baldy, and there was nothing they could do about it, but now both men and women doing that is ..." She held up her arms and made an X in front of her chest. "Isn't that what they mean?"

Then she continued. "It's never happened to me. Have you ever been sexually harassed?"

Chikako averted her eyes. "I don't know. Have I?" she responded without answering. For a moment she seemed to be deep in reflection.

Kyoko found this reaction from Chikako, who usually spoke directly and in an unadorned manner, to be unexpected. She didn't press her.

Mistress Koharu

That day, Kyoko had left Rosebud and went home along the backstreets to the east of Hakusan-dori. When she turned at the corner of the Ohara Bookkeeping School near her apartment, the phrase "The time is ripe" suddenly flashed through her mind.

Shall I stop by Rosebud one more time this Friday? Isn't it about time I meet him face-to-face. We only met once at the family party at the hotel in Mejirodai two years ago, so he's probably forgotten who I am, so I can pretend it's the first time we've met and talk a little. As she ran through the mental calculations, she made up her mind.

Next Friday had come, but when it was actually time to set her plan in motion, thunder rolled and rain beat down. But presently, as she looked up at the sky, golden evening light pierced the clouds above the woods of Yasukuni Shrine. "Those are auspicious clouds, a sign of good fortune," Kyoko whispered to herself.

As she was about to turn back towards Rosebud, the screenplay for a Japanese movie displayed in the window of the used bookstore Yaguchi Shoten drew her gaze. The store specialized in plays and screenplays, and she had once seen the actual script used in the filming of the 1976 comedy movie *Tora-san's Sunrise and Sunset*, the seventeenth film in the *Otoko wa tsurai yo* series, for sale there. The script Kyoko now spotted was for *President's Journey*, the crown jewel of the *Company President* franchise of movies produced by Toho Studios. This had been put up for consignment by the actress Dan Reiko, who played a small part in the film.

Kyoko had read all three volumes of Sato Tadao's *Screenplays: Famous Works of Japanese Film*, thinking they'd be useful for her work; however she had never read through the screenplays of popular films like the *Station Front* or *Company President* movie franchises.

The *President's Journey* screenplay was reasonably priced, so after a moment's hesitation, Kyoko went ahead and bought it. She had complex feelings about the purchase that she couldn't quite put into words. It felt as though the book could be that one last push in preparation for meeting Akira tonight, but also like she wanted an excuse to kill time and get her mind off that upcoming encounter. Caught up in this tangle of emotions, she walked to Sarugakucho and opened the door to Café de Primavera, a coffee shop so retro it looked like it belonged in the Showa era. She sat in the middle of a three-seater bench near the back wall, where an imitation of "The Birth of Venus" and a plaster of paris relief of "Madonna of the Pomegranate" were displayed, and after ordering a coffee and toast, she immediately began reading the script she had purchased.

The *Company President* franchise was a series of thirty-three comedy films which came out in the 1950s and 1960s. Along with the *Station Front* franchise, the *Company President* movies were one of the main pillars of Toho Studios's box office success. The films, initially set in the immediate postwar period and then throughout Japan's explosive economic growth, portrayed with a light and witty touch the world of happy-go-lucky salarymen and Japanese corporations, which was underpinned by the three policies of lifetime employment, seniority-based organization, and company unions. This was also the period of increasing wealth and consumerism that saw the emergence of the three durable goods that came to be known as the "Three

Holy Products"—the black and white TV, the washing machine, and the refrigerator.

Set in various companies headquartered in Tokyo, the *Company President* movies starred actors such as Morishige Hisaya, Kato Daisuke, Miki Norihei, and Kobayashi Keiju, accompanied by performances by actresses such as Awaji Keiko, Aratama Michiyo, and Tsukasa Yoko. Dan Reiko, whose script Kyoko had purchased, played Kobashi Keiju's love interest in *President's Journey*.

The tenth film in the *Company President* franchise, *President's Journey*, was released simultaneously in every theater in Japan that carried Toho Studio films on April 25, Showa 36 (1961). The simultaneous release was a means of securing box-office prominence and defending themselves financially from the competition.

The screenplay was by Sasahara Ryozo, based on the novel *Mr. Traveler* by Genji Keita, and the film was directed by Matsubayashi Shuei.

Kyoko read through *President's Journey* in one sitting. The slapstick adventure that plays out between the company president, Morishige Hisaya, and his assistant, Kobayashi Keiju, on the Kodama bullet train was so incredibly funny that, worried what the café owner might think of her, Kyoko had to stifle her laughter.

At first, the two men sit on opposite sides of the aisle in the train, but when a beautiful young woman sits next to the president's assistant, the president tells him, "Hey, give me your seat."

Since the assistant is under strict orders from the president's wife to make sure her husband does not cheat during this trip, the assistant replies, "But your seat is by the window. You've got to check out the scenery. Apparently you can see Mount Fuji really well."

He tries his best, but unable to find an appropriate comeback to the president's line that "adults should look at adult scenery," he gives up his seat.

However, that beautiful young woman was only saving a seat for her grandmother, who shows up just before the train departs. The old lady explains, "You wouldn't believe how crowded the bus was," and takes the seat next to the president. The beautiful woman tells the president, "Please keep an eye on her for me," before exiting the train.

At Yokohama, the old woman asks the president to buy her some dumplings. After picking up the food along with some tea and returning to his seat, he notices a glamorous beauty now sitting next to his assistant, and so again he asks his assistant, "Sorry to do this again, but can I get you to trade seats?"

The assistant makes a grumpy-looking face and says, "If we keep changing seats all willy-nilly, the conductor's going to scold us. Rules are rules!" However, through a display of truly selfish logic, the president forces the assistant to trade seats again and begins a conversation with the woman.

"Where are you heading?"

"Osaka."

The assistant is reading a book while keeping an eye on the president—the book's title: *Forgotten Virtues*. Then when the president gets up to use the restroom, the assistant says to the woman across the aisle, "I'm terribly sorry, but would you be willing to trade seats with me? That man sitting next to you is

Mistress Koharu

actually president of my company, and if we're separated like this, well, it's a bit inconvenient."

"I see. Please, go ahead."

The president returns with two bottles of Bireley's orange juice, and when he sees his assistant sitting calmly in the seat where the beauty once was, he hands him a juice looking completely dumbstruck.

Kyoko found the conclusion of this scene, the president having to grudgingly sit next to the assistant for the remainder of their journey, to be a technically skillful example of scene writing, and she read this scene through twice.

Walking through the door to Rosebud just after 7:30 p.m., Kyoko locked eyes with Chikako, who seemed surprised to see her. She walked towards the furthest counter seat where Akira always sat, and, without any hesitation, took his seat. Chikako moved along the counter and brought her a wet hand towel.

"I'm sorry, but that seat's reserved."

"Oh no, don't worry. I'll sit here then," Kyoko said, moving one seat to the left as planned.

As Kyoko flipped through the pages of *President's Journey*, taking occasional sips of her Moscow Mule, all the remaining seats except for the one on her right filled up. Chikako was so busy she didn't even have the time to change the record; the same songs by Caetano Veloso kept playing through the bar.

When it hit nine, someone entered the bar and headed straight for the backmost counter seat. While she felt his presence, Kyoko did not look up and pretended to continue reading the screenplay. The man sat next to her and ordered, "Bowmore twelve, on the rocks," and seemed to have taken some sort of paperwork out of his shoulder bag and begun checking it, but he also seemed curious about the fact that the woman to his left was reading something that looked like a script. Tentatively, he asked, "Do you do work in theater?"

Kyoko raised her head slowly and replied, "No, this is a screenplay." Akira's face was right there, looking at her from point-blank range, and she smiled at it.

<u>6.</u>

The manga editor Okitsu Yasutaka, who had joined the publisher at the same time as Akira, had gotten married four years ago and settled in Kohinata in Bunkyo Ward. His wife worked in the research lab of a food company, and they did not have any children.

Okitsu developed an interest in cacti about two years ago, set up a shelf on their well-lit veranda, and derived much pleasure from arranging his planters of individual cacti.

Today was a day off as he had worked on a holiday, so he went for a walk all the way to the Koishikawa Botanical Garden, where he picked up a map at the ticket counter and began strolling the recommended path in search of the glasshouse which was filled with new and rare breeds of cactus. He noticed on the map an icon for the Chinese fringetree, and while it would be a bit out of the way, he decided to visit that first.

His curiosity about the Chinese fringetree had been stirred by a historical novel being serialized in a newspaper which contained several depictions of that tree. Okitsu had yet to see an actual specimen in person, but when he had looked it up in *An Illustrated Guide to Trees*, he found that it was "a large deciduous tree of the olive family (Oleaceae) that could grow over twenty meters in height. Trees flower in May, when they produce cylindrical inflorescences and pure white flowers. The fringetree is a rare species, spread across China, Taiwan, and the Korean peninsula. In Japan, it can be found in Kyushu (disjunct distribution in Tsushima in Nagasaki Prefecture), Gifu, Aichi, and one part of Nagano Prefecture."

The historical novel was set primarily in Tsushima, and the Chinese fringetree was described as follows:

"In May, the clusters of white flowers give off a smell similar to sweet-scented olives, and the area's many capes are painted white as if by snow. There is nothing of greater beauty than that blossoming reflected on the blue sea, and this phenomenon has acquired the name umiterashi, sea lighting. It was during precisely this season when the fringetrees bloom that the resplendent ships of a Joseon Tongsinsa from Korea arrived in Tsushima."

Okitsu, full of curiosity since this was a tree he could not see elsewhere in Kanto, cut through the grove of enormous metasequoias, and as he walked along a row of Japanese alders, he found the sign for the Chinese fringetree on a specimen in a shady grove by a small pond, set away from the other trees. It was a single, old tree, that looked to be nearing the end of its life. Disappointed, he turned north and went around the pond, climbing a path lined with logs to prevent slipping, through the laurel forest, and on to an open plateau.

Okitsu ordered an ice coffee at the café between the systematic garden and the medicinal herb garden, took a seat on a bench under a wisteria trellis, and wiped away his sweat. The area was enclosed by reed screens.

The older woman who brought him his ice coffee said she liked chatting with her customers and that it had been twenty years since she opened this tea house.

"I used to see Mr. and Mrs. Shirakawa quite often, the governor of the Bank of Japan. They live near here," she said, bringing up a quite unexpected name. "The day after he retired, they were sitting right there on the same bench as you. They got soft serve."

The governor of the Bank of Japan? Okitsu must have made a doubtful face, as she continued.

"Those five years as governor were really hard on him. The government went from LDP to DP back to LDP. It changed twice!"

"You mean this happened recently?"

"Two years ago. He quit on March nineteenth, and I saw him on the twentieth. He was always on TV and all that, so up until that day I had been too scared to actually say anything to him. That day though, that was the first time I talked to him. I said, you're Mr. Shirakawa, right? Thanks for your hard work these five years. Today your soft serve is on the house. He hesitated at first, but he accepted it in the end. I was so happy."

"What a nice story. I ..."

He was just about to say something when he saw a young woman appear near the plots where Newton's apple tree and Mendel's grapevine were planted. Okitsu watched as she crossed in front of the glasshouse and walked under the row of maple trees.

Okitsu recalled that he had recently seen this woman. Before going to work last Monday, he had gone to the art supply store Sekaido in the Ikebukuro Parco shopping mall. Then on the way to the office, he had exited the subway just after eleven and was passing through the underground walkway when he noticed Yano Akira about thirty meters ahead of him. About ten meters behind Akira walked a woman. She appeared to be following him, not getting any closer or further away.

When Okitsu rushed up the stairs in front of his office building, he passed by the woman, who for some reason had made a sudden U-turn and was now heading down the stairs. He remembered clearly that she wore glasses and had amazing proportions.

Okitsu immediately paid his bill at the tea house and set off to follow that woman.

After she stopped and stared up for a few seconds at the three large bushes of pampas grass planted by the stones once used to dry medicinal herbs, she walked quickly westward, passing through the camellia garden by a giant gingko tree. She moved in a straight line at tremendous speed, but she did not seem to have a particular destination. It was almost as if she was doing some kind of training.

Okitsu walked parallel to her route until he reached the monument to the Tokyo earthquake, and assuming that she would have to turn around and head back along the west side of the park, he decided to wait for her there and talk to her when she came back.

But the woman took a sudden left and cut across the grass down a hill toward one of the ponds at the south of the garden.

Okitsu rushed after her, but he could already see her passing through the grove of metasequoias and Japanese alders toward the ticket counter.

Just as she exited through the gate, he saw a female employee burst out from behind the ticket counter. When he asked what had happened, the employee explained, visibly angry, that the woman had entered the park without purchasing a ticket and then just left.

Okitsu watched her vanish into the distance down the hill of Odonozaka towards the Hakusan district.

After Tatsuya began showing up at Rosebud every Wednesday, Chikako gave him her phone number as requested. Now he was no longer just propositioning her at the bar, but also constantly texting her about recreating *Steamy Journey*. He even said he'd drafted a rough script and put together story boards.

He once sent a message saying something about how "powerful" and "cool" it would be if he edited together intercutting videos of a "double-header"—two or more steam locomotives running connected to each other—and a doggy-style sex scene. Chikako was stunned by this particular suggestion and found herself questioning his sanity.

However, while she maintained her refusal to take part in his plots, she continued thinking about whether she could get close enough to him to take her one-in-a-million shot.

In the middle of August, Chikako got a message from Tatsuya saying he was planning to take the following Saturday off work to photograph trains on the Tsurumi Line, and he asked if she would like to meet up at Yokohama Station that day at four. He said he could reserve a suite at the Bay Sheraton in front of Yokohama Station.

Long ago in a Suntory-owned bar in Hibiya, Chikako had met a middle-aged man who worked in real estate in Tsurumi

Ward in Yokohama, and she ended up dating him for about a year. He had a wife and kids, and his office was in the Toyooka Shopping Arcade connected to the west exit of JR Tsurumi Station. They would always eat and drink in some homey but delicious restaurant before he took her to a hotel in Kawasaki or Yokohama.

The ward of Tsurumi had so many different ethnic restaurants that it had been covered in a magazine under the headline "Welcome to Multicultural Eats." In particular, in the area past Shiozurubashi and Shiomibashi, from 1-chome to 4-chome of Honchodori and 1-chome to 3-chome of Nakadori, there lived many Okinawans and people from South American Nikkei communities. Brazilian, Peruvian, and Bolivian restaurants lined the streets.

When she found out about his plan to shoot the Tsurumi Line, the first thing that came to her mind was the izakaya called Kokudoshita under the tracks of Kokudo Station on that same line. She recalled that it opened at 4:30 and their yakitori and bitter melon stir-fry were to die for. When she had arrived there once with her real estate agent companion, all the shops besides Kokudoshita on either side of the tunnel under the tracks had their shutters down, and the area was dark and damp—the whole place felt abandoned. No one was around. They had a little time until the shop opened at 4:30 p.m., so she and the man walked past the restaurant, passed under the tracks, and strolled along the embankment of the Tsurumi River. There had been absolutely no one around them, and the near side of the river was lined with dilapidated fishing vessels moored at the docks. These boats, abandoned there and half sunk, left a particularly deep impression on her. The river was about a hundred meters across, and the water had seemed pretty deep. On the other side of the river's mouth were huge fuel tanks, steel plant furnaces, and thermal power plant towers—the Keihin Industrial Zone.

If she could just lure Tatsuya into those abandoned ruins ... She imagined herself standing next to him at the river's edge. Completely deserted, the only sign of life the Tsurumi Line trains occasionally rattling across the bridge over the river fifty-meters upstream. It wouldn't seem particularly suspicious if an accident were to occur in such a place, and Tatsuya did not look like he would be a particularly strong swimmer. Grisly thoughts began squirming around in Chikako's mind, and as she began putting together a detailed plan, she found herself muttering, "I'll have to scope the place out."

As always, she did not reply to Tatsuya's message suggesting they meet at Yokohama Station, but when he showed up to the bar the following Wednesday evening, she asked him something, which was quite out of the ordinary for her. "Have you ever been to Kokudo Station on the Tsurumi Line?"

Tatsuya, thrilled that she was finally seeing things his way, replied that he had gotten off and stood on the platform before but never exited the station. "So, the Bay Sheraton. Okay?" he asked.

Three days later, 3 p.m. Saturday afternoon, Chikako stood near the dim, unmanned exit of Kokudo Station waiting for Tatsuya. The archway supporting the tracks formed a cave-like pathway, and sunlight leaked in weakly from the walkways on either exit of the tunnel.

Mistress Koharu

She had told Tatsuya that there were some photogenic tidal flats near the mouth of the Tsurumi River and that she wanted to stop by an izakaya after walking along the river and feeling the breeze. Tatsuya said they didn't have to go to an izakaya, he just wanted to shoot the industrial park and trains passing over the railway bridges and then go to Yokohama.

Tatsuya left the high-rise apartment building he lived in with his parents in Kiyosumi, Edo Ward just before noon. Wearing a T-shirt with the words "Enter the Dragon" on it and a fishing vest, a camera bag hanging from his shoulder, and pulling along a small duralumin suitcase full of camera equipment, he took the Hanzomon Line, the Toei Asakusa Line, Keikyu Main Line, and then the Nambu Line, from which he disembarked at the terminus, Hama-Kawasaki Station. As he left home and traveled west, the wind gradually swept away the morning clouds, and a blue sky showed itself. The temperature also rose, and now it was over thirty degrees. After leaving the unmanned gates of Nambu Line Hama-Kawasaki Station, Tatsuya, wiping his neck with a towel, made his way to Tsurumi Line Hama-Kawasaki Station. The Nambu Line and Tsurumi Line were both operated by the same railway company, JR, and both stations were named "Hama-Kawasaki," but they were forty or fifty meters apart.

He crossed a road busy with trucks that had no stoplights or crosswalks and then climbed an overpass. Standing on the platform, he waited for the 14:03 train headed for Ogimachi. In the afternoon, the train between Tsurumi and Ogimachi came just once every two hours. He had checked the times carefully and planned to shoot the Tsurumi Line starting from Ogimachi, the final stop on the line. Like a fish swimming upstream, he'd pass through seven stations and then arrive at Kokudo Station. There, his leading actress, Chikako, would be waiting for him. It felt almost like a fairy tale. He was very pleased with this plan.

The train arrived. One passenger got off and Tatsuya boarded. The man who got off wore a black suit and a red necktie. Passenger trains on the Tsurumi Line ran on a single track, with several lines for freight trains on either side.

At Ogimachi, the station was surrounded by freight yards, and beyond them in one direction was a canal. His next train would depart traveling in the opposite direction in three minutes. Leaving his suitcase on a seat of the train, he exited to the platform and took several photos of the area around the station, the white smoke of the chemical plants rising up in the background.

After departing, the train would stop at Showa, Hama-Kawasaki, Musashi-Shiraishi, Anzen, and Asano, and then he would arrive at Kokudo Station at 14:25. He would arrive thirty-five minutes before their agreed-upon time.

Kokudo Station was, except for Tsurumi Station, the only elevated station on the Tsurumi Line with side platforms. Also, as the platforms at Kokudo were not straight but built on a curve towards Tsurumi Bridge, there was a wide gap between the train and the platform. Just before arriving, they warned you about it repeatedly on the train announcements. He would get to Kokudo Station first and film the moment when Chikako, after overcoming her shock at the gap between the train and platform, fearfully leapt over it. He planned to place that shot at the beginning of their movie.

The train stopped only briefly at each station for just over ten seconds. There was no time to get off and photograph, so all he could do was take a few quick snaps from the window.

At Anzen Station he recognized five or six train aficionados, standing with their cameras at the edge of the platform. He noted there was a girl among them.

A brick red diesel engine pulling a long line of green Taki 1000 gasoline tankers slowly approached on a freight track. It was a freight train commonly known as the Beitan, carrying jet fuel from the US Navy Fuels Distribution Center south of Anzen Station to the Yokota Base.

Since the railway lines at the US Navy Fuels Distribution Center were not electrified, only diesel trains could make that leg of the trip. So here at Anzen Station, the load would be transferred to an electric train. The Beitan, now filled with jet fuel, would be pulled by an electric train from Anzen Station, along the Nambu Line from Hama-Kawasaki Freight Station, then along the Musashino Freight Line, rejoin the Nambu Line at Fuchu Honcho, and then passing through Haijima Station, arrive at Yokota Base. About half of the Musashino Freight Line runs underground, passing through tunnels below the Tama Hills, and whether on a street map or trainline map appears as a dotted line.

This was Tatsuya's first encounter with the Beitan. And as the Beitan normally runs only twice a week on Tuesdays and Thursdays, he doubted his eyes and blinked repeatedly before reaching for his duralumin suitcase and forcing himself through the train door just as it was about to close.

The DE10 diesel car, hauling over ten Taki 1000 tankers full of gas, transferred on to the secondary main freight line and waited. Then almost immediately, a deep-blue EF210 electric train from Yokota Base appeared, pulling empty Taki 1000s. The EF210 released the empty Takis, and then after eventually connecting to the full Takis, waited for the signal to depart back to Yokota Base. Similarly, the DE10 changed lines and connected to the empty Takis brought from Yokota and headed off back towards the US Navy Fuels Distribution Center.

Tatsuya was so absorbed in watching the Beitan he didn't realize that the 14:37 train for Tsurumi had already departed. He now waited anxiously for the following train at 14:58, which would mean he'd arrive at Kokudo Station at 15:05. His plan to get to the station early, film Chikako disembarking the train, and use it as the first scene of their film had fallen apart. Though he was only going to be five minutes late, he was overcome by impatience and a violent desire to skip their walk by the riverside, check in to the Bay Sheraton even just one second earlier, and shoot hours of indecent footage in their reserved suite.

When he arrived at Kokudo Station, he himself had to leap the almost thirty centimeters between the train and platform upon disembarking.

The ticket gate of Kokudo Station was directly below the opposite platform. From that platform there was a long set of stairs with a midway landing that headed straight down to the ticket gate. The stairs from the platform where Tatsuya stood stopped about six meters above street level, where they turned to a concrete bridge of about fifteen meters long which connected to the landing of the opposite stairs.

Tatsuya ran down the stairs from the platform, began to cross the bridge, and, recognizing Chikako's figure standing by the ticket gates, stopped.

Mistress Koharu

She was dressed casually, with a cerulean-blue striped shirt and slightly short beige pants, navy sneakers, and a straw hat. Facing the National Route 15 highway, the Daiichi Keihin, she had a tote bag on her shoulder and a cooler bag in her hand.

Tatsuya observed her from diagonally above, thinking she had a tight, sharp silhouette. Saying to himself that soon she would be all his, he pointed his camera at her and took three photos. The strobe light flashed.

Chikako turned around in surprise. She was worried about witnesses and had immediately started thinking about how it would be bad if someone photographed her meeting with Tatsuya, but she quickly recognized the person holding the camera was Tatsuya himself and smiled in relief.

Once he had raced down the remaining stairs and grabbed Chikako's arm, unable to suppress his feelings of excitement, he said, "Let's go straight to Yokohama."

Chikako gently shook off his arm.

"Don't rush. Right now, I want to walk along the banks of the Tsurumi River with you. We'll talk, and we'll build a connection, and we'll have a little alcohol to help us relax, and then, after that, we'll want to do something that feels good."

Tatsuya had no choice but to nod in agreement.

"I'm not rushing." He let out a little laugh to hide his embarrassment.

The pair passed through the dark tunnel under the tracks and climbed up the steep stairs to the Tsurumi River embankment. Before their eyes, the whole of the mouth of the Tsurumi River stretched out.

A few days prior, Chikako had come to scout the location.

She walked under Tsurumi Bridge, along the right bank of the river to the Kaigarahama tidal flats, and then turned around. As she made her way back, she checked each and every pier.

Only the right bank of the river had these small piers, and she had counted twelve in total, spreading from the flats up to near Rinko Tsurumigawa Bridge. At each pier were two or three fishing boats in the ten to twelve-ton class, moored with their bows facing upstream and cordoned off with iron fencing or chain link, with signs showing permissions from the Ministry of Land, Infrastructure, Transport and Tourism's Keihin Kasen Office.

Each sign had an itemized list of permissions: PURPOSE OF USE, AREA OF USE, USER NAME, NUMBER OF MOORED VESSELS, BOLLARD/ELECTRIC/WATER RETAINMENT. This was the first time Chikako had ever seen the word "retainment."

The gate to each pier had a solid-looking sliding bolt and padlock. Chikako had checked all twelve piers and discovered two or three gates that were bolted but only had a padlock hanging there, not actually snapped shut. Confirming no one was around her, she had then removed one of those locks and entered.

On the other side of the gate, Chikako found something like a prefab hut, with the side facing the river closed off with a vinyl sheet. Damaged fishing poles and other rusted fishing equipment, a broken cupboard, cracked bowls, and empty beer bottles were scattered about, and it was clear that the place had been abandoned.

At the edge of the pier were steps leading down to the sterns of the boats. Both of the boats docked there were out of service. With damage to their sides, they were half-sunk. A wooden bench for two or three people was placed at the side of the steps, and when she sat down, her feet were just above the water. There

Mistress Koharu

was about one and a half meters between her and the boat in front of her. The cabin and wheelhouse of one of the boats cut off Chikako's view of the opposite shore.

As she was about to leave, she noticed under a prefab kitchen sink a potted geranium. It was full of bright red flowers.

Chikako placed the pot into the sink and tried to turn on the faucet. When she found that no water would leave the tap, she poured the rest of the water from the plastic bottle she had brought with her on the plant.

Upon returning home, she had checked the tides for the mouth of the Tsurumi River on her computer, took a shower, and got a little sleep before getting dressed and heading to the bar.

Chikako and Tatsuya walked towards the tidal flats. Tatsuya turned to a seagull with a yellow beak perched on a bollard and snapped a photo. By the time they arrived at the flats, the tide had begun to rise little by little.

"It's pretty barren," Tatsuya said. He wanted to turn back to the station.

Chikako tried to get him to pay attention to the boats moored at the piers.

"You don't want to photograph an abandoned boat?"

"Abandoned boats? No, but I'd shoot abandoned tracks," he said bluntly.

"The piers are all locked," Chikako said as they walked upstream. "Oh. This one's open." She stopped. "Let's go in."

Checking that no one was standing around them, she removed the bolt and opened the door.

Tatsuya took a quick look and said, "It's got a deserted vibe.

Should we shoot a kiss scene here?" He reached for his duralumin suitcase to take out his camcorder and tripod.

Chikako hurriedly stopped him, saying, "Let's rest a bit first. There's a perfect bench for it right there."

Tatsuya, having just come from photographing the Tsurumi Line from Ogimachi, did feel a little thirsty. Once they sat on the bench, Chikako took a flask out of her bag and poured Rowan's Creek bourbon into paper cups. She added some cold water from a thermos to make a quick whiskey and water. Tatsuya gulped it down.

Tatsuya had a sweet tooth; he always enjoyed the granola and baked goods Chikako served at the bar. Chikako pulled some Haagen-Dazs vanilla ice cream out of her freezer bag, took a small bite herself, and then making sure to dig into the part with the 0.25 milligrams of triazolam, scooped a big spoonful from the cup and carried it to Tatsuya's mouth. He swallowed the ice cream without even tasting it.

When she took these sleeping pills she had gotten from Akira, she'd fall asleep in fifteen or twenty minutes. How would Tatsuya react? The speed probably depended on bodyweight. Would it kick in faster or slower if it was his first time?

Chikako minded her watch. While she pretended to sip on her weak whiskey and water, she observed him, but even after five minutes, nothing happened. As he drank his second drink, he narrowed his eyes saying the wind felt nice. Even after ten minutes, he did not show any signs of sleepiness. Chikako glanced at the geranium on top of the sink. She spotted a small spider on its leaves. It stretched its long legs and slowly made its way to the flowers. One cluster of flowers was illuminated by a slanting beam of light. Chikako's attention returned from the spider, and she looked at her watch. Fourteen minutes had passed.

As Tatsuya's paper cup looked ready to slip from his hand, the alcohol within spilling into the river, Chikako said, "We had better get going." His eyes were closed and his head drooping.

Chikako quickly looked around, and she took his smartphone from his vest pocket.

"What's wrong? Can't you stand up?" From behind, she put her hands under his armpits and tried to move him.

Just as Tatsuya drowsily stood halfway up, Chikako shoved his back as hard as she could.

He sunk deep into the water, then floated up, thrashing. Trying to reach the steps, he splashed along the side of the boat while bobbing up and down. Just when he finally grabbed hold of the edge of the steps, Chikako aimed for his head and threw his duralumin suitcase at him. There was a dull thump, and then Tatsuya once again sank into the water.

Chikako climbed down the steps and threw Tatsuya's smartphone and camera bag into the water. After checking to make sure she wasn't forgetting anything, and after returning the geranium under the sink, she left the pier, bolted the door, and closed the padlock. She walked about fifteen meters along the riverside and looked towards the gap between the pier and the fishing boat. Tatsuya was there floating face down, unmoving.

Chikako did not go back to Kokudo Station on the Tsurumi Line, instead she quickly passed under the tracks and took a narrow street along the Keikyu Main Line towards Keikyu Tsurumi Station.

Part Three

<u>1.</u>

One of Kyoko's favorite pastimes was exploring different cafés. She had picked up this hobby soon after she started working as a freelance subtitle translator, when she happened to visit ARGO, the library café in Kojimachi. About a five-minute walk from Hanzomon Station, the café was on the ninth floor of a highrise building. The café premises, shared with a French restaurant, overlooked the moat of the Imperial Palace. On the café's shelves were approximately one thousand art books, which customers could browse for free. The windows also offered a bird's-eye view of the Renaissance-style building of the British Embassy and their English garden. Kyoko had experienced a lovely time there at ARGO, just what she needed to lift her mood.

She later took detailed notes on her impressions of this café and began writing up "memorandums" about the many different cafés she visited. Now she had in her possession three Kokuyo Campus notebooks she titled "Best Cafés in Tokyo."

Since moving to Nishi-Kanda, she had continued visiting various cafés, primarily around Jimbocho. In addition to long-standing shops such as Sabouru, Ladrio, Milonga Nuova, and Café de Primavera in Sarugakucho, she had recently found two unique cafés. One was Klein Blue in Jimbocho 1-chome. Regardless of the time of day, one could order coffee, alcohol, and light food, and the café also had a semi-private room, the windows of which offered a view of the traffic of Yasukuni-dori.

The other was Café Hinataya in Ogawamachi. To reach this café, one had to take an elevator with a manual door to the fourth floor, whereupon entering the shop, one was sure to be shocked by the large windows that let in so much light they made the space almost too bright and somehow carried the bustle of the outside right up to the fourth floor. However, for some people hoping to do some deep thinking, this kind of busy environment could actually be just perfect.

After exchanging phone numbers with Akira at Rosebud, Kyoko wanted to immediately go on a date with him to one of her favorite cafés, but she thought it would be easier to invite him to a place with proper food and drinks, so after thinking over many options, she decided on CAFÉ&WAZAKE N3331.

The bar had opened two years ago in Maach Ecute Kanda Manseibashi, a shopping complex built in what was once Manseibashi Station, located between Chuo Kanda Station and Ochanomizu Station. The elevated platform had been transformed into a walkable terrace, and on the Ochanomizu side of that terrace stood N3331. Apropos of a bar that described itself as "the closest bar in the world to moving trains," customers could experience the thrill of watching trains pass by the windows on either side while enjoying sake and wine. Not only could they see the Chuo Line but also the Sobu Line as it passed over the bridge on the Kanda River, and, if they turned around, they could see the Keihin Tohoku Line, the Yamanote Line, and the Tohoku, Joetsu, and Nagano Shinkansen trains passing each other by in the distance.

Akira hesitated at first to reply when a message came from Kyoko the Monday after they had met, but he was pleased. She wasn't a beauty, but she spoke clearly and seemed like she'd be a fun woman to talk to. Akira felt she was acting somewhat reservedly at Rosebud, but maybe in a different time and place she'd be a bit more outgoing.

That Thursday at eight, he headed out to Manseibashi as they had agreed. It was his first time visiting this red brick building that once served as an elevated rail support before being transformed into a shopping complex. When Kyoko suggested this location, he had found it surprising, and he was further surprised by the fact that Kyoko showed up in a kimono. After staring silently, stunned by how well she wore the kimono, he asked, "Is that pongee?"

"It's called tozan. It's a plain weave of very fine cotton."

"It doesn't look like cotton at all. It's shiny and smooth like silk."

Kyoko was wearing a simple, striped kimono, patterned with fine lines of blue, yellow, white, and red, tied with a hemp summer obi of wisteria purple.

Akira first explained what he did for work, adding that it suited his personality and that he had no plans to move from the editorial department. Kyoko, judging the level of his interest in the topics she raised from his eyes and responses, steered the conversation accordingly, and skillfully told him all about the world of subtitling.

Work requests sometimes came directly from distributors, but most were from production companies. She primarily worked on movies and TV dramas, and the ratio of subtitles to dubbing she did was about seven to three. The majority of her work was feature films, but she did things like special features for DVDs as well. On principle, she didn't turn down any job. She did all her work on her computer using software called SST. They called chopping the script and narration into blocks for subtitling "boxing," and once that was finished, she always printed out the text and read it over on paper. It was easier to understand the continuity of the story and the flow of time that way.

It's said that viewers can read four Japanese characters every second on the screen, and things like contracted sounds count as half characters.

Akira leaned forward and asked, "What about question marks and exclamation points?"

"We don't count them."

"And commas?"

"In general we don't use them."

"I see. Ellipses?"

"They're one character."

Akira said he wanted her to tell him about a recent project she was proud of. He wanted to watch it.

"A project I'm proud of?" Kyoko hesitated. "This isn't my work, but the thing I was most moved by recently was the subtitles to *Interstellar* by Anze Takashi-san. The movie came out last November. Actually, I had read the script and really wanted to do it, so I put my name out there right away, too."

"I think I saw that right when it came out."

Interstellar was a 2014 science-fiction film by Christopher Nolan. In the near future, when climate change threatens humanity's existence on Earth, a man is tasked with the mission of finding another inhabitable planet and travels to another galaxy.

At the end of his journey through the pitch black of time and space, he returns home to reunite with his family, but …

Akira told Kyoko that the line repeated multiple times by Professor Brand, a NASA scientist who supported the relocation plan, "Do not go gentle into that good night," that line of poetry or something, was very impactful and must have come from or been inspired by something. Kyoko replied, "I was so curious about that poem, too! I mean, it's repeated four times, at each break in the film. When I looked it up, I found the author was Dylan Thomas, a twentieth century poet. He's a major figure in English, or Welsh, poetry. 'Do not go gentle into that good night' is the first line of one of his most famous poems. 'That good night,' refers to the night someone dies. This is a quote from Anze Takashi's subtitles, but the next part goes like this."

Kyoko took out her phone, opened the notes app, and showed it to Akira.

Oitemo ikari wo moyase / Old age should burn and rave at close of day;
Owari yuku hi ni okore okore kieyuku hikari ni / Rage, rage against the dying of the light.

"This poem is also in Shibata Motoyuki's anthology of translations of English poetry, *The Emperor of Ice-Cream*, published by Kawade Shobo Shinsha."

Kyoko scrolled down the screen and found Shibata's translation.

"Shibata translates 'Do not go gentle into that good night' as 'Ano yoki yo e otonashiku hairanaide.' And 'Rage, rage against the dying of the light' as 'Okoritamae hikari ga shinde iku koto ni okaritamae.'"

Then two Chuo Line rapid service trains, one heading in each direction, passed them by on either side of the café simultaneously, making a great racket. The light thrown off the trains struck Kyoko, who was waxing passionately on English poetry, and cast a sparkle in her eyes. Akira was captivated by that glimmer and suddenly found his heart racing.

After leaving the bar having promised to see Kyoko again, Akira gave himself over to his pleasant tipsiness and excitement as he headed home towards Suidobashi Station.

Once home, before going to bed, he couldn't help but surrender to the desire to tell Koharu about the spellbinding woman he had met that night.

"I've never met a woman like her before. She's fun to talk to, and sometimes my heart just starts racing. Maybe if I meet her again I'll be able to see more clearly what kind of woman she really is. I feel like I was overwhelmed today."

"Is she beautiful?" Koharu asked.

"No, she's pretty ordinary looking."

"Ordinary?"

"Yeah."

Until now, Akira had never talked to Koharu about a woman he was interested in. He had purchased Koharu for his sexual gratification, but she had provided him several other unexpected benefits. He was grateful for that, but he had avoided thinking about her feelings towards him and how those feelings might have changed in the time they had spent together.

Since Koharu asked about her looks the second Akira started

talking about Kyoko, he realized he might have said something he shouldn't have and began thinking about what he could do to make it right.

Akira went silent for a moment. "Sorry to change the subject, but you know, there really are very few truly beautiful women in this world. And even if she were one of those rare women with unnatural beauty, she'd gradually get old and her looks would fade. That's just the way people are," he said. "But you're different. If we could get past the oil issue with the silicone, if there were a technological revolution, you'd be able to keep your beauty forever."

"Forever?"

"Yes. For eternity."

"Giuseppe," Koharu said with a very serious look on her face, "always used to use the phrase 'memento mori.'" She spoke as though she was talking to herself.

Akira closed his eyes and tried to think of something else. He tried to remember the last line of the Dylan Thomas poem he had heard earlier.

"Rage, rage ..." The 'r' sound's so powerful. "Against the ..." What does that mean? What is he mad about? He's fighting against death, so ...

As he drifted off to sleep, he reached his hand out to Koharu's breast and whispered, "Dying of the light."

Having now realized her relationship with her long desired Akira, Kyoko judged that not only was it no longer necessary for her to continue staying in Nishi-Kanda 2-chome but to do so would expose her to unnecessary risk, and in order to move to Higashigotanda as she had planned, she made a visit to a real estate agent in front of Gotanda Station. Out of several available locations, she chose a 1LDK in a building named Heights Shimazuyama in Higashigotanda 3-chome. It was a third-floor apartment with a balcony in a four-story reinforced concrete building, and it had almost the same layout as her place in Nishi-Kanda but was about ten square meters smaller.

The apartment building was on the eastern side of a hilltop and was built as close to the edge of the cliff as possible. Below her balcony spread houses and wooden apartment buildings tightly packed along the steep hillside.

This area located on the southeast side of the Musashino Plateau, containing the districts of Kamiosaki in Shinagawa Ward and Higashigotanda, was divided up into a complex of hills and valleys, the differences in elevation ranging from twenty to thirty meters, by many small, branching rivers, giving it quite the unique geography. Those hills were euphemistically referred to as "yama" or "mountains," and each was named after the owner of the estate that once sat upon them—the hill on which the Shogun Shinagawa Goten had his home was called Gotenyama, the hill on which the Shimazu clan of Satsuma had their home was Shimazuyama, and there were also Ikedayama, Hanabusayama, and Yatsuyama. All together the five hills were referred to as Jonan Gozan, meaning "Five Mountains South of the Castle," and the area was well established as one of Tokyo's wealthier residential neighborhoods, known for its luxurious mansions, though none of the five "yama" names nor the collective name Jonan Gozan were ever registered as official place names.

Even back when she lived in Kitashinagawa 2-chome near Shimbamba Station, Kyoko had always liked Shimazuyama, and if she had not met Akira, she expected she would have moved there sooner.

After Kyoko moved to Heights Shimazuyama, she began walking around Jonan Gozan, and it brought her great pleasure to discover that within the Seisen University Campus there remained a building designed by British architect Josiah Conder, who had also designed the Rokumeikan and Nikolai Orthodox Cathedral in Kanda.

Downhill from the entrance to the university on the left, she found a hamburger shop called Franklin Avenue and was drawn in by its pleasant ambiance. The outdoor terrace seating was fine, but what was especially charming were the small, round tables in front of the upright piano in one corner inside. She saw the waitress encourage a couple, a man and a woman, to sit at one of those tables in front of the piano, but Kyoko didn't know whether there was going to be a show. The many varieties of hamburgers available and the extensive selection of wine were enticing, and Kyoko pondered inviting Akira here for a Sunday lunch. Or maybe they should do dinner at the French restaurant Ne Quittez pas, which was just to the left of Franklin Avenue. She vaguely remembered from some TV program that their spécialité was inshore fish soup.

At the beginning of July, after taking Higa Katsuyuki to Gallery Hitogata, Akira had invited him to a wine bar in Noge, and while Higa's talk of death and dolls did make Akira a little anxious about his relationships with Chikako and Koharu, it had not inspired him to throw away what he had and seek out some young woman with whom to start playing the game of love.

Akira was partly sincere in his belief that his relationships with Koharu, the love doll he spent big bucks on, and Chikako, whom he left an envelope full of cash every time he visited, were, precisely to the extent that they were monetized, free from the complicated and messy feelings of love and romance and thus better for his mental health. Because of that, even though he found Kyoko absolutely magnetic, he did not want to go all in and take the initiative in their courtship.

Kyoko couldn't know for sure, but having seen him through her binoculars absorbed completely in *Eyes Wide Shut*, and seeing the interest he expressed in the lines from *Interstellar*, she imagined that film might offer her a way in, so the second time they met, she asked Akira directly what films he liked. And, as expected, she found that he liked American movies, so she recommended him films by European directors.

"What about Fellini?" she asked.

"I've only seen *Amarcord*," he answered. "The scene where all the townspeople get into their little boats and go out to see that great passenger ship was amazing."

So she recommended *La Strada* starring Giulietta Masina, and it apparently did a number on him, as he texted her, "The last scene where proud clown Zampano breaks down in the surf was the saddest, most heart-wrenching thing I've ever seen."

Next, Kyoko lent him DVDs of *La Dolce Vita*, *Nights of Cabiria*, and *8 1/2*. She also included director Kurahara Koreyoshi's *Glass-Hearted Johnny*, saying, "This one's on the house."

"Ashikawa Izumi's the heroine?" Akira asked. The makeup artist he had hired to do Koharu's makeup had brought up this woman's name. He remembered her saying that she wanted to give Koharu a bit of her soft and innocent look.

"This is a Japanese remake of *La Strada*. Gelsomina is played by Ashikawa Izumi, and Zampano is Shishido Joe," Kyoko explained.

After that she recommended Tarkovsky's *Stalker*, Clément's *Gervaise*, Godard's *Pierrot le Fou*, and of the later recommendations, the film that Akira was most overcome by was Bergman's *Wild Strawberries*. That suggestion especially strengthened his trust in her as a guide to the world of film.

Kyoko took the initiative; she held the reins in her relationship with Akira, and at some point, while listening attentively to another of his reactions to one of her film recommendations—his comments were always frank and direct—she sensed that he was beginning to have romantic feelings for her, and while she continued listening to him, she feigned obliviousness to this development.

They discussed not only movies, but also shared their opinions on books they had read, and once Kyoko talked about the anarchist Emma Goldman.

"This woman was born around the beginning of the Meiji era, and she immigrated from Lithuania to America, where she lived her whole life as a radical activist," she began. "It's said that at one of her speeches promoting women's liberation, she got the crowd so riled up it turned into a riot."

Kyoko had learned of Emma Goldman from the third-wave American feminist Naomi Wolf, known for her book *The Beauty Myth*, but she was most intrigued by Goldman's belief that she had a secret she had to keep from the whole world.

"At thirty-eight, she first came to know the pleasures of sex, but she worried that this discovery ran contrary to her life as an activist. She stood up against unjust laws and customs, but she wrote in a letter to her lover that she felt as helpless as a crewman on a sinking ship tossed into the roaring ocean.

"Something about her, this woman's rights activist who argued that men's oppression caused so much strife in women's lives, struggling with this tension between love and her political movement, feels so human. I can feel the full depth of her humanity. It's strange for me to say this about another woman, but I thought she was wife material."

While it would be an overstatement to say this was a sort of "sentimental education" for him, Akira did find himself gradually awakening emotionally as he listened to Kyoko's stories. He also noticed himself wanting to accept the things she made him feel.

However, what would happen if she somehow learned about his own secret he had to keep from the world? He hadn't before been able to imagine what dangers would await him if that secret came out, but now he began to understand exactly what he would have to face.

Kyoko always chose the places they would meet, but when she suggested the café mentioned in the detective agency report, Espace Biblio in Surugadaiue, he said, "It's a cool café, right? But when I sit somewhere surrounded by so many books, I always get into work mode and can't relax," and rejected her suggestion to meet there.

The pair saw each other at the beginning of every week, first meeting up somewhere between Jimbocho and Awajicho or around Ogawamachi, like the Portuguese restaurant and bar Piripiri, the Italian restaurant Anti Heblingan, or the casual dining bar Mimasuya. Occasionally, they'd visit Japanese-style Western food restaurants like Ponchi Ken.

Even as he met more and more with Kyoko, Akira never stopped going to Rosebud on Fridays. Having completed her mission, however, Kyoko stopped showing her face in Chikako's bar.

Akira began to discover the pleasure of letting the woman take the lead and invite him on dates. And while he found something refreshing about this new arrangement, he was also aware that some might say he was being bossed around by his woman, and he did somewhat resemble a husband who joyfully complained of being henpecked.

At the beginning of October, Akira suddenly made an uncharacteristic proposition.

"I'm going to Osaka for one night and two days, the first Thursday and Friday of November. Do you want to come?"

Kyoko had been waiting for this sort of invitation, but she did not say yes immediately. She paused for a moment, and then said the first thing that came to mind. "There's a theater near Nihonbashi that's specialized in bunraku puppet theater, right? I want to watch a performance there one of those afternoons."

"Nipponbashi." Akira corrected her pronunciation, a smile bursting across his face.

2.

Chikako paid tireless attention to the newspapers and the TV news. She took particular care checking the crime and accident pages of the morning and evening editions of several daily papers, sports papers, and evening tabloids. And whenever she saw a headline such as "Strange Corpse Washes up on Karekinada Coast" or "Body of Deceased Man Found in Naka River," she would look up the name of any river or coast she didn't recognize and research its location.

In mid-September, when she spotted the headline in gothic font reading "Body Found in Keihin Canal" near the bottom of a page in the crime and accidents section of a morning paper, her heart began pounding furiously.

"On September 13 at 11:30 a.m., a man fishing on a boat reported a 'person floating' near Ohashi in Ogishima in the Keihin Canal. The fire department performed a rescue operation, but the man was confirmed already deceased. The man was in his 50s or 60s. He had no obvious wounds and appeared to have been dead for several weeks … The Kawasaki Rinko Police Department is advancing investigations and considering the possibilities of both accidental death and foul play. They hope to identify the victim and cause of death soon."

Chikako continued to search attentively for information on the case, but there was never a follow up report.

The third meeting of the Paranormal Activity Research Committee, originally scheduled for August, was delayed until the middle of September, and not a single member expressed any interest in Kondo Tatsuya's absence.

Aside from Tatsuya, there was one other thing that bothered Chikako.

Akaneya Kyoko had first showed up at her bar in the middle of June. At that time, when Chikako asked if she lived nearby, Kyoko had averted her eyes and said she lived in Kitashinagawa. She remembered thinking immediately that Kyoko was a terrible liar and wondering why she would try to hide where she lived.

Kyoko had come in again sometime in the first half of the following week and became a regular after that, coming every week, usually on Tuesdays. At the end of July she had come in on a Tuesday as usual, and they talked about the Equal Employment Opportunity Law. Kyoko had asked Chikako if she had ever experienced sexual harassment, and Chikako had dodged her question.

However, that following Friday, Kyoko had showed up again. She had come sometime after 7:30 p.m. and went directly for the counter seat furthest in the back, and when Chikako said it was reserved, she had moved one seat over. Chikako wasn't totally sure, but she seemed to have been waiting for someone.

Akira had arrived sometime after 9 p.m. and sat next to Kyoko. Chikako had watched them, and they clearly seemed to have been meeting for the first time. Logically then, there was no way Kyoko could have been waiting for Akira.

Kyoko left thirty or forty minutes after Akira appeared. Her objective must have been to get Akira's phone number, and with that accomplished, she had no need for a long conversation. But what importance could that number have had to Kyoko then? Chikako could not figure that out.

From then, Kyoko had stopped showing up at the bar. For Chikako, who had watched many customers come and go, something about this sudden patronage and then absence, especially at a bar like Rosebud, struck her as fishy.

Chikako's intuition told her that the key to understanding Kyoko's disappearance was her meeting Akira here and, additionally, that meeting was in some way connected to the shady Kitashinagawa address.

Then, on Tuesday, September 1, Kyoko showed her face for the final time. At the far counter seats were two men. Kyoko took a seat near the door, acted as though she hadn't had a near month-long absence, and talked casually about how she had just picked up film critic Ogawa Tetsu's book *My American Film History* from Yaguchi Shoten. She was going to go through it from beginning to end and watch every major postwar American film she had missed. A lightbulb flashed in Chikako's mind. She told Kyoko that she'd seen a really interesting postwar Japanese film. Kyoko asked what it was.

"*Blue Mountain Range*," Chikako answered.

"Why'd you see such an old film? It must be from over seventy years ago."

"You met that guy here once, right? Yano-san, who works at a publisher. He's very knowledgeable about movies too. He recommended it to me so I rented it."

Chikako observed Kyoko's reaction, but her expression was blank. She just nodded.

Chikako pushed.

"The lead actress, the buxom beauty ..."

"Hara Setsuko?"

"Yeah, that was her name. When I told Yano-san that I had borrowed *Blue Mountain Range*, he told me that the first time he saw Hara Setsuko, he was surprised to find that Japan had actresses like that too."

This time, Chikako did not let the darkening of Kyoko's eyes escape her.

Mistress Koharu

She was clearly interested in Yano Akira. After having met him just once at the counter here for a short time at the end of July? But there was no need to dig any deeper than this. It would be easier for her to gather information from Akira.

Sunday, two weeks later, Chikako and Akira met at the Tawara-machi Station intersection and headed to an okonomiyaki restaurant called Sentaro they had talked about long before.

A young woman wearing glasses was tailing them at some distance.

She walked the area around Sentaro and waited for the two to leave the restaurant, the whole while imagining the Great Hall of Higashi Honganji replaced by Matthias Church atop Buda Castle Hill. Once they left, she headed back to the intersection and after watching them both go into an apartment building, descended the subway stairs.

Koharu had identified where the "ordinary looking" woman who set Akira's heart racing lived.

Akira and Chikako showered together and then, clad in only bath towels, drank Isami shochu from Kagoshima before getting into bed.

Chikako timed it perfectly. When she saw that Akira, a little bit drunk, was looking sleepy, she took his penis in the palm of her left hand and sucked on his nipple. And then, strengthening her grip, she licked the base of his neck. His body responded with a quiver, but his eyes continued to wander the air.

Chikako made her voice sultry as she spoke. "I feel like recently I've had a lot of single customers."

"Men?"

"Women, too. The bookstore manager who always comes by herself, she said she got divorced."

"The one with the Armani glasses?"

"Yeah. And there's this woman Akaneya-san. She's always by herself. Do you remember her?"

Akira did not respond. He pulled her head in with his right hand, kissed her, and stuck his tongue in her mouth. After he pulled away, he said, "She's a subtitle translator. She said they don't have anyone else to check their work, so typos are the translator's responsibility."

That wasn't what Chikako wanted to know.

"She's fun to talk to, right?"

"Yeah. She knows a lot, unexpected things, too."

Having gotten what she wanted, Chikako changed positions, and with a handy use of her lips and tongue, put a condom on Akira's penis.

Even having learned that the two were meeting outside of the bar and getting closer, Chikako still somehow got the sense that their relationship was not yet physical.

The beginning of the following week, the owner of a real estate agency on Hakusan-dori came by the bar, his face deeply tanned, saying he had just been to Okinawa to play golf. After a bit of conversation about the souvenirs he had brought back, it emerged that the girl sitting near the entrance a couple of weeks ago had found a place through his agency.

"Oh, really? She told me she lived in Kitashinagawa."

"Nope. Nishi-Kanda. It was one of my girls who took care of her, but I remember her coming by the office, maybe fall of last year."

Mistress Koharu

Chikako had never been to Akira's place, but she remembered that he lived in Nishi-Kanda 2-chome.

She asked, "Nishi-Kanda. Does she happen to live in 2-chome?" and the man nodded.

Chikako was confused, and she went silent trying to put her thoughts together.

"Your customer, that guy Yano-san? I found him a place a while back, right? The place she's renting is right in front of his building."

The man felt he had already said a bit too much, so he did not tell her that Kyoko had recently ended her lease at the Leopalace and moved.

Akira and Kyoko had been living right across from each other since fall of last year, but the two just met at the end of July? While Chikako wanted to find some sort of logic to make sense of this curious story, she did not want to ask Akira directly. She had a feeling that asking would cause a definitive rupture in their own relationship. After all, he assumed that she did not know about his dating Kyoko.

Chikako loved Akira, and while she would never be able to marry him, she hoped to continue their physical relationship indefinitely. A powerful rival had shown herself, so what should she do? If she considered what was best for Akira and his life, the right choice would be to fall back.

She recalled the scene in *Blue Mountain Range* where the geisha, Umetaro, drunkenly bewails her unrequited love for Dr. Numuta, saying "I'll give up, I should just give up." She saw herself as Umetaro losing in love to Akaneya Kyoko's English teacher Shimazaki Yukiko—the feeling was unbearable.

As the rays of the sinking sun slipped through fragments of cloud and streamed through her window, Chikako left her apartment and headed to the northeast corner of the Kotobuki 4-chome intersection

There, she crossed Kokusai-dori heading west, turned in front of Sanzendo, the Buddhist alter makers, and continued over Asakusa-dori. There was Exit 2 for Tawaramachi Station. The stairs of Exit 2 led directly to the gates to the platform for trains heading in the direction of Ginza and Shibuya. This was the route Chikako always took to work.

Tawaramachi Station had three exits, numbered one to three; all three had stairs, and none escalators. The sole elevator was rather removed from the intersection, near Inaricho, and Chikako rarely used it.

But today she walked past Exit 2 and continued south along the west side of Kokusai-dori towards Kuramae.

Koharu was standing on the southeast corner of the Kotobuki 4-chome intersection, in front of the Asakusa Hanko Center, staking out the entrance to Chikako's building.

When she saw Chikako unexpectedly walk past her regular path down Exit 2, Koharu began walking along the opposite side of Kokusai-dori, matching her pace.

Having traveled just over three hundred meters, Chikako crossed Kasuga-dori, which intersected Kokusai-dori, and entered a bakery a few doors down from the corner.

Koharu stopped and stared at the bakery's large door, a combination of Nashiji patterned glass and zelkova wood. She and that door were separated by a wide road with three lanes of traffic running in either direction. Koharu checked there were no oncoming cars and then raced onto the road; she jumped over the azaleas planted in the median, crossed three more lanes, and then hid in the shadow of the planters on the sidewalk.

Leaving the bakery with a paper bag in hand, Chikako walked quickly back along the road she had come down. The bag contained the nut and fig granola she served at Rosebud, along with coconut macaroons and pecan cookies.

Koharu stepped out from the shadow of the planters and followed Chikako, keeping about ten meters between them. Once she could see Exit 2, she increased her pace and closed the distance.

The forty-two steps down the stairs of Exit 2 were quite steep. They did not descend straight down; there was a fan-shaped intermediate landing halfway where the stairs turned to the right. Because of that, one couldn't see the lower half of the stairs from above.

The area around Tawaramachi Station was quiet from 3:30 p.m. in the afternoon to about 5 p.m., and Chikako, who regularly commuted to work at this time, often climbed down these stairs without seeing any other people.

Today, too, Chikako briskly descended the deserted upper stairs, and as she crossed the landing to the lower stairs, she sensed someone sneaking up behind her and was about to turn around. Just then, a mother and child appeared at the foot of the stairs, and distracted by them, she headed to the ticket gate without looking behind her.

The mother who had passed Chikako on the stairs saw a young woman standing completely still on the midway landing and, giving the woman a suspicious glance, pulled her daughter's hand close.

Recently Chikako had been sensing people watching her when she went out. Whenever she felt someone's eyes were on her, she stopped where she was and scanned her surroundings, but she never saw anyone who looked the part tailing her—there was never, for example, a middle-aged detective-looking man anywhere to be seen. Yet she could unquestionably sense the faint energy of someone's gaze. She could feel it.

A month and a half had passed since the photoshoot on the Tsurumi Line. Since then, there had not been any media coverage of the incident. This disinterest, this lack of reaction, irritated her.

She felt that if one day out of the blue a man showed up at Rosebud, took a seat at the counter, declared himself to be Tatsuya's father, and asked if she knew anything about his son's whereabouts, then she might just be able to get a handle on her unmanageable emotions and even be able to play dumb. She was not quite Akutagawa, but the way things were, she felt her "vague insecurity" would only worsen.

When she arrived at Rosebud before work, she would first check on her pride and joy, the bathroom. She would give it a quick cleaning, and after looking over her whole body in the bathroom mirror and getting herself ready, she would proceed to prepare the rest of the bar. One day in the middle of October, she found the floor between the tank and the toilet was wet. Was there a leak?

After wiping it up, she left the bathroom and went behind the counter but was overcome by the impossible thought that the liquid might have been brackish water from the mouth of the Tsurumi River. Once this thought occurred to her, she could not rid it from her mind.

Mistress Koharu

Water continued appearing at irregular intervals on the bathroom floor, sometimes emitting the smell of tidal flats and occasionally a smell that reminded her of the rusty iron odor of the abandoned ships along the riverside.

Chikako imagined Tatsuya standing in the bathroom, waiting for her to open the door, and it sent shivers down her spine. And while she never saw his shadow on the walls or shelves, she remained constantly tense, bracing herself in expectation of some eerie noise that would surely make her jump; she lost her appetite, gradually grew thinner, and began to look visibly worn out.

3.

Akira had planned to depart from Tokyo Station together with Kyoko, so he purchased two tickets for the premium Green Car seats on the Nozomi Express to Shin-Osaka Station. But as she accepted the ticket, Kyoko said, "I'll get on at Shinagawa. If I meet you on the train, we can pretend we've got something to hide."

Kyoko had explained to Akira that she had recently moved within Shinagawa Ward from Kitashinagawa to her current apartment in Shimazuyama. However, there was a secret stretch of time between her stay in Kitashinagawa and Shimazuyama she didn't want Akira to know about—from the end of last year till this August when, for over eight months, she had lived in the Leopalace in Nishi-Kanda 2-chome before taking that seat next to him at the counter of Rosebud at the end of July, all under the pretense of coincidence.

Kyoko had previously thought that once she had got together with Akira, the eight months she spent spying on him would be forgiven; when they had gone grey together, she could confess to it as a humorous story. But now she was sure this was the one secret she would have to take to the grave.

On the day of their departure, it was raining in Tokyo. Light rain alternated with patches of clear sky all the way until Nagoya, but the second they passed through the Sekigahara Tunnel, the sky turned blue and there was not a single cloud in sight. They arrived at Shin-Osaka Station at 10:30 a.m. and took a taxi to the center of the city. Completely new to Osaka, this was Kyoko's first time crossing the Yodo River. Akira explained how the Yodo River started at Lake Biwa, and she nodded, an expression of surprise on her face.

They checked into the Imperial Hotel in Tenmabashi, dropped off their luggage, and took up the window-side seats they had reserved for their buffet lunch at The Park on the first floor.

The Park had a twenty-four-meter-long atrium, and the windows of gently curving glass filled the space with natural light. Through the windows, one could see up close the river and the nature trail running along the riverbank.

"The buffet lunch is good here. Especially the roast beef and paella. Don't even try anything else until you've had those," said Akira

Through the window, Kyoko watched the joggers on the nature trail constantly coming and going and two four-man row boats gliding in parallel across the surface of the river, their oars glimmering with drops of water as they slid upstream. She

couldn't hear what was said, but the coxswains shouted something through megaphones. A man and a woman in a scull
moved languidly down the river in the opposite direction, as if
to take the place of the row boats.

"This is the real Yodo River. People call it Okawa, as in big
river, the same name some people use for the Sumida River."

"Then the river we just crossed was?"

"Technically speaking, that's New Yodo River."

They gently clinked together the rims of their glasses of white
wine.

"On the right bank a little bit downstream from here is the
path to the Japan Mint Head Office. That spot is famous for
their yaezakura cherry blossoms. Even further down, the river branches into the Dojima River and Tosabori River, and
there's a sandbank in the middle, then they come back together
to become the Aji River, which enters Osaka Harbor. On that
sandbank called Nakanoshima, there's the Museum of Oriental
Ceramics ..."

After lunch, the two split up, Akira heading to Minoh to
check on his father and Kyoko, at Akira's recommendation, to
the Museum of Oriental Ceramics.

Last May, when his father was struggling with early-stage
dementia and finding it difficult to live alone, Akira had filed
the paperwork to put him in a private senior living home in the
Nishiyodogawa Ward of Osaka, but his father hadn't liked it
there and ended the contract. However, his father did agree to
be moved to another facility in Minoh City.

Then at the end of September, Akira was contacted by the
home and informed that his father's level of necessary care had

been elevated from low to moderate and the facility wanted to talk to Akira about how to proceed.

As this facility was designated by the local government as a "Special Facility for Assisted Living and Nursing Care," nursing care services would be covered by long-term care insurance, and the manager of the home said he wanted to discuss the details of those services together with Akira and his father and the facility's care manager, and he specified the afternoon of Thursday, November 5, for their meeting.

Additionally, a big developer planning a large-scale housing development had reached out saying they wanted to purchase his father's currently empty house in the middle-class neighborhood of Hyakurakusou in Minoh City. The paperwork was forwarded to Akira by his father's care home. If he were to sell, he'd need his father's permission. His father may have dementia, but Akira still needed to talk this over with him.

Akira and Kyoko took a taxi from the hotel to Umeda, and from there Akira took the Hankyu Line while Kyoko got on the Midosuji Subway Line.

"A taxi's the fastest way to get to the Museum of Oriental Ceramics, but I want you to see the Osaka subway, especially the retro-ness of Yodoyabashi Station. It opened in 1933 and there are lacquered archways and twenty or so chandeliers. On the platform there's even an overhead concourse," Akira said, handing her a memo he wrote on the hotel's notepad. There were hand-drawn maps along with directions on how to get from Yodoyabashi Station to the museum and then from there to Ebisubashi Bridge in Dotonbori, where they were to meet back up.

Getting off the train at Yodoyabashi Station, Kyoko walked

the overhead concourse, looking up at the chandeliers hanging from the arched lacquered ceiling, confirming what Akira had described, before passing through the ticket gate and exiting the station. She crossed Yodoyabashi Bridge and followed along Tosabori River to the Museum of Oriental Ceramics.

Akira's memo also functioned as a guide. "On the left you will see a three-story baroque stone building with a brass-shingled dome. That's Osaka Nakanoshima Library. Next, there will be a red-brick building with an arched roof in a neo-Renaissance style, the Central Public Hall. After that, the chic and angular two-story building of brown, unglazed tile you'll see one road over in front of the camphor and zelkova trees is the Museum of Oriental Ceramics," and so on.

The Osaka Municipal Museum of Oriental Ceramics was born out of the downfall of Ataka & Co., a company which once held a place of prominence alongside Mitsubishi Corporation, Mitsui & Co., and Sumitomo Corporation as one of Japan's big ten trading companies.

In 1975, Ataka & Co. suffered major losses due to the first oil shock. So in 1977, Ataka Eiichi, the eldest son of founder Ataka Yakichi, oversaw the transfer of management of the Chinese and Korean pottery collected by Ataka & Co., known as the "Ataka Collection," to Sumitomo Bank, which was handling the liquidation of Ataka & Co.'s assets. Then, in 1980, the twenty-one corporate members of the Sumitomo Group donated the Ataka Collection, a total of 965 pieces valued at approximately 15.2 billion yen, to Osaka City, and in 1982, the city established the Museum of Oriental Ceramics at Nakanoshima in the center of the city. After that, the museum's collection grew thanks to donations from benefactors such as Dr. Rhee Byung-chang, a Zainichi Korean who donated an additional 301 pieces of Korean pottery in 1999. The museum now held approximately four thousand pieces in total, including two national treasures and thirteen pieces of important cultural heritage, making it one of the world's preeminent museums and research centers. As the expression goes, "Refined is the script of the third generation's HOUSE FOR SALE sign" (though Ataka Eiichi was only second generation). The Museum of Oriental Ceramics could be called the gift of a profligate son left in charge of the family business.

Kyoko followed the designated path through the softly lit museum. It began with ash glaze pottery from the Shang dynasty, also known as the Yin dynasty, of China circa the 16th to 11th centuries BC and passed through approximately 1,700 years to the late Han period, when true celadon began to appear.

The glassy, colored glaze of celadon pottery let through and reflected light, producing colors with tremendous depth, such as a blue that does not exist in the world of plants or minerals. The Later Tang poet Lu Guimeng wrote that the glaze "stole its color from a thousand peaks of jade." Yue ware, celadon pottery from Zhejiang Province, was referred to as "mysterious color porcelain"; it served as vessels for offerings to the emperor and use by retainers and commoners was prohibited.

White porcelain followed celadon. True white porcelain first appeared in the Sui dynasty, and in Korea during the Joseon dynasty, where it was particularly valued, this sort of pottery came to be known as "imperial vessels."

While the ceiling of the room focusing on Chinese celadon pottery was particularly high and filled with bright light, the area for Korean white porcelain had a low ceiling and the lighting was more restrained, producing an intimate atmosphere. Kyoko was charmed by the beautiful colors and shapes of the vessels that adorned the whole of human history.

On the second floor, there was an area to view pieces in natural light let in through a skylight. Kyoko spent a long time here standing in front a piece of Tang Sancai pottery named "Figurine of a Lady," staring at it engrossed.

The statue was of a shapely woman with plump cheeks showing just a hint of rouge; her neck was tilted and a slight smile graced her lips. She looked as though she were listening to the song of a small bird (though there was no sign of the bird) alighting on the tips of her slender fingers.

In another display stood beautiful thin-mouthed vases of olive-green celadon. One sign read, CELADON WITH ETCHING, LOTUS PATTERN, PLUM VASE (GORYEO PERIOD, 12TH CENTURY). According to the explanation, "plum vase" referred to vessels with narrow necks and a rounded upper section, which then tapered down towards the base.

Kyoko further read that recent underwater archeological research found that these vases were used to preserve and carry honey and sesame oil, and upon learning that they were not "mysterious color porcelain" or "imperial vessels" used to make offerings to the emperor, she suddenly felt herself relax, allowing her to fully enjoy the rest of her viewing experience.

After making one pass through the viewing rooms, she stopped by Café Salon on the first floor for a rest. In the small café, light filtered in through the leaves outside the ceiling-high windows, and the surface of the Dojima River could be glimpsed beyond the trees. Kyoko was surprised by the thickness of the menu she received from a silver-haired waitress and the variety of offerings contained therein. When she looked carefully over the coffee selection, she read, "Enjoy your coffee in a Royal Copenhagen cup." Alongside the black tea, green tea, and every other item, the names of pottery makers were also listed.

When Kyoko ordered a Kilimanjaro roast, she asked the waitress about their rose jelly, and she replied that they got their rose extract and petals from a rose garden right here on Nakanoshima.

Kyoko decided that she would have to make a new Osaka section in her "Best Cafés in Tokyo" notebook and write about Café Salon there.

The couple were to rendezvous at 4:30 p.m. at Ebisubashi Bridge. Akira had finished his visit to his father and had arrived earlier than expected. He stood on Ebisubashi Bridge for the first time since its reconstruction in 2007. The bridge had been widened and the center made into something of a public square. As he wandered about, he found a plaque lodged in the granite railing on the bridge's north-western side.

Inscribed there was a poem by Osaka's preeminent senryu poet, Kishimoto Suifu: "Ebisubashi / love that scatters / blotting papers."

To the left of the poem was a picture, beneath which read, "Tanizaki Junichiro, *Some Prefer Nettles*, Image by Koide Narashige." Further towards the bottom left corner in small font was written, "March 2008. Donated by the Osaka Ebisubashi Lion's Club." *Some Prefer Nettles* is a Tanizaki novel that was serialized in the Osaka Mainichi Shimbun and Tokyo Nichi Nichi Shimbun from December 4, 1928 to June 19, 1929, and Koide's images published alongside the novel are said to be masterpieces of modern illustration.

Near the beginning of the novel is a scene where the main characters, a husband and wife, go to the now defunct Benten-za Theater in Dotonbori to watch a bunraku puppet play. The couple, who live in Toyonaka, take the Hankyu Line to Umeda, then get on a taxi to Ebisubashi Bridge. Koide Narashige's illustration depicts the couple through the window of the taxi as it arrives at Ebisubashi Bridge, the lively crowd on the bridge in the background.

Kyoko arrived a few minutes late, and when she got out of the taxi on the south end of the bridge, Akira was standing right in front of her.

He led her to the center of the bridge and leaned over the railing.

"This is the infamous Dotonbori River. It's only thirty meters across. Look, that's the famous Glico sign, 'Three hundred meters per piece.' This year, it's like festival season all year—there are a bunch of events to commemorate the four-hundredth anniversary of the river's widening. Those pleasure cruises are always running up and down the river, and there are over 1,200 paper lanterns set up on the streets on either side of it. Once it gets dark they all light up at once."

Akira lightly placed his hand on Kyoko's elbow as they passed under the landmark moving crab sign for the restaurant Kani Doraku and entered the bustle of Dotonbori.

Between the Starbucks and a neighboring building was a small stone monument that said "Takemoto-za Memorial."

"This is where the bunraku theater Takemoto-za used to be. This area used to be called the Five Theaters of Dotonbori, and there were rows of little playhouses. Now it's full of arcades and these trashy animatronic signs telling you to eat yourself broke. But those moving signs also apparently have their roots in the puppet theater. The playhouses used to use the puppets in their advertising."

They took the narrow Ukiyo Roji alleyway by the side of the udon restaurant Imai, walked through Hozenji Yokocho Alley, and after splashing water on the Mizukake Fudo statue at Hozenji Temple and saying a quick prayer, arrived at the Sennichimae Shopping District and passed through the noren curtains of okonomiyaki restaurant Mizuno.

They took a narrow flight of stairs to the second floor and were shown to their seats. At the table they ordered yam okonomiyaki, house-style okonomiyaki, and green onion okonomiyaki. A friendly middle-aged woman quickly spread batter on the teppan hotplate, and as her two metal spatulas rang out pleasantly she told them, "Our hotplates are three and a half centimeters thick. The batter and ingredients are important, but this thickness is the real secret ingredient. You all are from Tokyo? I went to Sentaro in Asakusa once a long time ago. You know, know your enemy. I was shocked they charged extra for bonito flakes!" She didn't say anything about how it had tasted.

Akira nodded without saying a word and poured beer into Kyoko's glass.

When they left the restaurant, the sun had set and all the lanterns on Dotonbori River, emblazoned with the names of local businesses and individuals, were lit up, the illumination on both

Mistress Koharu

sides of the river gleaming gaudily on its surface. They returned down Dotonbori-dori to Ebisubashi and descended from the bridge to the pathway below, walking downstream under the bridges of Dotonboribashi, Shin-Ebisubashi, Daikokubashi, Shin-ribashi, and arrived at the Minatomachi Pier next to Ukiniwabashi.

Here, they boarded the Tombori River Jazz Boat. They had reserved seats for the 6:30 p.m. cruise and planned to enjoy a jazz performance as the boat traveled upstream for about half an hour, before turning around at Nipponbashi and returning to Minatomachi. The cruise had been operating since 2013.

The band was named South Side Jazz Band after Osaka Mina-mi, the south side of Osaka where they performed. It was a quin-tet, consisting of a clarinet, trombone, trumpet, tuba, and a banjo.

Akira and Kyoko sat on a two-seat bench on the bow of the boat, with other couples taking seats on the stern, and the band was positioned in the middle of the deck. The bandmaster was an older man with a red goatee, and he held a clarinet. The trombone and trumpet players were young women, and both the tuba and banjo players were young men. After introductions, they began with a performance of "Somebody Stole My Gal" just as the boat launched.

In the wakes of the pleasure cruise ships passing along the river, the lantern lights reflected on the surface twisted like a giant snake diving into the water.

"Oh, it's the lantern for where we just ate," Kyoko said pointing.

In a row of names including Sushimaru, Hozenji, Kigawa, and Futomasa, there was the restaurant name Mizuno. The per-formance continued with "On the Sunny Side of the Street," fol-lowed by "All of Me."

The jazz melodies, the lantern lights, the crowd, in addition to the slight tipsiness from the drinks at Mizuno put Akira into a pleasant mood, and this mellow feeling had him gabbing one-sidedly at Kyoko.

"The economist Nishibe Susumu wrote in an essay that … an essay asking what it was that made life good …"

He kept talking, not pausing to ask if Kyoko knew who Nishibe was.

"He answered one good friend, one good book, one good memory, and one good woman. Apparently it was Chesterton who originally said this. But anyway, I had always thought that the last one, a good woman, would be impossible for me to get."

Akira stopped talking and looked deep into Kyoko's eyes.

"But now, I feel like I've finally met a good woman."

Kyoko had never seen, not even in the movies, such roundabout flirting. Regardless, the feeling Akira was pronouncing was clear enough, and she wanted to be grateful that her long wait had finally paid off.

Just as "When the Saints Go Marching In" began, they shared their first kiss. The two of them on the bow could be seen clearly by people on the bridges and pathways on either side of the river, who whistled and jeered. The band also noticed, and the bandmaster's clarinet rang out through the night sky a tiny bit louder.

The boat turned around at Nipponbashi, and the pair got off halfway at Tazaemonbashi and took a taxi back to their hotel. After taking a shower and changing into his pajamas, Akira knocked on Kyoko's door.

Kyoko had been hesitant to share a room with Akira and was grateful that he had booked them two double rooms.

Mistress Koharu

She let him in with an enormous smile, and after taking a seat on the sofa, she spread out the ten or so postcards she had gotten at the museum.

"This big white porcelain vase from the Joseon period was given by Shiga Naoya to the head of Todaiji Temple, and it was cracked by a thief who tried to steal it. But they repaired it, and they say its original beauty has come back to life."

Akira reached out and touched her cheek with his right hand as he listened, ran his fingers through her hair, pulled her head in, and kissed her for a second time.

They got into bed, and as Akira settled his body beside hers, he noticed something unusual. While she tried to accept him, Kyoko simultaneously showed signs of resistance. He sensed some hesitation in her awkward and seemingly contradictory bodily reactions; she tried to hug him and shove him away at once. It was only after the deed was done that he realized the meaning behind her seemingly confusing actions; this was the first time Kyoko had sex with someone of the opposite sex. Akira, who had not expected her to be a virgin, looked up at the ceiling and said, "Unbelievable," in a soft voice.

Kyoko, who misunderstood and thought he was saying that the sex had been good, buried her face in his chest and said, "Me too."

The following day, they left their suitcases at the hotel and got a late breakfast at the restaurant Ueroku Shokudo, planning to make an 11 a.m. showing of a bunraku play. Over the years Akira had become accustomed to the flavors of Tokyo, and he was bothered by the sweetness of the small pot of sukiyaki he had.

Kyoko, who didn't know what Tokyo sukiyaki tasted like, said it was just like the sukiyaki in her home, Matsue.

They caught a cab in front of the restaurant and headed to the National Bunraku Theater in Nipponbashi 1-chome, arriving just in time for the performance. Right as they slipped into their seats, the tableau curtains were pulled to the side and the narrator's stage at the front of the main stage turned around, revealing the narrator and the shamisen player. Next, the black-clad stagehand appeared, who clapped together the wooden hyoshigi and introduced the setting. Then the narrator's voice rang out, accompanied with a low note played on the shamisen. Of the more than seven hundred seats, about a quarter were occupied.

"The love of a prostitute is deep beyond measure; it's a bottomless sea of affection that cannot be emptied or dried. By shell river …"

The play began with a lively night at Sonezaki New Quarter.

Akira had long ago seen *The Love Suicides at Sonezaki* and *The Courier for Hell* at this theater, and at the Tokyo National Theater on the Small Stage *The Woman-Killer and the Hell of Oil*, but despite the fact that his college thesis was on playwright Chikamatsu Monzaemon, this was his first time seeing Chikamatsu's *The Love Suicides at Amijima*. In bunraku theaters, each play only comes around once every few years, sometimes even taking over a decade to return. Furthermore, performances were held at the National Bunraku Theater in Osaka only in January, April, August, and November, and at the Tokyo National Theater on the Small Stage in February, May, September, and December—making it a challenge to catch a specific play. Akira had graduated without an opportunity to see *The Love Suicides at Amijima*, and since then he had not been to either theater in Osaka or Tokyo. He was attending this showing at Kyoko's request, and the fact that it happened to be this play was a coincidence of fate.

The Love Suicides at Amijima is a sewamono or domestic drama written by Chikamatsu Monzaemon, based on the actual double suicide of Kinokuniya Koharu, a prostitute, and Kamiya Jihei, a married man. In December, 1720 (Kyoho 5), a mere two months after the incident happened, this play was performed for the first time at Takemoto-za in Dotonbori. It was the last of Chikamatsu's plays depicting a double suicide with a prostitute—after this work, the performance of love suicide plays was forbidden by the shogunate.

"'Who has sent for me tonight?' She wonders, uncertain as a dove in the uncertain light of a standing lantern."

Koharu appears, approaching the dim light of the lanterns.

Kyoko had looked up the play online and knew the basic plot. However, actually seeing it at a theater, the stage felt far away and the heads of the dolls looked like little more than beans. She couldn't hear the narrator well, she found the shamisen to be simply annoying, and her body shrunk in the discomfort of the seat.

Akira had named the love doll he purchased at the end of last year Koharu, inspired by his old familiarity with the world of Chikamatsu. He knew the Koharu on stage would be chased, along with Kamiya Jihei, on a journey to their deaths.

Akira began to see the love doll in his bedroom as the bunraku doll playing Koharu on the stage, and this caused him to think of himself as Jihei. He gave his head a little shake to rid himself of those fantasies as quickly as he could.

Suddenly, Kyoko experienced a strange phenomenon of reversal. She could now understand the narrator, the shamisen began to make sense to her. This brought her right up next to the stage, and in her mind the dolls came to life.

The narrator's stage rotated, the narrator and shamisen player changed, and the second act began.

Koharu ends her relationship with Jihei, moved by a letter from his wife, Osan, begging Koharu not to let him commit suicide with her. Having saved Jihei and his wife, Osan, she resigns herself to be sold off to the villain Tahei and prepares to kill herself.

"Alas! I'd be failing in the obligations I owe her as another woman if I allowed her to die," Osan cries to Jihei, ready to do anything to prepare the money to free Koharu.

Kyoko pressed on the inner edges of her eyes, overcome by Osan's outburst of emotion.

After the play, the two walked west along Sennichimae-dori, turned south, and then, after browsing Kuromon Market, cut across Sakaisuji Street, entered the seafood restaurant Futomasa, and ate fugu sashimi while drinking hirezake. They returned to Sakaisuji Street, caught a taxi, stopped by the hotel to grab their suitcases, and then headed straight for Shin-Osaka Station, where they got on the 16:54 Nozomi bullet train to Tokyo.

The train made a racket as it passed over the Seta River but crossed it in an instant. The sky, filled with strips of cloud, was still bright. It was unclear where exactly the sun was in the sky, but given the time of day it must have been far in the west. The peaks of the Hira Mountains stretching from Mount Hiei were tinted purplish black, and Lake Biwa had sunk into their shadows.

The couple had cans of beer in their hands and watched the scenery pass by through their windows as they sunk deep in thought. Kyoko sat in the window seat, and her head was leaning slightly to the right. Her baroque pearl earrings, each about the size of a grain of rice, shook ever so slightly.

Back at Futomasa, Kyoko had very hesitantly asked if Akira wanted to live with her. Akira didn't answer directly and evaded the question by asking, "Where?" She responded by listing off the names of stations on the Chuo and Den-en-toshi Lines—either the Ogikubo/Nishi-Ogikubo/Kichijoji area or around Sakura-shimmachi/Yoga/Futako-Tamagawa—then added, "This is just hypothetical, of course."

She had simply said the names of places that came to mind from her city wanderings, where she had found cafés she liked. Now, capturing both the scenery through the window and Kyoko's profile in his gaze, Akira thought to himself that it would be nice to live in those parts of town, but—here his thoughts took a sudden leap—if they were going to live together, instead of renting, they could always buy a house. His thoughts jumped to homeownership because yesterday when he met with his father to ask about selling the house, he was told, "It's fine, take care of it. I'm not attached, and I don't really care. It's just the land anyway, right? That has any value."

This was the same father who, saying he was "searching for his mom," convinced the workers at the home to take him out in their car, got out in the middle of the road and wandered around town; the same father who went to the lobby of the

Minoh Kanko Hotel, and telling the staff he had promised his mom he'd meet her at this or that public bath, tried to take the elevator to the rooftop. But once they were talking about money, his father would suddenly perk up and come to his senses. It was hard to believe that his dementia was getting worse. This must have been what people were talking about when they said senility could come and go.

"If you're gonna get married, you can sell the house and use the money for your own down payment."

But there was an order in which things had to be done. First, they'd move in together and after that get married. Whether they had a ceremony or not, only then would they buy a house. At least that's what common sense dictated.

Akira had been thinking about marrying Kyoko even before their trip.

Kyoko always saw him in a positive light, and her unchanging acceptance gave Akira the courage to make the move. Whenever he tried to explain something personal, she immediately expressed understanding, as though she had come prepared to affirm him for who he was, and she showed a great depth of understanding and willingness to accept anything. It was the first time he had ever been with a woman like that, and he may never meet one again. He may have said some corny things on the Tombori River Jazz Boat, about finally meeting a good woman, but he did not regret it.

However, there were still two obstacles. One was his relationship with Chikako.

It was Friday, so when he arrived at Tokyo Station he thought he'd take a cab straight to Rosebud and after delivering the "551

Horai" pork buns he picked up in Osaka, bring up the subject of ending things. Chikako wasn't the kind of woman to get torn up about something like this and start crying or screaming. Of course, he wouldn't confess about his relationship with Kyoko. If Chikako needed a severance payout, how much would be appropriate?

The problem was Koharu.

He had been thinking that he could try to contact Gallery Hitogata. He had seen an advertisement on a love doll manufacturer's webpage saying they buy back used dolls, but Koharu was imported so he probably couldn't take her to them. At Gallery Hitogata they could replace the hole and maybe resell her.

But Akira felt a deep shame for coldly abandoning Koharu after she had been so devoted to him. She was not just a lump of silicone, and not just a tool for satisfying his sexual desires. She was a being who communicated with him, and she also served as a sort of tranquilizer.

But if he was going to start a new life with Kyoko, then he had to remove all traces of Koharu from his surroundings.

While the past few weeks he had planned to call the lazy eyed manager of Gallery Hitogata, he had hesitated and been unable to take the leap. During this time, he was made unpleasantly aware of the fact that he was a selfish egoist, lacking in decisiveness when it came to things like this.

He had up until now avoided thinking about what kind of feelings Koharu had for him. If he was going to go through with getting rid of her, it didn't seem that there was any need to try and find out about such things now, but still, he felt as though someone was barraging him with the question about whether his actions were really okay.

He took a sip of beer, looked at Kyoko's flushed face, and sighed.

The edges of her eyes faintly red, Kyoko watched as the late autumn of Omi Basin rolled past. In the forest stood a mix of yellowed leaves and evergreens, pierced by the late evening sun. There was a single winding road that led to the forest, and she daydreamed of walking that path together with Akira. Deep in the forest, building their own hut, living a self-sufficient life out there, just the two of them, unknown to the rest of the world. And then she thought of the book *Walden*.

Since last night, when her relationship with Akira suddenly grew much deeper, Kyoko calmly accepted that the future she had long desired was now coming into being. She decided that all she had to do now was focus on their marriage and that there was nothing to block their path to a happy wedding.

She was overcome by anticipation of happiness and stared at the ever-changing evening scenery with a smile on her face.

While Kyoko was in possession of a bright mind and a wealth of perceptiveness, she had believed unquestioningly in the flat and lifeless image of Akira depicted in the detective agency's report; she lacked the tools necessary to sense the darkness in his heart.

That report had made the fatal error of claiming that Akira "does not appear to be dating anyone" and "there are no rumors of ongoing relationships."

She wanted to know the details of him as a person: his education, work background, how much he made. However, she never considered exploring his humanity or interiority to observe the parts of him that couldn't have a price put on them, and she never felt any necessity to do so. She had not even once questioned whether a man about to turn forty in a year who was still single might be in possession of some strange proclivity, might be capable of incredibly selfish acts, or might have a tendency towards extreme narcissism. Kyoko was, in one sense, an innocent woman, and she was unable to muster an awareness of the danger that her unconscious belief in the innate and natural goodness of people would put her in.

The Nozomi bullet train passed through Maibara Station, and as it curved along the tracks to the right, an enormous mountain filled the window.

"It's Mount Ibuki," Akira said, pointing.

The foot of the mountain was already cloaked in grey darkness, but from midway up its slope to the peak, Mount Ibuki was dyed orange and deep red, blending with the sky.

The next instant, the train entered the Sekigahara Tunnel.

The previous week, Chikako had contacted a maintenance company to get them to check for water leaks in the bar, and because they were coming at 5:30 p.m., she left her apartment earlier than usual.

She hoped that a professional opinion and some routine work could help ease her paranoid delusions, but, on the other hand, she was anxious about what she would do if they found that there was nothing wrong with the toilet or its tank.

Chikako had also made up her mind to tell Akira her doubts about Kyoko and the information she had received from the estate agent, and she had been running through mental simulations of the conversation since the morning, contemplating the order in which to bring up topics if Akira showed up at the bar tonight.

Absorbed in these thoughts, she walked the streets but she was, so to speak, in a world of her own. She crossed in front of Sanzendo onto Asakusa-dori and headed for Exit 2 of Tawara-machi Station.

The steep upper stairway and the fan-shaped landing were abandoned as always, and Chikako paid them no mind as she rushed down to the station. Then, without making a sound as she stepped, a young woman suddenly appeared from below, passing Chikako on the landing.

After Chikako had begun descending the lower stairs, that young woman spun around and with tremendous speed went for Chikako. Sensing the young woman approaching, she paused mid-step and turned around. A beautiful woman she had never seen before shoved both of her arms under Chikako's armpits and with impressive strength threw her down the stairs.

Chikako floated in the air for a second and fell, her body tilted forward. Her arms did not extend fast enough, and her forehead hit the edge of a step. She lost consciousness.

The first person to find Chikako was a woman who worked at the Asakusa Hanko Center. She exited the ticket gate and was headed for the stairs when she spotted an enormous pool of blood, found a woman face down on the stairs, and frantically notified a station attendant. Chikako was taken by ambulance to Eiju General Hospital in Higashi-Ueno 2-chome.

Kyoko disembarked the bullet train at Shinagawa, and Akira took a taxi from Tokyo Station to Jimbocho.

Mistress Koharu

The shutters of Rosebud were closed, the LED sign in the window was off, and the standing sign not out on the road. In front of the bar stood a man Akira had talked to a few times at the counter. The man said, "Wonder why she's closed?" and then walked away.

Akira tried to call Chikako's phone but just got her voicemail.

He couldn't get in touch with her the next day either, so the following day, Sunday, he visited her apartment in Tawaramachi and tried to ring her room but did not get any response. Then the window to the building caretaker's room opened, and the caretaker stuck his face out. He recognized Akira, and he told him that yesterday the police came to ask about Chikako and that two days earlier in the evening, she was found having fallen down the subway stairs, that she was seriously injured and taken by ambulance to Eiju General Hospital. Akira headed straight to the hospital, but he wasn't allowed to see her and had no choice but to head back home.

Chikako was diagnosed with a fractured skull and a brain contusion from a strong blow to the forehead by the edge of the subway stairs. It was hard to say how her condition would progress. While her life might not be in danger, there was a possibility that she might not regain consciousness and remain in what's known as a vegetative state.

Based on the testimony of the woman who found her and the security footage, the police believed that the injury was caused by Chikako missing a step and falling down the stairs, and they judged the possibility of foul play to be highly unlikely. Since the security footage did not show the lower stairs, the moment she was attacked from behind was not caught on film.

Chikako was identified and her address discovered by way of the National Health Insurance card she had on her person. And since her older brother's name was listed as her guarantor on the rental contract provided by the building management company, he was contacted by the police three days after the accident and came to the city from Takatsuki-cho in Shiga Prefecture, rushing to Eiju General Hospital.

4.

Two weeks had passed. Akira had phoned Eiju General Hospital and confirmed that, while her condition remained stable, Chikako had still not regained consciousness.

Monday was a holiday, and as it had been some time since he'd last done so, Akira planned to take some of Koharu's clothes to the cleaners before work Tuesday morning. He was putting her miniskirt, wide-leg pants, and raincoat into a paper bag when he noticed a small bulge in the chest pocket of her red blouse.

Inside the pocket, he found what seemed to be some sort of fruit, about one and a half centimeters in diameter. Examining it more closely, it appeared to actually be a kind of flower cluster. It had a spherical center from which pale yellow-white flowers radiated, making it look something like a model of a firework exploding. The sphere was still attached to a stem, so it didn't seem to have just fallen into her pocket—she must have picked it, put it in that pocket, and then forgotten about it.

Akira took a picture of the flower cluster in his hand before remembering that he had an app where he could search by image. He put that strange flower on the table and after taking another photo in the app, pressed the search button. The first result to appear was "big sea urchins," along with reference photos.

Sea urchins photographed with their shells open certainly did, from a distance at least, resemble the flower.

He wrapped the foreign object in tissue paper, put it in his bag, and decided to search through the plant reference books in his company library for it. He didn't want to raise it with Koharu.

While he was walking from his apartment to Suidobashi Station, he considered the possibility that Koharu had received the flower from someone. If that was the case, that would mean she had some sort of relationship with some third party unbeknownst to Akira. Either way, whether she had gotten it from someone else or picked it herself, that meant she had left the apartment and gotten it somewhere outside, as Akira was certain that he hadn't carried it into the apartment stuck on something he was carrying.

If she was going out while he wasn't home, what was she doing about the lock? Was she opening the door from the inside, leaving it unlocked when she walked around, coming back, entering through the unlocked door, then locking it again from the inside and waiting for him to come home like nothing had happened?

He realized she may have been using one of the two spare keys he kept in the dresser in the closet, and he decided to check when he got home.

In the library room at his office, he looked through *Okino Color Encyclopedia of Plants, A Color Encyclopedia of Japanese Plants—Grasses Volumes* 1-3, *Kaki Color Reference Guide*, and so on, but he could not identify the name of the flower. It could have been a rare foreign plant, and without even a basic knowledge of botany, he felt it would probably be impossible to dig through such a vast quantity of pictures and references to identify this one flower.

Then he remembered meeting one of his high school classmates, Miyata Naoki, at a reunion they had in Tokyo three years ago. He was an assistant professor at Tokyo University of Agriculture and Technology in Fuchu City in Tokyo, and if Akira recalled correctly, he had said he researched the DNA of edible plants. He might know what this was.

That night after getting home, Akira checked the drawer and found there was only one spare key.

The next day, Wednesday, Akira went to work after taking down Miyata's office phone number from a New Year's card. He contacted Miyata and made plans to meet at the dining bar Donzoko in Shibuya 3-chome that night.

After first catching up on rumors about their classmates while drinking dark beer, they ordered Żubrówka Bison Grass.

Saying he wanted to ask about it before they got drunk, Akira took out the tissue paper with the strange flower. Miyata picked it up, pinching the stem, and after staring at it for fifteen to twenty seconds said, "You found something really special. This is *Sinoadina racemosa*. I believe it's a deciduous tree, part of the madder family. They're found in the southern part of Kyushu, Okinawa, Taiwan, and China."

"But this was by my house. I'm in Nishi-Kanda."

"There's only one tree on Honshu."

"Just one?"

Mistress Koharu

"Yeah. At the entrance to Koishikawa Botanical Garden there's a ticket gate, right? If you turn left at the ticket gate instead of following the main path, two or three minutes away, on the right side, between the Japanese alder and metasequoias is this tree. It's pretty big, and in summer the whole tree is covered in flowers."

That night, Akira sat on his couch with a glass of Tachibana Genshu sweet potato shochu in one hand and stared at the TV screen. One by one, people who had been shot to death were being carried out of a concert hall.

He was watching a special on the simultaneous terror attacks in Paris on November 13, where 130 people died. Islamic State claimed responsibility. Akira felt he couldn't take it anymore; he grabbed the remote to turn off the TV and placed his glass on the table. He took the sinoadina flower out of his bag, and after staring for a moment at the tiny, shriveled flowers, he began to wonder how many times exactly Koharu had left this building on her own.

Akira believed that what the makeup artist had told him, that he "shouldn't let anyone else see her," was the truth, and he had believed that he had kept Koharu like a bird in a cage, but Koharu had easily slipped out of her imprisonment and was flying free in the world outside. He could never have imagined that she would go all the way to Koishikawa Botanical Garden.

He felt betrayed, but he also realized that this would allow him to finally reach a decision on the topic of her disposal, which he had been so hesitant to make up his mind about.

Thursday evening, he called Gallery Hitogata in Koganecho and asked the manager if he wouldn't take back Koharu.

The gallery manager was single. He lived with two love dolls and enjoyed a ménage à trois each weekend; he thought to himself that he could take Koharu in secret from his boss and begin a weekly ménage à quatre, but he did not say a word about that. Instead he simply said emotionlessly, "I see. We charge a small fee for disposal, but if that is all right with you, we can take her."

Akira was calmed, promised to pay fifty yen, and said he would come by car at one o'clock on Saturday afternoon.

After work, Akira got off the train at Ochanomizu Station and headed for Hilltop Hotel. He entered the first floor bar and ordered a bourbon and water, noticing the soft mood music playing in the background. As he brought the glass to his lips and listened to the music, he couldn't recall the title of the song that came on after "The Water is Wide." Opera or something, he thought. And then, suddenly, the title "Lascia ch'io pianga" came to him.

After phoning the manager of Gallery Hitogata, he had felt as though one of his problems had been taken care of, but after some time passed, there came a fluttering in his heart and unease began to creep in. He had come to a hotel bar he didn't usually visit for a change of mood, but the moment he remembered the name of that song, he realized that he felt like he wanted to cry. The words "it's not fair" echoed through his head.

He planned to take Koharu to the gallery on Saturday afternoon without ever questioning her about her secrets or the fact that she held on to a spare key. He had found an excuse to get rid of her, but he would not be able to explain that reason to her before handing her over to the lazy-eyed little man.

Mistress Koharu

He hated himself for pushing forward with this heartless act; he was mad at himself, but at the same time he was well aware that there was no good alternative, and because of that he was now in a hopeless, "Lascia ch'io pianga" kind of mood.

Regarding Chikako's ordeal, he was worried about whether or not she would recover, but he also thought the situation would be a good reason to end things with her. It was unfair of him to think such heartless things about Chikako, who had never wavered in her support of him. Would the joy he'd share with Kyoko help him forget the debts he owed to Koharu and Chikako?

Akira drank several whiskeys at a quick tempo, and on his way home, walking along a street lined with horse chestnut trees, he missed a step descending the hill of Onnazaka and almost fell backwards.

He took a shower, and after heading to his bedroom and getting in bed, he cuddled up next to Koharu as always. She pressed her breasts against his left shoulder and with her left hand softly stroked his penis through his pajamas.

"Let's go for a drive the day after tomorrow."

"Where are we going?"

"Around Yokohama."

Koharu nodded.

"Once you talked about meeting a girl like none you'd ever met before, who made your heart race, right? Have you seen her recently?" Koharu asked casually.

Akira responded, "Who?"

"With average looks."

Akira realized she was talking about Kyoko.

"I saw her last week. She had just gotten a job working on some Disney animation or something. She was very excited."

Koharu twisted her body, pulled it away from Akira, and looked into his face. Akira didn't realize she was surprised.

"I asked how much she makes. It's quite a ... quite a ..." he started to say, but then dozed off. Koharu brought her body next to his again and asked Akira in her mind, *Then who was she? Who was the woman in that apartment?*

<u>5.</u>

Akira arrived at the gallery at one o'clock on the dot. When he showed up in front of the door carrying a sleeping bag, the manager, who had been waiting, said, "Thank you for going through all the trouble," and wringing his hands, gestured for Akira to come inside.

As soon as he placed the sleeping bag on the sofa in the display space, Akira let loose a rapid-fire explanation that due to unavoidable circumstances he had to let go of the doll and handed over an envelope of cash. "Thank you," he said, and tried to rush out of the space.

Caught by surprise, the manager watched Akira's back as he made for the door. "What circumstances ..." he asked.

Without turning around Akira replied, "I'm getting married," and continued to the exit.

Akira had no inclination to explain to the manager that Koharu had the physical strength to walk from Nishi-Kanda to Koishikawa and back, or that she could communicate with humans. He thought that if he did, the manager might be alarmed and refuse to take her. He also did not say anything to Koharu upon their separation. If he were asked why he remained silent, he might have said he wanted to do all he could to avoid a crying scene, but the truth was he had no words for the situation. Koharu may have been a love doll, but he could not forgive himself for treating her this way, and at the same time, he could not confess the truth to her either.

After seeing Akira off with a suspicious look, the manager began running through the possibilities. Though they must have grown close over the past year, he had left without even removing her from the sleeping bag. Maybe he had tried to take her apart and failed. The gallery manager hesitantly unzipped the sleeping bag, preparing himself for the worst.

He sat Koharu on the sofa, and then his eyes grew wide with disbelief. He had known she had ideal proportions, but her face also had transformed into a thing of great beauty, exactly the sort of visage which the Japanese adore. Excited, he began talking to himself. "You look just like ... What was her name? The actress. This is amazing, too amazing. Can't waste something like this on a foursome."

There was a very talented makeup artist working for Orient Industry, and once, when he went to visit the factory, he had seen her work. Maybe this was her doing as well.

Koharu was wearing a long cashmere cardigan, and beneath that the slightly faded dress with embroidered flowers she had on when she left the showroom. The manager spent a moment lost in thought before removing her cardigan.

After fully undressing her, he took a Nikon digital camera out from the drawer of his desk, put Koharu in a provocative pose, and began photographing her. After taking over twenty shots, he looked through the photos on the camera and then, satisfied, checked the softness of her breasts before heading for his computer.

He left Koharu on the sofa, completely naked.

As he searched for a certain man's email address, he plotted how he would rake in some cash without reporting any of it to the gallery owner. How much would that man be willing to pay for this doll? If it was less than a million yen, he could contact other collectors as well. It all depended on whether that man made a generous offer.

In Yamate in Yokohama, near Ferris University, was a large, white mansion with an enormous yard. An old American man lived alone in that house. He was in his mid-seventies and managed a mid-sized advertising company that made commercials to sell Japanese products overseas. He was known in that business as one of the best.

That old man was a love doll collector, and one room in his mansion, a room even his maid had never entered, was his dedicated collection room.

When he had visited Gallery Hitogata, he'd told the manager about a "one-of-a-kind sex doll" he had in his secret collection. In the movie *Blade Runner* directed by Ridley Scott, there features a replicant named Rachel; he had made a special order to Abyss Creations in California to create a doll that looked identical to that android. It was produced in absolute secret so as to prevent any squabbles over copyright, and its face was handled by a Hollywood special effects expert using photos of Sean Young, the actress who played Rachel. The old man suggested the manager come see it some time, but he had yet to take him up on the offer.

After finding the old man's email address, he immediately began composing an email in English. "Just today I have acquired a doll of rare beauty. I'm about to begin contacting major collectors in Japan and arrange an auction, but before that I wanted to make a private offer to you. What price would you put on this doll?" He attached the photos he had just taken to the message.

From when she woke up that morning, Koharu had found Akira's behavior to be strange. He barely spoke, had a cold attitude towards her, and avoided eye contact. After driving her to Yokohama, he had left her in the gallery in the sleeping bag, and there was no sign of him coming back.

Koharu was terribly confused to find herself being photographed nude by that crooked-eyed man she had never wanted to see again, and she was overcome with anxiety that she might once again be lined up here with other dolls, exposed to the curious glances of various men. Gradually, that anxiety transformed into a silent rage.

To her back right stood a doll, named Ayana, in lingerie with white lace flowers. Koharu decided that the first thing she would have to do is get out of the gallery, and after taking a quick glance at the manager, whose back was turned to her and his attention focused entirely on his computer, she stood up, careful not to make a sound, and approached Ayana. Picking her up, she carried Ayana under her right arm and snuck quietly up to the manager's desk.

After finishing his message, the manager stretched his back and then moved his neck in small circles, preparing to get up.

Koharu wound up, took aim at the side of his head, and swung Ayana as hard as she could. Without so much as a yelp, the manager fell from his chair and lost consciousness.

A train passed noisily overhead. Koharu placed Ayana on the ground, and after dressing herself and putting on her shoes, she took a glance at the collapsed manager. Crossing the imitation wood flooring of the gallery, she then descended the wooden stairs. On the street, she checked left and right, confirming no one was around, and followed the road running alongside the Ooka River until she came to a wider street and began walking northeast.

After leaving the gallery, Akira went home, parked his car, and then walked along Hakusan-dori toward the Jimbocho intersection. He wanted, above all else, to get this Koharu situation out of his head.

He went into a bookstore on the corner of the intersection and bought a weekly magazine and two paperbacks. Then, he headed to a place in Sarugakucho that Kyoko had told him about, Café de Primavera.

As he sipped Jamaican Blue Mountain coffee, he read an article in the magazine about STAP cells.

The title of the article was "STAP Cells Do Exist: Obokata Haruko Now," and it touched on the recent rescindment of Obokata's doctorate for supposed scientific fraud, describing her life since the scandal. But in his mind, a vision of Koharu lined up again in that gallery appeared, and Akira lost focus.

He left the café and stopped by the izakaya Kagiroi, which he had visited once before, and took a seat at the counter. Ordering

Mistress Koharu

the grilled miso eggplant, he downed a shochu on the rocks but couldn't seem to get drunk.

Koharu crossed the Hinodecho intersection, turned onto Route 16 just in front of Sakuragicho Station, and followed the sidewalk alongside the elevated railway of the JR Negishi Line until Takashimacho, where she cut under the JR Negishi Line tracks to Route 1. At the Aoki-dori stoplight, she turned again onto Route 15 (Daiichi Keihin National Road) and sensing that this road continued northeast, increased her speed.

Continuing on Route 15, she passed by the Koyasu Highway and Namamugi Station entrance and under the tracks of JR Tsurumi Line Kokudo Station. The sun, already far in the west, illuminated the fibratus clouds spread high in the sky and stained the sky gold with specks of dark red.

Near the Tsurumi Tax Office, Koharu passed two high school boys casually peddling along on their bicycles.

"What was with her? That woman?" one of them yelled, eyes spread wide with shock.

"Was she running?"

"No, she's walking, but fast, like a power walker."

The two pedaled more intensely to catch up with her and then biked alongside. They were full of curiosity about this beautiful woman walking at an unbelievable speed and considered talking to her, but they were overwhelmed by her powerful gaze, glued straight ahead, so they just followed along silently.

At the Tsurumi Bridge south intersection, the moment the crossing light was about to turn from yellow to red, Koharu raced into the road and over to the opposite sidewalk. The boys, failing to make the crossing in time, continued to bike along with her still but now with the road between them. Once they reached the gentle slope of Tsurumi Bridge, they gave up and turned around.

It was high tide, and the surface of the Tsurumi River bulged; the wind off the river carried a hint of ocean tide as it played with Koharu's hair. There were small piers visible on the left bank, and on the stern of one of the fishing boats docked there was a single man with his line cast.

Koharu crossed the Tsurumi Bridge. Upon seeing a large white Akita dog led by a middle-aged woman standing confidently beneath the red light at the Gomu-dori entrance intersection, she rushed to the sidewalk on the opposite side of the road.

She arrived at Kawasaki. Each time she saw a Land Cruiser, she stopped, her heart filled with vain hopes that it might be him.

Rokugo Bridge now came into view, passing over the Tama River. A few hundred meters before the road transformed into a bridge, Route 15 became an elevated road for cars only, leaving its sidewalk behind.

A service road ran parallel to the main road for some distance, but that ultimately disappeared, and Koharu lost sight of any way onto the bridge. As she stood there at a loss, a mother on a bike with her two small children in child seats appeared from an intersecting alleyway, crossed the road, and then stopped in front of a short building. In the seat in front of the handlebars was a boy of one or two, and in the back seat, a girl of three or four.

Mistress Koharu

The mother got off the bike and, pushing it along, turned at the corner of the building. As she rounded the corner, the girl turned around to face Koharu's direction and waved.

Koharu followed the bike. When she made her way around the corner, she found in front of her a long set of gently inclining stairs. In the middle of those stairs was a narrow ramp along which the mother pushed her bike.

The stairs eventually connected to the same bridge as Route 15. The bridge was tall and continued far into the distance. Traffic was backed up in both directions, and there was such an unending flow of people and bicycles traversing the wide walkway that it made one wonder where they manifested from. It was as lively as a town center. An ambulance's siren sounded, and the paramedics wove between cars as they shouted through the ambulance's loudspeaker for drivers to clear the road. About three hundred meters upstream of the Rokugo Bridge, the Keikyu Main Line, Tokaido Main Line, and Keihin Tohoku Line trains ran in both directions across the river, the lights from inside the trains and the shadows of their passengers spilling from their windows and across the river's surface as they went.

The sun sank rapidly as though rushing Koharu, urging her on. However, she couldn't move as freely as she had up until now. She kept bumping into people, finding her path blocked by bicycles and their noisy bells. The red glow of the setting sun struck the surface of the river, its reflection shining silver and stretching forever against the flow of the water.

The sun finally set. The sky, now a deeper shade of red, grew darker by the instant. And though darkness was approaching, Koharu had still not crossed the bridge.

The moment Akira opened his door after returning home from Kagiroi, he noticed a familiar pair of low-heeled pumps left at the entrance. He stood there stunned and whispered, "Impossible." He turned on the lights and peeked into the bedroom. Koharu was sitting on the bed facing the side of the room. She did not turn to look at him.

Akira was at a loss for words. In shock, he fled to the living-dining-kitchen, and after sinking once into the couch, he got up, took a can of Guinness from the refrigerator, and paced as he drank.

"How did she get here without any money? It's too far to walk."

The phone on the closet next to the wall was blinking. On the display was a missed call notification and the number for Gallery Hitogata. He tried to call back, but the manager didn't answer and it went straight to voicemail.

Akira sat back down on the couch and remembered the time when, in the year he started elementary school, he had found a puppy on the way back from school and brought her home with him. His parents said he could keep her on the condition he took care of her, but two or three days after her first heat, she vanished. He walked the neighborhood searching for her to no avail, and just as he was about to give up, the dog reappeared, filthy and exhausted looking. His father made a sullen face and didn't say anything, but that dog vanished a second time, and this time never returned.

Now he could easily imagine what had become of that poor dog. Koharu worked much faster than her, returning to him like a boomerang.

Renting out a storage space and leaving her there might be

Mistress Koharu

crueler than giving her over to the manager of Gallery Hitogata. And, what was more, he wanted to avoid keeping a secret like that from Kyoko.

He had to find a way to end their relationship.

Long ago he had read an essay collection titled *Until the Bodies Are Taken Care Of*, but could he "take care of" Koharu?

Akira felt guilty for abandoning Koharu, and as he was unable to rid himself of his feelings of pity for her, he had up until now been unable to imagine any particularly grizzly solutions to his problem. Besides, when it came down to it, if he were to try to cut her up and throw her out with the trash, or dig a hole and bury her, or throw her into the river or sea from a bridge or a boat, if, in the middle of that, she were to beg for her life, he wouldn't be able to follow through with it. And if anyone witnessed him, they'd assume him to be a murderer, and they'd contact the police. All this despite the fact that Koharu was not even alive, and thus, it would not even be possible to murder her.

Akira remembered the story he had heard from his friend Higa about Kokoschka. The artist had made and then lived with a life-sized doll modeled after another man's wife, and then one night he cut off her head and defenestrated her into the garden below. It was a true story, and Kokoschka had claimed that action had set him free from a curse, but Akira was not haunted by Koharu. Given the situation though, it was apparent that if he didn't take Kokoschka-level action, he would not be able to rid himself of Koharu.

Take her to a deserted place and make sure she can never come back. He would have to make sure she couldn't leave, but rather than tying her up, maybe it would be faster to hang her.

What was the English word again? For a tree to hang someone. A hanging tree?

Akira, both drunk and shocked by Koharu's return, was overwhelmed and began to feel dizzy. He also came to the conclusion that Koharu might have other special powers he had not yet noticed, and he began to fear her. His guilt and pity vanished without a trace.

He had promised to visit Kyoko in Higashigotanda the next morning at ten. By then, he needed to put an end to this problem. All he would need for this drastic step was a single rope. Well then, the question was could he get enough strong rope to do the job at a convenience store at this hour?

Luckily, he managed to procure the rope at a 7-Eleven in Misakicho. He also figured out where he could do it, and he began searching for a map on his computer.

Five years ago when he moved to this apartment, right after he purchased his Land Cruiser, he went on a drive to the town of Hakone. After visiting the Hakone Open-Air Museum and the Pola Museum of Art, he stopped by the outlet mall in Gotemba. After getting on the Tomei Expressway, just past the Ayusawa Rest Area, there was a stretch of highway full of tunnels passing through towering mountain ranges and tall bridges over deep valleys. In particular, the densely forested mountains and steep valleys around the Tsuburano Tunnel left a deep impression on him.

He printed out a map and some information about the Yamakita, Tsuburano, and Ashigara areas, and after reading it over carefully, took the rope he had just purchased out of the plastic bag.

It was sixty meters long, six millimeters in diameter, with a label claiming, "Strong and slip-resistant. Easy to use narrow type." It was made of polypropylene, and the attached instructions said it "does not release poison gas upon combustion" and that it was "for packing only" and not for "use for anything besides the intended purpose."

Akira cut ten meters of rope, tied a noose, and slipped the other end through it; then he bundled it up and tied it with a rubber band and put it in his shoulder bag.

It was fifteen minutes before midnight. Akira checked what time the sun would rise tomorrow, set his alarm for 3:30 a.m., sunk into the couch, and closed his eyes. He heard no sounds from his bedroom.

Akira got up from the couch even before his alarm rang. After washing his face, gargling, and brushing his teeth, he went to the bedroom and called out to Koharu.

"Let's go out for a bit."

He changed her into a sweatsuit and put on her sneakers. As he locked the door, he thought about where she could be hiding the spare key she must have taken, but he decided to forget about it. At such an early hour, he wouldn't run into anyone in the hallways or elevator. Placing Koharu in the front passenger seat, he belted her in. She was silent the entire time and did not resist.

He traveled from Nishi-Kanda to the Shuto Expressway Route 5 then took the Inner Circular Route to Expressway Route 3. Even before making it to the Tomei Expressway, he encountered traffic from a rear-end collision, some road work, and reduced lanes due to a service inspection. So even though there were very few cars on the road at this hour, he was already twenty minutes behind schedule when he finally crossed the Tama River. However, despite this, and despite the fact that he was flanked by trucks doing one hundred kilometers per hour, he kept to the speed limit of eighty. He had to do all he could to avoid an accident or getting a ticket.

As he crossed the Sagami River, the wind was so strong it shook the car. Far above the silhouettes of Mount Oyama and Mount Tanzawa twinkled a handful of stars. Around the time he passed the Hadano-Nakai Interchange, the darkness began to fade. Koharu stared straight ahead without so much as blinking.

Akira's car left the Tomei Expressway at the Oi-Matsuda Interchange and then got on Route 246, which passed through Gotemba. Route 246 eventually met the JR Gotemba Line and then ran parallel to it heading west. After passing through the towns of Matsuda and Yamakita, the road grew narrow and mountainous and began sloping upwards, and the towns faded into the growing light behind them.

Akira pulled his car over to the shoulder, checked where the entrance to Tsuburano was on his map, and started the engine again.

The Sakawa River twisted through the valley depths. At the stoplight before the Yasudo Zuido Tunnel, Akira turned right off of Route 246. The moment he made that hairpin turn onto an even narrower and steeper cliffside road, he was illuminated by the rising sun, and the trees of the valley and cliff face were painted crimson. For the first time since they'd left the apartment, Koharu blinked.

The road split in two, one stretch leading to Onoyama and

the other to Tsuburano. Akira turned his steering wheel left, to Tsuburano, and after passing through a sparsely housed area, the road continued through a patch of cleared forest and led under the elevated Tomei Expressway. The road continued to wind up the cliffside, but the view suddenly opened up, and the Tomei Expressway appeared again, now below them. Akira could see the two dark mouths of the Tsuburano Tunnel, with trucks and buses slowing down as they entered and exited.

Akira checked his location on the map. The road would split again up ahead, and if he went straight, he would arrive at Yamakita Tsuburano Park, and if he took a left he'd enter the Tsuburano Forest Road. He took the Forest Road. Akira rolled down the windows and was struck by the cold mountain air, causing him to scrunch up his shoulders and pull in his neck. The road was paved, but if a car traveling in the opposite direction appeared, he would have to reverse to let them pass, and even then he would just be able to make enough room.

Endless switchbacks led deeper into the forest. The planted forest of cedar and cypress trees gave way to a natural forest of camphor, itajii, oak, and ash trees. He could see only patches of sky above the treetops, and the light that did make it through only dimly lit the dark stone of the cliff face beside him.

About twenty minutes along the Forest Road, his route was blocked by steel pipe barriers. There was a sign reading, NO CARS BEYOND THIS POINT —YAMAKITA-MACHI FOREST SOCIETY. He could see a small path through thick underbrush stretching out beyond the barriers.

Akira took Koharu out from the passenger seat and, taking her hand, walked down the path. The wind blowing through the branches, the sound of their footsteps on fallen leaves, and the fluttering of the wings of birds were in perfect harmony, and it felt as though they were just out for an early morning hike. They walked deeper into the forest, Akira appraising each individual tree as he went. They stopped beneath a camphor tree. But Akira decided it was too close to the road, so they went searching even deeper in the forest. Further down the path they found another small path leading uphill and took it. Akira kept an eye on the scenery below them to keep track of their location; he pulled Koharu along with his right hand, using his left to part the brush as they climbed.

After walking for about an hour, the trail ended. They could hear the sound of water somewhere far below. They must have been at an elevation of about 350 meters. Akira checked his watch and whispered, "This should be good enough."

Akira wound around towards the other side of the slope, which was not visible from the path. He saw white haze winding its way up through the forest below and ascending towards them. It must have been river fog rising from the bottom of the valley. He moved a bit further downhill and tried to decide on a tree. The mist had reached around their feet. Through the canopy of trees, there was a perfectly clear, blue sky. He looked down and happened to see a moss-covered stone buddha peeking out of the brush. After spotting the first statue, he then saw another further along. Unbeknownst to himself, Akira had entered the Okuyamaga Road, a road once traversed back in the Edo period.

How bizarre. It almost feels like I'm on a journey, like in the michiyuki scene of a play.

"This is not a love suicide. Like hell I'd do that."

Mistress Koharu

He made a point to say it out loud, not to anyone in particular. Koharu followed along silently, making no moves to resist.

They found a large itajii tree. It stood straight up on the steep slope of the mountain, its thick, sturdy branches reaching out in all directions. When Akira started walking towards that tree, Koharu said something to him. But Akira couldn't make out what she'd said. When he turned to look at her, a questioning look on his face, she repeated herself.

"Don't abandon me."

"I'm not abandoning you. I'm sadly, very sadly, giving you up."

Akira was curt, his words simply an excuse for himself.

When they arrived at the base of the tree, Akira took the rope from his shoulder bag, double-knotted one end of it to give it weight, slipped the noose around Koharu's neck, and tightened it until it cut into her throat. Koharu stared sadly at the ground.

Akira threw the rope up over one of the branches about four meters high, grabbed the knot that came down over the other end, and began pulling, forcefully but slowly. Koharu's feet gradually lifted from the earth.

When he had raised Koharu's feet one and a half meters off the ground, he wrapped the rope several times around the trunk of the tree.

After tying a final knot, he hurried away from the tree. He felt like a murderer as he stumbled back down the path he had come from. Even hikers wouldn't come this deep in the woods, so no one will find her for years, he thought. And even if she is found, the Forest Association and police will just send her to the dump, of course. Eventually, Koharu's silicone will lose all her oil and transform into a hard lump. She must.

Akira did not at all consider the possibility that she might come back again.

Akira got lost. He couldn't find the route that led back to his car. The thick layer of cedar leaves covering the sloping ground made it slippery as ice, and he fell backwards landing on his rear several times. After one such fall, as he rose, turning his gaze upward, he saw, far at the end of the deep V of the valley, Mount Fuji capped with snow. The mountain was lit by the morning sun. Akira was blown away, and, completely still, he stared for a moment at the mountain's beatific form.

Once she could no longer see Akira, Koharu took the rope in both hands and pulled her body upwards, climbing until she could get her right hand on the branch; she then removed the noose with her left and jumped down to the earth. She ignored Akira, who was gazing in awe at Mount Fuji, and raced downhill. After easily making her way back to the pipe barriers, she slid herself face up under the car. Koharu spread her arms out across the bottom of the car to grip the stainless-steel frame below the running boards and wrapped her legs around the two bars of the main frame that ran from the front to the back of the undercarriage.

Akira finally made it back to the car, completely exhausted both mentally and physically. He started the Land Cruiser and got on Route 246. The whole way to the Oi-Matsuda Interchange, Mount Fuji, far in the distance, was reflected in his rearview mirror.

Akira exited the Tomei Expressway for the Tokyo Interchange, and when he got on Tamagawa-dori, he stopped his car and called Kyoko.

Mistress Koharu

"I'm heading over now. I should look for Seisen University?"

"You're coming by car? There isn't any parking around here. It's a bit of a ways, but can you park at the Tokyu Store next to Gotanda Station? Then walk up the hill in front of the university. Call me and I can come meet you."

After parking his car, he walked away from Gotanda Station, took a left, and went up the gently sloping hill, as Kyoko came down from the top of it. The two met right in front of the front gate of Seisen University. Kyoko was wearing an orange sweater over a button-down shirt with jeans and loafers.

They climbed to the top of the hill and entered the grounds of a small temple. From some distance behind, Koharu watched them.

They passed through the temple grounds, took the first right, then took a left downhill at the next intersection, before finally arriving at a set of steep concrete steps.

"I might not've been able to find this place if you didn't come get me," Akira said as they climbed down the stairs. "Several of these houses look abandoned," he added.

A two-story white, wooden house stood on the right side of the slope.

"This one's become a hoarder house, but a Russian newspaper reporter apparently used to live here before."

The garage, which took up half of the first floor, had two shutters, and the right one was open. Piled up inside were dried-up potted cacti, tables and chairs with missing legs, and old tires. Peeking out from the piles of trash was the hood of a foreign-looking convertible. There was no license plate, and both the headlights were smashed.

Kyoko turned around and said, "I live here," pointing to the four-story apartment building diagonally across from the abandoned house.

The outer walls of the steel-reinforced concrete building were covered with thin, black steel panels patterned with waves. There was no elevator, and the stairs with aluminum handrailing led up to the open-air hallways of each floor.

Koharu watched them walk down the hallway of the third floor and enter room 303 before sneaking into the garage of the abandoned house and hiding behind the closed shutter.

Akira took a seat at the dining table, and Kyoko lit the alcohol lamp of her siphon coffee maker and started brewing coffee.

After standing up and opening the curtains, Akira stared out the balcony's glass door. He went to Kyoko's desk, where her laptop was left open. On the screen was a scene from the new Disney film she was subtitling, *Alice Through the Looking Glass.*

As he sipped his coffee, Akira asked, "Is this mail order?" looking at the coffee maker.

"I first saw this kind of alcohol lamp siphon coffee maker at Café Do near Meguro Station, and since then I'd always wanted one."

Kyoko had, this spring, checked out the Futako-za Street Market held once a week at Futako-Tamagawa Rise Shopping Center and found this in a shop specializing in Western antiques. "I splurged on it," she said, laughing. She added that she had also stopped by the Spanish bakery that had just opened, Mallorca, and could not forget the taste of the white wine she had there, Fan d'Oro.

"The Seikado Bunko Art Museum in Futako-Tamagawa has a

Yohen Tenmoku tea bowl. It's a national treasure, and there are only three left in the world. The other two are also not in China, their country of origin, but Japan. Daitokuji Temple in Kyoto and Fujita Museum in Osaka, I believe. The pottery museum you went to in Osaka had a national treasure, a Yuteki Tenmoku tea bowl. That's also Jian ware from the Southern Song dynasty."

Here he goes mansplaining again, Kyoko thought to herself, but instead of commenting on that, she replied, "I don't remember. I wonder if I missed it. Maybe it's not part of their permanent collection?"

They had planned to go out and look at places where they might want to live together, but Akira explained that last night something suddenly came up and he had to go to Gotemba, so he'd just returned to the city this morning and hadn't slept. He asked if it would be okay for him to head home and come back later.

Kyoko said that was fine and suggested, "Why don't you go to work straight from here in the morning?"

After seeing Akira off, Kyoko went back to her work but almost immediately stopped her fingers on the keyboard and began daydreaming about their new life together.

If they were to live together and get married, whether or not they had a ceremony, she wanted to go to Europe for their honeymoon. She had already planned several itineraries for traveling through Italy, and currently she felt that rather than the common option of starting from Rome and heading north, going south seemed more appealing.

Kyoko took the *Thomas Cook European Timetable* off her bookshelf, stared at the boot-shaped train map, and daydreamed about getting on the Italo express train from Rome, changing trains in Napoli, and heading for Palermo in Sicily.

They could also stay in Napoli for two or three days, and maybe visit Amalfi and the remains of Pompei. Just as she was returning the timetable to her bookshelf, her intercom rang.

When she looked through the peephole, she saw a young woman in a sweatsuit. Kyoko had a feeling she had seen her somewhere and assumed she was someone who lived in the building. She answered, "Yes?" as she opened the door.

With Koharu on his back, Akira climbed a mountain ridge. He was surrounded by thick fog and could only see one or two steps in front of him. The love doll on his back grew heavier and heavier, and it was becoming difficult to walk.

He thought of the line from the Soseki story, "The child on my back suddenly grew as heavy as a stone jizo statue."

Koharu gleefully sang a sort of nursery rhyme. "*Akira / Starts with A / Anjuro / Ants a-hoisting / Aren't they? / Aren't they?*"

It was the song his grandfather had taught him.

Her arms were wrapped around his neck and began choking him. He couldn't stand. His knees hit the ground and he screamed. Would it finally kill him, this doll's curse? He had stepped into a terrifyingly ghastly world, and there was no turning back. Realizing this, he woke up.

The time on his alarm clock was 5 p.m.

Akira showered, changed, and after gathering his things for work the next morning, called Kyoko. She didn't answer, and as he walked to Jimbocho Station, he tried her again, once again getting her answering machine. As he rushed from Gotanda Station along the route they had walked that morning, he felt a fluttering in his chest.

He tried Kyoko's intercom, but there was no response. He knocked on the door, but there was only silence on the other side. He placed his hand on the doorknob and tried to turn it. For some reason, it was unlocked.

Leaving the door open, he placed his shoulder bag down in the entryway and carefully opened the door to the right that led to the living-dining-kitchen.

Between the kitchen counter and table was a woman lying on the floor. She was wearing a sweatsuit. Akira reached for the light switch to the right of the door. The lights went on, and he realized it was Kyoko. Doubting his eyes, he froze in confusion. Kyoko's body was twisted unnaturally—she didn't look to have merely passed out.

He went toward her, and as he carefully took his first step, he sensed someone behind him and turned around. There, in front of the bathroom door, in an orange sweater and jeans, stood Koharu.

Why is Koharu here? And why is Kyoko on the ground? Still unable to comprehend the situation, he was visited by a premonition of destruction, which instantaneously exploded in him into a feeling of rage.

"What are you doing here?" Akira suppressed the anger in his voice and squeezed out the words.

Koharu had taken Kyoko's place. She spoke calmly. "Don't abandon me."

She repeated the same line she had said in front of the itajii tree.

Akira slowly backed up to the dining table, took the alcohol lamp in his hand, and screaming, "You monster," threw it at Koharu.

The unlit lamp struck the left side of her chest and shattered, shards of glass and alcohol falling to the floor below.

This did not satisfy him. He grabbed the copy of the *Japan Times* on the edge of the table, ripped off a page, lit it with the lamp lighter, and threw it at Koharu as she advanced towards him.

The sweater, now covered in alcohol, went up in flames, and the fire spread to her hair. The burning paper which she had deflected with her hand fell to the ground, and fire spread across the floor as well.

Koharu jumped onto the table, and Akira, overwhelmed by the scene, backed up. Koharu dived straight for his chest. She tackled Akira to the ground, and as he fell, he hit the back of his head on the wall, knocking him unconscious.

Koharu spooned Akira, now unable to move, held his head with her right hand, and, as always, reached down there with her left.

The fire spread across the carpet to the wallpaper, and in an instant the curtains were up in flames, the tongues of heat lapping at the ceiling.

Smoke billowed out of the door which Akira had left open and into the open-air hallway. Upon noticing the smoke, a neighbor had called the fire department, and as the fire approached the wall where the two were lying, a siren wailed in the distance.

Koharu got up and lifting Akira up from behind by the

armpits, dragged him out to the hallway, and then she turned back towards the burning room and paused. The neighborhood residents who had gathered in front of the apartment building let out startled cries upon seeing a half-naked woman standing in the third-floor hallway.

She stared at Akira's paling face and said, "Viszlát, kedvesem," goodbye, my dear, and returned to the burning room.

The air outside roused Akira; he lifted his head, opened his eyes a sliver, and watched Koharu walk away from him surrounded by a halo of crimson flames before shutting his eyes again. He lost consciousness once more just as he heard the footsteps of firefighters racing up the stairs.

Translator's Note

Before I began translating *Mistress Koharu*, I did not imagine I would actually visit Orient Industry's gallery. In fact, I did not believe the gallery really existed. I do not mean I was in disbelief of love dolls or that some such gallery existed somewhere in Tokyo. I simply mean that, in the time between first reading *Mistress Koharu* and beginning the translation, due to some bias of my own, I had assumed that within a novel—even a novel I was fully aware abounded with references to old films, cafés, restaurants, documentaries, mockumentaries, and types of shochu—the love doll gallery had to be fiction.

But almost immediately upon embarking on this translation and attempting to concoct a plausible sounding translation for the Japanese name of this love doll manufacturer, I discovered I had looked right past one of the most important references in the text. Orient Industry was real. Just as described in the novel, it was Japan's leading love doll manufacturer. In fact, the only thing that seemed to be different was that their Okachimachi gallery no longer required reservations.

Thus, one October afternoon in 2023, me and a few friends, there for both moral support and out of their own curiosity, took an elevator up to the third floor of the sort of unremarkable building called zakkyo biru in Japanese—a mixed use building that could house offices, residences, and/or commercial facilities. We passed through a door as nondescript as the building itself and were met with three love dolls—two of which were replicas of children—clad in gorgeous kimono and posed as an oiran dochu, a procession of the highest rank geisha and their retinue. Next our eyes went to the recreation of the classic Katsushika Hokusai print, *The Dream of the Fisherman's Wife*, the wall behind it covered with copies of ukiyo-e depicting intercourse between women and various animals. We paid the one thousand yen entry fee to a cheerful old man who was quite hard of hearing. This man would be our guide.

The tour itself was an interactive experience. As we made our way through the gallery, we were instructed to squeeze, prod, and even sniff the product to better understand the quality of the materials and craftsmanship. Our guide was incredibly knowledgeable, and his nonchalance around the dolls was intimidating. This combined with his boyish enthusiasm made it somehow impossible for us to disobey his instruction. When he, for example, directed us to try their newest product, Mon de Normu, a mammillary drink server made of silicon that dispensed liquid from the left nipple when the right breast was squeezed, he looked at us with a genuine eagerness that made it perfectly clear the tour would not continue until we complied.

The uncanniness of this experience was of course compounded by the dolls themselves and their truly startling closeness to human appearance. Each doll is manufactured with such great care and attention to detail that I hesitate to call them "products" or "things," yet they are also produced for consumption (another word that doesn't quite seem to fit) in a way that makes it hard for me to use the word "art." I guess the adjective that feels most accurate to me is probably "artisanal." And on this tour we were

Mistress Koharu

faced with at least a dozen of them displayed in various states of undress and degrees of dismemberment.

But maybe the strangest part of this experience for me was the odd familiarity I felt. So much of what we were told on the tour—the properties of silicon, the workings of love doll frames, how you can detach and change their heads—I found myself nodding along to, knowingly.

After the tour, we took group photos in front of both the love doll oiran dochu and the recreation of *The Dream of the Fisherman's Wife*. Our guide was not a great photographer. Many of the photos he took for us were obscured by his thumb, and one captured none of us, only a love doll mounted by a stuffed octopus.

On the way out, I mentioned that I was translating a book that features Orient Industry, and he tried to sell me a DVD of a film starring one of their love dolls.

My trip to the Orient Industry gallery was the first of several such research trips. None were quite as impactful as the first, but each was uncanny in a similar way. I always set out to get a clearer mental image of what was being described in the text, to better picture the detailed descriptions of roads and stairs and train platforms. And yet, despite my belief that I was visiting these various sites because I couldn't fully visualize what was on the page, I often wound up with a sense of seeing double. It was as if the shadowy visions I had formed in my mind had been projected into the world. The text had become a sort of Borgesian map, projected over physical reality. On occasion, the descriptions in the text turned out to be so detailed, I could use the novel to navigate—I followed Koharu's path from Kanda 2-chome to Yanagimori Shrine not with Google Maps open on my phone, but a PDF of the novel.

As I continued translating, the map became more and more real to me. Piecing it together felt something like getting used to the Tokyo railway map. At first, all the lines and station names are overwhelming, the colors more distracting than helpful when trying to pick out the route you need. But over time you see patterns; the code starts to make sense.

Mistress Koharu is full of evocative images, and the plot is thrilling. But it is the book's obsessive citation that links everything together. All the references trace out the characters and the world they live in, both physical and cultural. They also provide the reader a seemingly infinite selection of overlapping paths to wander, each offering a new view of something in the text you thought you understood.

My job as translator then was to recreate this map in all its glorious excessiveness. I had to capture to the best of my ability this wide range of references and make them legible to an English-language reader, to give them the tools to peel back the layers of reference and see what they can find in this strange nesting doll of a book. The references didn't need to be (in fact they shouldn't be) too blatant. That would rob the reader of the mystery and the opportunity to explore. But they did need to be there and be accessible enough to be found with some effort.

At times I felt the facticity of the work made my job as translator easier. I was freed from the responsibility of having to name things—I just had to find out what their names were. More frequently, I wished I could just make it all up. It is frankly exhausting to google across two languages to find correspondences, to track down and then compare the Japanese and English versions of obscure texts, to decide which of two existing translations is more appropriate. And often, the end result feels slightly messier, slightly more awkward in English than what I would have chosen.

Translators are always researchers and fact-checkers, but never before have I had to give myself so thoroughly over to those roles. Google, especially Google Maps, was an indispensable tool in this research, as was Tabelog, "Japan's No. 1 Restaurant Listing and Reservation Site." I relied heavily on my neighborhood libraries, Archive.com, and my many amazing friends who helped me translate Russian street names and find pirated versions of Discovery Channel documentaries with Japanese subtitles. And of course, I am eternally grateful for editors who both indulged me and pushed back when I left paragraphs as uncontextualized lists of proper nouns. That said, I take full responsibility for any errors that did make it through to the final text, and am sincerely sorry for any names I might have gotten wrong.

I have employed a range of approaches in order to make references accessible to English-language readers. I handled decisions about how to translate on a case-by-case basis, and some may fault me for inconsistency—I prefer to see it as a wealth of strategies for handling a wealth of challenges. I sometimes chose to transliterate rather than translate when a TV show or magazine was easier to identify by its Japanese title. Other times I chose to supply my own translations to fit within the context—if there was a pun, for example. I have tried to find canonical translations when available. I have also retained a plethora of

Japanese terms that I considered important for their specificity, occasionally adding glosses or manipulating context where I felt necessary. I tried my best not to assume a familiarity with Japanese culture, but I did assume an openness to the unfamiliar and a willingness to explore.

For geographic formations, I tried to make it clear what something was. Yodogawa is the Yodo River, Hiei-san is Mount Hiei. Some may be irked with reduplication across languages in the names of temples, shrines, and bridges (Kenchoji Temple, Ebisubashi Bridge), but I felt these additions necessary for readers less familiar with the Japanese language. Throughout the text, I have consistently followed the Japanese system for addresses using block numbers called chome (pronounced like cho-may) so curious readers can go on their own fieldtrips, and I tried to maintain intersection, block, street, and district names as presented in the original text. Names of highways, graciously, tend to have standardized English translations, though I have transformed the "Parking Areas" of Japanese highways to "Rest Stops."

It is important to note that while the map presented in this novel is frozen in amber, Japan is not. As of publication we are already separated from the time of the novel by not just ten years but also a global pandemic, and many of the smaller restaurants and cafes mentioned in the text have shut down. As the Japanese map shifts, the English one also might lose its stability. Despite my best efforts to pick the most accessible translations, my selections may fall into obscurity in the near future.

Even the most central references are not immune to change. On August 21, 2024, Orient Industry announced that they would end business operations and their galleries would shut

Mistress Koharu

their doors in September of that year, just under a year after I visited. They have since reversed this decision, so as of publication, you can still visit their Okachimachi gallery.

The home to Gallery Hitogata, the book's other love doll gallery, has already changed its name. The complex of shops, art studios, and galleries that goes by The New Studio Beneath the Rails in the novel was already over ten years old when I began working on this translation. It's no longer new, and maybe for that reason it now goes by Site-A Gallery Beneath the Railways. Working on this translation, I found several English translations of the old name, but they were all slightly different. Part of my mission in trekking out to Hinodecho was to see if I could find an official translation of its old Japanese name lingering anywhere.

I had another motivation, though. I could not locate Gallery Hitogata anywhere online. I needed, for my own sake, to confirm if this love doll gallery was also real. After all, my gut was wrong about Orient Industry. There was no reason I couldn't be wrong about Hitogata as well.

I followed Akira's path from Koganecho Station down the riverside, checking every posted bit of text along the way. I found the description of the establishment of Koganecho Area Management Center and plenty of postings about ongoing projects, but had no luck in finding out what the place was called in English ten years ago. Still, I continued on, as if pulled by some strong magnetic force. I reached the end of the building beneath the tracks. There, in the furthest point from Koganecho Station, was Artbook Bazaar. I climbed the wooden stairs and followed along the glass wall. There, at the top of the stairs, I thought, I would find my answer.

honfordstar.com